All quotations from *Consolations of Philosophy* taken from the open-source online Gutenburg version. Thank you.

To the Allen Brothers

Aka

The Fan Club

The Kinglet

By Paul Goulding

Philosophy gently touched my breast with her hand, and said: 'There is no danger; these are the symptoms of lethargy, the usual sickness of deluded minds. For a while he has forgotten himself; he will easily recover his memory, if only he first recognises me. And that he may do so, let me now wipe his eyes that are clouded with a mist of mortal things.'

Boethius

Civilisation is a hopeless race to discover remedies for the evils it produces.

Jean-Jacques Rousseau

Personae

The Monastery
Jordanes
Owen, his man
Abbot Basilius
Brother Arminius
Brother Anacreon
Brother Isidorus
Brother Josephus
Brother Uldin
Brother Paulinus

The Barbarians
Theodoric, King of the Goths
Theodoric Strabo, a rival king
Odovacar, a barbarian usurper of the Western Empire
Pitzias – a general of Theodoric
Mammo – a general of Theodoric
Tulum – a general of Theodoric
Theudis – friend of Theodoric
Augofleda – wife to Theodoric

The Italian Court
Faustus – a Roman courtier
Festus – a Roman courtier
Liberius – a Roman civil servant
Cassiodorus – a Roman statesman
Boethius – a Roman statesman
Symmachus – a Roman patrician
Ennodius – a priest
Cyprian – a Roman patrician

Constantinople
Zeno – Emperor of the Eastern Empire 474-491
Anastasius – Emperor of the East 491-518
Castalius – a disreputable bookseller
Justinian – heir-apparent and future Emperor of the East 527-564
Theodora – his consort and future wife
Narses – Justinian's chamberlain

Ass on a Mule

This very place which thou callest exile is to them that dwell therein their native land.
Boethius

'By Saint Saba!' I exclaimed.

I leaned against the crumbling rock-face that had caused the problem, and picked yet another stone from the space between my foot and the insole of the sandal.

And yet again, I asked myself why I was not mounted on a horse and accompanied by a retinue of servants. I was now, whether I liked it or not, Bishop of Crotona. And however cash-strapped the members of my flock might be, I was sure they would rather see their shepherd processing through the south of Italy in a style that proclaimed to the world their civic pride and religious duty.

But all is as God wills. Apparently.

In the last month of the year of our Lord of 550, the good Pope Vigilius, who had so recently consecrated me, was held captive in Constantinople by the equally pious Emperor Justinian. Rome was besieged by civilised Greeks and defended by barbarian Goths. The world was turned upside down. And then there was the plague on top of all the rest. So I had to content myself with a Bruttian mule and a British retainer, both of doubtful pedigree and perverse humour.

After I had tiptoed past the defile that had caused me to dismount in the first place, I got back in the saddle. Then glanced over my shoulder to check that Owen was keeping pace and had not, yet again, been waylaid. Either by the imposing mountains that rose to our right – 'did you ever see such royal peaks, your worshipfulness?' Or by the precipitous drop down to the roiling waves on our left – 'you wouldn't wanna take a dip in that, wudger?' Or simply by the desire for a chat with any foot passenger that was more ready than myself for conversation.

I needn't have worried about Owen.

'All right there, squire?' he asked, with a finger salute to the brim of his hat. The man had more honorifics for me than a Byzantine courtier, and none of them were correct. He also had a habit of affixing most of his sentences with, what were to me, incomprehensible tags. 'Wudger' was a favourite. I was not sure what it meant. Perhaps it was an obscure British honorific.

I nodded and looked up. It had grown very dark. The sky now touched the mountains and I could hear the sea beat with increased fury against the rocks beneath us. The only humans foolish enough to be out in the bitter blast from the Adriatic were the bone-headed servant and his foolish master.

A mule on an ass, and an ass on a mule.

All the signs pointed to the onset of a storm. Sure enough, I felt the first drops of rain prick my face and pulled the folds of my *paenula* more closely about my body. All that was needed now was for my mule or his ass to throw a shoe.

'Begging your honour's pardon,' Owen shouted.

I looked around. He was standing beside the pack mule and holding up its fetlock.

'We had best find shelter,' I conceded, adding 'you cretin' under my breath.

The rain had turned to daggers of ice. My clothes were already sodden and my skin frozen. I raised my hand to shield my eyes while I tried to scan the road ahead for signs of habitation.

The route we were travelling from Brundisium – where we had landed – to Scylletium, our destination, appeared to be one of the least trafficked of the Calabrian peninsula. And with the exception of the lights of Crotona that we had seen below us some time ago, we had seen nothing more than peasant hovels since we left Tarentum. Not that there had been many of these. The few houses we had passed had either been boarded up or the shutters had closed as we went by.

The plague itself was fading. Memories of it had not.

So I held little hope that we should find anything better now.

Of a sudden I heard Owen yell once more above the howl of the storm. He was pointing to the slopes ahead of us. I could see nothing more than rubble obscured by the slanting sleet. Then I saw my man walking his ass ahead of me and beckoning me to follow.

I dug my heels into the belly of the mule. A little later I was able to make out a faint glow on the hillside in front of us. Then, a few hundred feet farther down the road, I could hear the repeated creak and slap of a wooden board as it swung against a wall.

Under the arch of the stable entrance, I dismounted and threw the reins over the mule. As I did so, there was a howl from the hills. A dog, perhaps. Or a wolf.

Owen took charge of the reins. He had a broad smirk on his face.

'Years of training,' he said. 'Smell a tavern a mile away.'

'Without a word of exaggeration,' as he might have added. And indeed did so when we were sitting in the relative comfort of the inn itself, warming and drying ourselves before a fire. 'Always allowing for wind direction.'

'Looks like it's settled in for the night,' observed the landlord as he emerged from the shadows. Startled into silence by his sudden appearance, I answered only with a brief grunt of agreement. Owen, curse him, was more forthcoming.

'Wouldn't throw a tyke out on a night like this, wudger.'

Now it was the innkeeper's turn to reply with a grunt. He was no doubt wondering whether 'wudger' was an insult of some kind.

'You'll be wanting some tucker then,' he said, giving up the effort of interpretation. 'And a doss for the night, I guess.'

I looked in desperation at Owen. He grinned at me before answering.

'Hit the nail on the head, entcher. Bowl of broth and some bread and cheese, chased down by your best red. Followed soon enough by a couple of flea-free palliasses.'

He has his uses. His Latin is eccentric from a purist point of view. But he has a fine grasp of idiom. This is more than can be said for my understanding of the language, which is largely limited to the written form, aspires imperfectly to the Classical and was gleaned from a monastic primer. So I had had no idea what the landlord was talking about until Owen provided a gloss.

I leaned against the wall of the hearth, letting the warmth revive my frozen limbs.

The tykes in the night were us. Owen was an exotic Celtic hybrid. Somehow he had found his way from the Islands of the West to the ancient centre of Empire. I assumed he had been taken as a slave and manumitted by Vigilius, before being passed on to me as a gift on my consecration as bishop. Or offloaded, perhaps.

As to the exact nature of Owen's lineage, I had to take his own word. Which was that he hailed from the south of Anglia and was the product of a union between a Celtic seamstress and a Roman soldier. A centurion, of course. Which did leave open the possibility that he was, in fact, telling the truth when he claimed to have travelled to Italy to find his father.

As for me, I was of Goth and Alan descent. Which made me at least as much of a barbarian as my servant, even if I chose not to broadcast the fact. But then, who wasn't a mongrel these days? At least, I had had my brutishness purged by repeated doses of Christian doctrine and classical education. Which was more than could be said of my man.

*

Most of the vapour had steamed out of my clothes and some feeling been restored to my limbs by the time the landlord returned. He brought with him a young woman laden down with the tray of 'tucker'. The host himself was carrying a jug of wine and three beakers. He indicated where the plates and food should be set down before depositing his own load. Then he beckoned to us and took a seat himself.

I suppressed a sigh. I was not given to small talk at the best of times. But at least we tykes had *not* been thrown out into the night. So I summoned up as much grace as I could manage, and rose to take my seat beside the other two.

I studied the broth for a moment, before I committed myself. It consisted mainly of water with some grains floating on the surface. They looked like barley and smelt of mould. The bread was of rye and smelt similar.

Or perhaps the fetor emanated from our host. By the glow of the oil-lamp, I studied his face as he poured wine into our tumblers. Scrofulous, certainly. The lumps stood out on his neck like angry molehills. Some other malady had infected his face, causing inflamed patches that left islands of hair on his scalp and jaw. Meanwhile his lower lip drooped to the right, allowing a surplus of spittle to gather. Occasionally, he hawked and spat to remove it. The rest of the time he spluttered the surplus across the table at us and our food whenever he opened his mouth.

On the other hand, his clothes seemed freshly laundered. I put this down to the offices of the woman that waited upon us. So it was probably the soup and the bread that actually smelt rotten. A wet harvest and a damp autumn, no doubt. I only hoped that I would not fall victim to ergotism before fulfilling my commission. Or before taking up my post, for that matter.

My eyes shifted back to the bread and cheese. These at least I could scrape the mould off. Unfortunately the landlord had noticed my inspection of him and regarded it as an invitation to open a conversation.

'Come far?'

'Brundisium,' I replied.

'Before that, Constantinople,' Owen added, no doubt seeking to impress.

The landlord whistled through his remaining front teeth. Then nodded as if this explained a great deal.

'Where the Big Feller lives,' he said.

I shot a warning look at Owen. He was already looking at me. There was some sense in him, then. He knew when to shut up. The landlord could be pro-Roman or pro-Goth. Or he could even be a supporter of the bandits of the wasteland that Italy had become after these years of warfare between the Gothic kingdom and the Eastern Empire. It was safest to wait and see.

'The Emperor Justinian. Yes,' I replied. Not a 'big feller' in terms of physical stature. But great in his opinions, not least of himself.

I took a small sip of the wine. A pleasant surprise. It was full and deep, if a little musty.'

'Fuck you want to come here for then? Leave a nice cushy number for this hole.'

A question was safer than an answer. The man could also be a misguided follower of Arius, and thus a heretic. And I, despite my Gothic origins, was now a Catholic prelate.

'Business bad, then?'

He snorted, this time depositing his phlegm on the table top.

'Always was a bit off the beaten track this place. Since the fucking wars started, the only passing trade we get is the armies. Then there was the fucking plague. Though that seems to have run its course, thank God.'

He crossed himself.

'So now we're just left with the military – first Goths traipsing through, then the Imperials. Back and bloody forth all the fucking time. One lot as bad as the other. None of 'em much good at settling their bills. To be fair though, the Babas at least go through the motions.'

Neither pro-barbarian, nor pro-Roman, then. More concerned with making a living. No bad thing that, either. These days, the best you could hope for was to make do.

'And the last lot to pass by?'

'The Baba King. Heading south.'

So Totila, the latest in the short line of Goth rulers, was in Sicily, I assumed. If Imperial troops had landed there, then that was surely nothing but a diversionary tactic. And one that the Goth King had fallen for. The mainland itself would now be open to invasion.

If so, the end might be in sight. That at least would be a blessing, however little I cared for Justinian. He had, after all, started the war by invading Italy, claiming that this was to avenge the murder of the rightful heir to King Theodoric. It had always seemed to me that this was little more than a cover for his own ambitions, even if it meant ridding the Empire of barbarian, and no doubt barbarous, rule. I suspected Justinian wanted to go down in history, inter alia, as the Emperor that had reunited East and West Rome and thus restored the integrity of the Empire. And the Devil take the cost in human suffering. Even if it meant, in the long run, the restoration of civilised life.

Fortunately, the innkeeper's curiosity about current affairs seemed purely local. He didn't enquire further into Constantinopolitan politics, or my own opinion of them. Instead he ran his eyes over my *paenula*, as if noticing it for the first time.

'Nice fabric,' he said. 'Black twill's my guess. Tarentum wool?'

A pause for a response that was not forthcoming.

'Man of the cloth,' he said. I decided to take this as a statement and, again, said nothing.

'Your new bishop, entit.'

I looked sideways at Owen and kicked him sideways beneath the table.

The landlord whistled and nodded again.

'Missed your turning, did you then?' He pointed over his shoulder with his thumb. 'Crotona's back thataways.'

Owen looked at me. I wasn't sure if this was because he didn't want to be kicked again or because he did not know how to answer.

'I have an errand to carry out first.'

Another nod.

'The monastery,' Owen explained.

'In Scylletium,' I added.

'The ponds.' The landlord raised a scabby eyebrow. Then threw his head back and drained his beaker. The monastery was named Vivarium after the lakes that had been excavated and stocked with live fish.

11

'Fuck you want with that bunch of weirdos? Pardoning my Scythian, your lordship.'

The landlord had no better grasp of the honorifics than Owen had. And his use of the vernacular was even cruder.

This time I had no intention of answering. And my servant couldn't. I limited myself to mumbling something about private business.

'Tour of inspection, then?'

'Something like that.'

I took another draft of the wine. Strong too, I decided.

When I looked up at him, the landlord was smiling at me.

'Good, eh? *Aqua nigra*, we call it. Black water. Secret of the south. Laid down before the plague wrecked the harvests.'

I smiled, my heart warming to him. Not such a bad chap, perhaps. After all was said and done.

'Your secret is safe with me.'

*

I lay awake for a while on the coarse mattresses that Owen had given over to my sole use while he slept on bare boards. The two palliasses had been stitched together in a parody of a bridal bed. I suppose he had his good points. His heart was in the right place even if his brain was in mid-Atlantic.

A god-forsaken land, this. Both Italy itself and especially, from what I had seen, my new diocese. I had thought the blight of war might have passed the area by, since there was little to attract conquerors in this rocky desert. But that turned out to be a forlorn hope.

Still there might be some prospect of peace. Even if Totila survived the new invasion, there was talk that Germanus, Justinian's cousin, was on his way. With him, he would bring his new wife, the granddaughter of 'great' Theoderic. There was an even chance that the match would be acceptable to both warring parties. If so, Totila would surely make Germanus his heir and the *Pax Romana* would eventually be restored.

It was a resolution worth praying for. And I did so, before I closed my eyes in sleep.

The Ponds

Honour cometh not to virtue from rank, but to rank from virtue.
Boethius

Our destination was, as might have been expected, at the top of a hill. The mule had refused to move when faced with the last steep incline, so I arrived on foot outside the entrance to the monastery – dusty, dishevelled, short of breath and temper, and hauling the mule along by brute force.

I looked over at my man. He had somehow managed to coax his donkey where my mule had declined, apparently by whispering unintelligible endearments into the creature's ear. Now I waited for him to summon the porter. Instead he avoided my eyes, and swinging down from his saddle, began to busy himself with the baggage straps.

I heaved a sigh and rapped on the door myself. This made little noise and less impression. The only sound I heard in response was a polite cough from Owen. I looked round and saw him pointing to the bell-rope hanging to the right of the doorway. Taking a moment to glare at him, I swung the rope to the side and rang the bell.

A few minutes later came the sound of footsteps. Then one side of the door creaked open to reveal a man a little older than myself. His shoulders were rounded and his head bowed with age or care, or both. But he was still a man of considerable height and patrician bearing. If the porter looked like this, I marvelled, then I must have arrived at a gentleman's fraternity rather than a monastic community.

The fellow looked at me. There was momentary confusion in his eyes, before this was replaced with what appeared to be relief. This look, in turn, proved to be fleeting, since it was soon replaced by a worried expression. This last turned out to be the natural set of his features.

'How can I be of service?' he asked.

For some reason this inspired my mule with panic and I regained the reins only with difficulty. Summoning up what dignity I could while standing beside a mutinous mule, I requested to be admitted to the presence of the abbot.

A look of confusion again.

'Speaking,' he replied.

I heard a snicker from behind me and flushed. Given he had to answer the door himself, presumably this abbot shared my misfortune in being master to a British servant.

'I have the honour of being your new bishop, Father Abbot.' I almost said 'Brother'. The habit died hard.

'Excellency.' The abbot hesitated a moment before bowing his head. 'Welcome to our humble establishment.'

I bowed my head a little less in return and hoped I was learning behaviour becoming my new status. At least I had been awarded a correct honorific. For what it was worth.

'To what do we owe the pleasure…?'

My response was a demonstrative shiver.

The abbot took the hint.

'Forgive me, Excellency. Please follow me in.'

Throwing the reins of the mule in the direction of Owen with an air of triumph, I was rewarded with another chuckle. Then I entered the monastery.

It had been difficult to make out much of the complex on our approach, since the buildings lay in the shadow and lap of the surrounding hills. But, as I walked through the portico and into the entrance hall, it was plain to see that the monastery had not been purpose-built.

I am not sure whether 'plain' is the right word. Nor can I claim much experience of what a monastery *should* look like. My knowledge of such communities was limited to the one of which I was a titular member. I visited it seldom, only in the intervals allowed by my secular duties. But even in these brief interludes it was difficult to detect any of the faded splendour that adorned the walls of the passage here.

My first impression was one of colour only – terracotta ochres and burnt earth reds, relieved by dashes of verdigris. Then I paused to study the paintings more closely. As I did so, I heard yet another dirty laugh behind me. Clearly Owen had finished tethering the animals and was enjoying my confusion and subsequent discomfort as the subjects of the murals became clear to me.

Initially I took it be a pedagogic guide to the torments of hell. But on closer inspection, it was obvious that the wall paintings depicted fauns and nymphs engaged in the various stages and positions of a Bacchanalia. Either Vivarium had served as a brothel in a previous incarnation, or the owner had been a debauchee with a leaning towards the pederastic.

Morbidly fascinated, I tried to decide exactly what a cucumber was doing in a picture that otherwise did not seem to devote much space to the virtues of simple and healthy cuisine. When the truth came upon me, I jerked my head back in shock and disgust and looked around to see if anyone had noticed my discomfiture. Needless to say, Owen had a broad smirk on his face. The abbot, on the other hand, looked deeply perturbed.

'I trust you don't think…,' he began.

'I will try not to,' I replied.

'The fact of the matter is, the monastery was originally the summer house on the estate.'

Not a brothel, then. Something to be grateful for, at least.

'Unfortunately, the Master has not as yet had the leisure to make the changes appropriate to the new function of the complex.'

I wondered, in the meantime, whether the members of the monastery used these images as salutary reminders of the wicked world they had renounced. Or for other, less worthy purposes.

I took one last look before moving on and was forced to admit that the painter had shown considerable skill. However repellent the subject-matter, he had an understanding of anatomy that our more spiritual age seemed to have lost. The saints and martyrs that were the more acceptable subjects of the visual arts these days most often looked as though they had hung too long on a washing line. As we passed on through the atrium, I noted to my relief that the designer of the floor mosaics had limited himself to representations of wild animals and circus slaughter.

I had assumed that the abbot would escort me to his own house for our interview and fancied this would be situated outside the main building and set in pleasant grounds – overlooking the coastline, perhaps. But as soon as we had passed through the atrium into a cloistered area, he veered off into one of the wing-rooms. The chamber was furnished as a small office and, going by the reek of rancid fat, lay close by the kitchens.

'Your study?' I asked, examining the spartan walls and general lack of fixtures.

The abbot's cheeks coloured.

'The parlour. I have no office of my own.'

I raised an eyebrow. This was an alien concept to me. In my experience, the rules of an institution were usually written by and for the convenience of those that headed it.

'We consider all things to be held in common here,' he went on.

'A commendable spirit of renunciation.' I said, hoping the same was not expected of bishops of the diocese. I needed some comforts to make up for the unenviable nature of my posting and my own lack of interest in it.

The abbot gave an absent nod.

'So in what way can we be of service to our Lord Bishop?'

As I explained the nature of my commission, a look of perplexity appeared on the abbot's face.

'I regret to say that the Master is not in residence.'

Now it was my turn to look confused.

'Is not the abbot, by custom and rule, the executive head of the monastery?' I asked. Though, in fairness, the idea of cenobitic monasteries was relatively new to the west, and I supposed the rules were still evolving. 'I had assumed the Master was merely the former owner of the property.'

'In this case, ah....' He cleared his throat. '...the Master combines both roles.'

That agreed with my own experience. Of the secular world, at least. To ride two horses, you need first to own two horses, as the Goths say.

'And when will the Master grace us with his presence?'

'He is expected daily,' the abbot said with an uncertain smile. Then added, 'and has been for the past few years.'

'He has never visited?'

'Not recently.'

I was surprised, to say the least. Whether the monastery was designed as atonement for a dissolute life or whether it represented a genuine act of piety, I would have thought that its patron would be interested in witnessing the result.

The abbot seemed to sense my incredulity.

'He has been otherwise detained.' With a gentle smile. 'And what with the ravages of the plague....'

I returned him a sage nod.

'Render unto Caesar....'

'I am, however, sure that he would have no objection to Your Grace consulting the open stacks of our humble collection.'

Well, we would have to see how far the humble open stacks managed to satisfy His Grace's curiosity. For the moment I gave a shallow dip of the head to signify my acceptance.

'In the meantime, I am sure you will wish to familiarise yourself with our facilities and in due course with your own quarters.'

He glanced across at Owen who was leaning against the door post, picking his teeth with a long fingernail.

'And those of your companion…,' he added, a question in his voice.

Understandably so. Even during our brief relationship, Owen had shown an enviable ability to make himself at home everywhere he went. Not least by adopting an air of familiarity with new surroundings and new acquaintances that I, though I had had more years of practice, had never managed to achieve. It was not surprising, then, that the abbot had mistaken the nature of our mutual standing.

'Owen,' I said by way of clarification, 'when you have stabled the animals, please bring in the bags.'

He stood to attention and mock-saluted.

'No sooner said than done, squire.'

I smothered a sigh. I had not wished for a servant, even though I realised it was expected of my new position. Indeed I had never had a retainer of this kind and was unsure how to address one with the required admixture of familiarity and authority.

True, in an earlier life I had been in the habit of barking commands to low-ranking officers and private soldiers. But this did not seem to work with a 'personal attendant', or whatever we should call him. Initially, when I had tried this approach, Owen had just stared at me, bemusement written in capital letters across his face. It was only when I moderated my voice that he recovered his understanding.

Now, when he judged my tone too peremptory, he would slip into the role of a chirpy but brainless batman as if in parody of my own military background. Not for the first time, I cursed the good Vigilius under my breath. He might at least have given me the choice of my own man. I am sure I could have sought out a former NCO who would have been happy in the post, and cheerfully obliging in the fulfilment of his duties. Instead I had an insolent Briton foisted on me from the Papal pool of surplus labour.

As the abbot showed me round the monastery, my attention drifted off, sometimes alighting on the interior decoration of the building, sometimes on the abbot himself. Both belied their present function. As before, images of the sacred scarcely concealed the profanity of their surroundings. A crucifix, for example, carelessly hung between the breasts of a preternaturally well-endowed nymphet.

Meanwhile, the Father Superior himself seemed similarly out of place. His humble manner, though doubtless sincere, seemed under constant strain, as if it were in conflict with years of breeding to a position and sense of privilege. Occasionally this conflict erupted through the surface meekness, taking the form of verbal or physical tics – a sudden irrelevant contraction of the lips, a fleeting shadow of some indefinable emotion across his brow and eyes, a nervous jerking at the sleeve of his tunic.

'And this is the library.'

My guide's hand described a vague parabola, doubtless intended to indicate the profusion of books, before coming to rest on the sleeve of the opposite arm and holding on to it for dear life.

In truth, I was surprised at the number of volumes and wondered how the monastery had managed to acquire such a prodigious collection.

'The gift of the Master,' the abbot explained, 'and others. Over many years.'

I nodded my appreciation and moved closer to the shelves. My eyebrows shot up as I recognised again the discordant juxtaposition of the pagan and the Christian. Here Aristotle sat beside Augustine of Hippo; Hesiod, of all people, hobnobbed with Origen of Alexandria.

'The Master is convinced that even the most pagan of texts will allow of orthodox Christian exegesis.'

I was impressed and nodded my approval. The presence of the awe-inspiring Augustine was assurance of the soundness of the enterprise.

I turned to look at the abbot. His twitches were now in full flow, as if he were trying to restrain himself from uttering an opinion on the subject. All of a sudden I felt a pang of pity for him.

'What is your name, father?' I asked, assuming a gentler tone.

'I still carry my lay name of Basilius. Decius Basilius Venantius.'

'As pious a name as any, Father Basilius.' And a most aristocratic one by the sound of it. An explanation for his comportment and mode of speech. And his spasms, perhaps, if his present position represented a fall from grace. 'I see no reason to change it, do you?'

The man's expression suddenly brightened, and a timid smile flitted across his face.

'I am here to be guided by my superiors,' he said.

'We are all equal in the eyes of God, my son.' I uttered this below my breath. I wasn't entirely convinced. My background led me to doubt the truth of the platitude, even if my present position did not officially admit of such equivocation.

I returned my attention to the open shelves and skimmed rapidly along the titles. What I was looking for was not in immediate evidence. But a more careful inspection was required. I wondered where the closed stacks were located, and what they contained. If Hesiod was on open view, I could only guess what might be hidden.

*

The *scriptorium* proved less interesting. There was a solitary young monk at work, laboriously copying out a text. Like a child mastering its alphabet, he licked the tip of his quill at regular intervals, blackening his tongue and lips. He was so absorbed by his task that he failed to notice he was being watched. Eventually he looked up with a cast eye and smiled an idiot smile before bending back to his work.

'Brother Anacreon is a novice, I am afraid,' Basilius explained with an apologetic smile.

'*Scriptoria* are places of learning,' I consoled him, 'regardless of the capacity.'

'In that case, we can regard the monastery as a veritable Lyceum,' the abbot observed with a nervous giggle.

'How so?'

'Sadly even many of our more seasoned brothers lack even the rudiments of an education.'

This was surprising, to say the least. While it is true that I had taken holy orders to improve my scholarship, it had been a precondition of entry that I should at least be literate.

'The Master assures me that he will be bringing more qualified copyists and illuminators with him when he eventually honours us with his presence,' the abbot added.

I checked for signs of sarcasm on the abbot's face and, finding none, lifted an illuminated text off the desk next to the cretin with the black tongue. The writing was ornate and the illustrations gorgeous. I held the open manuscript up for the abbot to see.

'*Someone* here is indeed gifted.'

He blushed.

'I also sometimes try my inadequate hand.'

'I would urge you to try your very adequate hand more often,' I replied. 'The work is magnificently executed.'

The abbot bowed his head to conceal his pleasure. As he did so, a bell tolled from the rear of the main building.

'Sext,' Basilius pointed out redundantly. I was familiar with the hours. 'The monks will soon be arriving in the *refectorium* for their lunch. If you don't mind postponing the inspection of your sleeping accommodation until later, perhaps you would care to share our simple fare?'

I inclined my head. I had not eaten since the evening before. And since then, the hostelry food had played havoc with my intestines, creating a vacuum that demanded to be filled.

As we walked out into a large and splendid courtyard at the rear, the abbot pointed out the *lavatorium* and accompanied me to a series of basins lining the outside of the building. They were situated in the midst of and were presumably supplied from the same source as the crystal-clear cisterns that gave the monastery its name. The whole layout was exquisitely landscaped. And like the gardens, the sanitary arrangements were far superior to any I had encountered in Constantinople.

Basilius washed his hands, then looked up.

'Your man will be joining us for the meal?'

'I expect he will have preceded us,' I replied.

*

In which I was soon proved right. When we entered the hall, I could see Owen was in full thespian mode. He held his audience of monks rapt with dramatic gestures designed, I imagine, to compensate for the deficiencies of his verbal communication.

I sighed and looked over at a table on the podium at the far end. Instead Basilius led me in the other direction. We eventually seated ourselves at the corner of the bench from which Owen was holding court.

'Are we, by any chance, expecting important guests?' I asked the abbot with a touch of asperity and a meaningful glance at the vacant high table.

His cheeks reddened and he lowered his eyes.

'The seat of honour is reserved, Excellency.'

'Let me guess. For the benefit of the ubiquitous but strangely absent Master?'

'And guests of his invitation. To my mortification.' He bowed his head.

'So you do have a Rule here, then?'

'The Rule is of and by the Master himself.'

This was not *The Rule of the Master* I was familiar with. I had to content myself with casting my eyes over the collection of monks that faced each other down the length of the table.

I was confronted with rows of open mouths, displaying teeth in varying degrees of decay in faces of either moronic or villainous aspect. Or both. The mouths were open, needless to say, not in salivating anticipation of the dire food we were shortly presented with. But rather in mirth at the performance of my servant. Had I excess of self-love, I might well have taken offence at being thus upstaged. Having but a moderate dose, I limited myself to another sigh and turned back to my dining companion.

'You seem to have summoned up the dregs of humanity to join you in your devotions,' I commented with more than a modicum of pique.

The abbot flushed again, this time with a touch of anger, perhaps.

'We are all God's creatures,' he replied. 'These creatures have been abandoned by everyone else.'

'Aah!'

'Is not the provision of sanctuary one of the highest functions of any consecrated building?'

I felt rightly chastened and sought to moderate the sharpness of my tone. Not wholly successfully.

'I take it this function is not elaborated upon in any greater detail in the Rule of Your Master.'

Basilius averted his eyes.

'Not in any greater detail, no.'

I shifted uncomfortably in my seat. An all-too-long sojourn in Constantinople had made me grow unfamiliar with true charity of heart. Clearly I had much still to learn about the subject. I could make a good start, perhaps, by studying the abbot's behaviour more closely.

'You feel perhaps that the Rule should be interpreted liberally. In a spirit that our true Master would have approved of.'

As I mentioned our Lord and Saviour, the abbot's eyes grew moist.

'I am sure our more immediate Master will approve when he hears of the hardship of these people's lives and sees the haven we have provided for them.'

'We?' I wondered.

Nonetheless, I detected an opening.

'I am equally sure that he will approve of my consulting the *whole* of your library when he hears of the importance of my mission.'

Basilius glanced nervously at me for a moment, then away again.

I decided to press my point home.

'Every house I have had experience of,' one to be precise, 'invests total authority in the abbot of the order.'

'This House is unique then, I suppose,' the abbot replied with an attempt at a shrug.

'But even so, the Master surely delegates authority to you, *in loco parentis*, as it were.'

'The Rule is unequivocal in that respect, I regret to say,' he muttered, then attempted to suppress a tremor. 'I would suggest you take it up with him when he arrives.'

'And when might we expect him then?'

'Daily.' A shudder ran through his body again. 'As I think I mentioned.'

I looked forward to meeting him. In the meantime I would fulfil as much of my commission as I could, just he in case he turned out to be of a less charitable nature than his deputy.

The Instalment Plan

To each thing God hath given its appointed time.
Boethius

The abbot called the after-dinner lull 'a time for reflection'.

We were walking back through the grounds at the time. As I did my best to reflect on what in the name of the Almighty I was doing here, I noticed a grand house partially obscured by flowering shrubs and trees. Despite the vegetation, it was obvious that it occupied the most desirable position, overlooking as it did the spectacular coastline.

'You have a fine view to reflect upon,' I observed.

The usual look of confusion pierced the usual frown.

I pointed to the mansion house and his brow cleared.

'The Master's?' I decided.

He nodded.

The abbot, as it turned out, did not even care to award himself the semi-luxury of the private accommodation he had allowed myself and my servant. At least I was not required to sleep in the *dormitorium* with the rest of the monks, which is where Basilius rested, and meditated.

So, things could be worse. Nonetheless, as I later looked round my cell, I admired the frugal functionality of the room and thanked the Lord that I did not live here.

I glanced across at Owen. He had sized the room up briefly with an approving eye, before claiming 'it'll do the trick nicely, wunnit' and settling his square frame onto the palliasse at the foot of my bed. He then proceeded to interpret the 'period of reflection' as an opportunity for a 'kip'. If I had been inclined to meditate on the transitory nature of existence, I would have had to negotiate Owen's snores before venturing into the upper ether.

I studied his broad face and flat pugilist's nose in repose. His lips slipped into a cretinous, Morphean smile, while a sliver of saliva trailed down to the mattress. It struck me that if Owen were to devote as much time and effort to satisfying my wishes as he did to gratifying his own physical needs, then our relationship would be a lot more cordial.

As he slept, a gold-crested bird, what we call the kinglet, flew in through the unglazed window and alighted close by. Unconcerned by his presence, it foraged on the floor of the cell. Perhaps I should reflect instead on the bird, I reflected. There was surely more to admire in the handiwork that had gone into the creation of this gem of miniaturist art than in the crude hackwork that had shaped my manservant.

The kinglet paused in its work, suddenly aware it was being studied. It swivelled its head to the side to gaze at me with jet-black eyes, cocked its tail, then flew with a whirring of wings and guttural clucking sound into a crevice in the wall.

The abbot might indeed have a point with this period of meditation. It had been some time since I had focused my attention so closely on one of God's creations. My heart filled with wonder, and, to my irritation, my eyes with tears. Suddenly I felt a surge of resentment. Why was my servant more favoured by God's creatures than I was? My lips tightened into a smile. No doubt it was because he was closer on the scale of being to the beasts than to the angels.

I was feeling less than angelic myself. The monastery put me out of sorts for reasons I could not work out. Moreover, the weather had worsened since my walk back to the main building after lunch. Otherwise, I would have been tempted to walk off my ill-temper along the valleys and ridges of this inhospitable country. A closer inspection of the room did little to raise my spirits. If there had ever been licentious murals here, they had been whitewashed over, doubtless to prevent the mind wandering during the prescribed periods of contemplation. Meanwhile, the furnishings were Spartan to the point of self-flagellation, consisting of:

Item – one mattress on the floor (now occupied by comatose Briton);

Item – one mattress on bedframe (occupied by bored Roman citizen);

Item – one lectern, also of questionable pedigree (unoccupied for the foreseeable future).

And that was it. Little else to do but meditate. And pray. Which was probably the idea.

Once again I looked over at the figure of Owen as he lay on the floor. He had a smile on his face and his pelvis was grinding the air. It was not difficult to judge what he was dreaming of. Not for the first time, I thanked God for the blessing of civilisation, even if it hadn't worked with the British. To be honest though, I felt a touch of envy at his simple pleasures. The sight of such pleasure in action, however, did not lend itself well to my devotions. So I decided to leave him to his succubus and headed back to the library.

There I could browse at leisure and in private. After all, a deal was a deal. And I should make at least a token effort to fulfil its terms. So I began to browse along the so-called open stacks. I dreaded what would happen if I failed to find what I was looking for. For I was not sure whether the absence of the final volume of Cassiodorus' *History* would expedite my departure or delay it.

This was all the fault of that bastard, Castalius. Or rather my own lack of firmness in the face of his threats.

*

He had a shop on a back street across from the Hippodrome in Constantinople. I had first come across this dingy emporium a good few months earlier, when I had been touting my history of Rome. This had been written at the behest of Pope Vigilius, who was – then as now – detained in Constantinople, having offended the Emperor of the East on some doctrinal point that only the two of them understood. As for myself, I had not yet taken holy orders and was still engaged as a private secretary.

Unfortunately, since he was effectively living in exile, Vigilius' means were as modest as his station. When I had completed the work, I found he had not the wherewithal to finance its publication. Nonetheless, to my irritation, he claimed co-authorship on the basis that the idea had been his, even if the composition had not been.

I was reluctant to discard the manuscript after investing so much time and effort in it, so I hawked it around the booksellers of the capital. Few even looked at the text. Instead, they complained that books on the subject had flooded the market and, of course, they'd been left with 'piles of parchment they couldn't shift to save their lives'.

By the time I located Castalius' backstreet 'Antiquarian Bibliotheca', as the signboard fancifully announced, I was really just going through the motions. At least if I'd covered all the available outlets, I could at least sleep better. I hoped.

The turf was not promising. As might be expected of an area so close to the Hippodrome, the street was dank and the walls covered with graffiti. Many of the houses were still deserted and boarded up from the time of the plague. The bookshop itself was sandwiched between what was clearly a lowlife tavern and what looked to be an equally lowlife brothel. Indeed, it was mainly to escape the insistent sales pitch of both the innkeeper and the bordello bouncer that I decided to enter.

Inside the light was so poor that I almost walked into an individual wearing a greasy leather apron over a grimy chiton.

'I'm looking for the 'antiquarian',' I said.

The man bowed in the court fashion.

'At your service,' he said in a surprisingly cultivated voice.

I had still acquired no skill in the art of touting my wares, and was not sure how to begin.

'I have a rather odd request.'

He pursed his lips and ran his eyes over me.

'We have a room at the back for the more, how shall we say, esoteric tastes. If you would care to follow....'

By which I gathered that the range of material on sale was not limited to the strictly antique, the devotional or even the legal. I demurred politely and explained my mission.

Castalius proved to be both accommodating and well-informed. The name of Vigilius kindled his interest.

'Bishop of Rome, eh?' he commented.

That sounded encouraging.

'So you'll publish?' I asked.

'For the usual consideration.'

'Consideration?'

At this, he lapsed into some kind of quasi-legal gobbledegook to the effect that I would have to advance the cost of publication. When sales had reached a certain point, then all further proceeds would belong to me.

'Sure to sell like hog pasties on Palm Sunday, if you'll excuse the phrase. But we'll still need a down-payment as security.'

I took a deep breath. It was back to square one, in a sense. I had no more money to invest than Vigilius did, and much less interest. But Castalius was a silver-tongued devil. With his predictions of vast sums about to come my way, I ordered a preliminary run of 100 copies, and, after further haggling, paid only a token deposit. Then I put the whole matter of further settlement out of my mind, secure in the knowledge that I had fulfilled Vigilius' request and that there was a nice little rainy-day fund steadily growing and waiting for one of my life's many rainy days. If further manuscript runs were needed, I assumed Castalius would either get in touch or commission them on his own initiative.

It was only when a pair of brawny bookends appeared at my master's door that I fancied I might have made a mistake. They looked like bailiffs and had mumbled something about 'tabs to be settled'. Then demanded I accompany them immediately to deal with the matter. I ran my eyes over the considerable length and girth of each. Instead of necks, both had thick hawsers that extended from the shoulder to the ear. Both had tattoos on wrists and scars on biceps, which suggested to me that they had at some time served in the military. I decided that the safest course was to comply with their wishes.

But, despite my guess that they would convey me to the guards or the quaestors, they took me, in the first instance, to Castalius' shop. I ducked my head as I entered the portico between the brothel and what I now took to be a gambling dive, and wondered if Castalius owned the whole block. There seemed to be something of a theme going in the neighbourhood.

One last nudge from my escorts propelled me into the gloom of the interior and almost into the waiting arms of the proprietor.

'To what do I owe...?' I began.

''To whom do you owe' would be more to the point,' he replied.

I reminded him of the Palm Sunday metaphor. He pointed to a pile of dog-eared manuscripts occupying one of the many dark corners of his shop.

'But I thought...,' I began.

'We all make mistakes,' he replied. 'Yours will cost you 100 *solidi*.'

'A hundred...!'

I could not manage the rest of the sentence. In my present line of work, it would take me a year to pay that off. If I didn't starve in the meantime.

Castalius anticipated my next question.

'Not that I would have charged as much as one *solidus* per copy, you understand. But there's the question of interest.'

'Interest?'

'Capital bound up in that pile of garbage that could have been more gainfully deployed elsewhere.'

I stood up straight and attempted to recover my powers of speech.

'I regard it as *our* mistake,' I countered with more boldness than I felt. 'A mutual misunderstanding, if you like.'

Castalius smiled. Clearly someone had once pointed out to him that a genuine smile should extend to the eyes, but despite the attempt, he hadn't quite mastered the technique. The result was a rictus surmounted by narrow slots.

'I have nothing like that amount of cash at my disposal,' I added.

Still the frozen smile.

'The Pope…,' I began pontifically. Surely a reminder of the co-author's position would help.

'… disclaims all responsibility, not being party to the original contract.'

The episcopal ingrate had thrown me to the lions then. Or not quite, perhaps.

I pointed out that through the grace and favour of the man who had instigated the whole problem, I was about to take up a new post and anticipated a commensurate rise in my material worth.

'My felicitations. I could come up with a payment plan, in that case,' he said, and named another outrageous rate of interest. As he did so, he looked over at the grim twins. 'Premium to be paid weekly to these gentlemen.'

The gentlemen grinned grotesquely. One of them was picking his teeth with a small fruit-knife at the time and, as Castalius spoke, drew it across his throat.

I strove to conceal a shudder of both fear and distaste.

'May I make so bold as to enquire the nature of the post in question?' the bookseller asked.

'I have been appointed Bishop of Crotona.'

He bowed his head as if impressed.

'My congratulations. The Vigilius connection had its compensations, I take it. Grace and favour, indeed. Grace and favour.'

'I have truly been blessed,' I replied, although I had already been wondering whether the patronage was more of a curse than a blessing. I had heard that sending officials into holy orders was a milder punishment for offending the sensibilities of the Emperor. I wondered whether this applied to Popes too.

'And when are you due to take up your position?'

I explained that the consecration was scheduled for the following month, but that my actual relocation depended on the seas. As the year advanced into autumn, it could be months before the weather allowed.

'Whatever the case, Crotona poses a number of problems,' Castalius said after a moment's reflection.

'How so?'

'For the first, the cost of collection would be considerably more than the premium due.'

I gave a weak nod of acknowledgement.

'Apart from the fact that my esteemed colleagues have a distinct aversion to sea travel.'

'Ah!' I regarded the esteemed colleagues. It was good to know they found something in this world intimidating.

'The problem is not, however, insurmountable. We have… how shall I put it? ... local Bruttian affiliates that might be called upon. However, this alternative is hardly trouble-free.'

'Why not?'

'I've never visited the region in question,' he replied. 'But I have read much and also heard a great deal.'

He pricked my interest. I had read and heard next to nothing of the place.

'You are aware that most members of your future flock are likely to be troglodytes.'

'They still live in caves?!'

'Apart from a few mariners of a piratical bent, and fewer merchants that trade chiefly in stolen goods, that is.'

My expression gave me away.

'You understand that this is likely to have a radically negative impact on your earning power. Especially if they devour you, as rumour has it happened to your predecessor.'

I cursed Vigilius silently and wondered again if I had unwittingly offended him.

'Perhaps I could work it off instead?' I offered, although I wondered what form this could take. I had a vision of myself washing dishes until I left for Italy, until I realised that they probably didn't go in for such niceties in this establishment. Or any of the neighbouring properties, for that matter.

'I was about to suggest something of that nature,' he replied.

I had the feeling that I had waded from a quagmire into a quicksand.

'You wish to commission a further work from me?' I asked.

I was uncertain whether to be incredulous or apprehensive. The lack of success of my previous effort made it unlikely that Castalius would see me as a commercial proposition. On the other hand, the kind of subject matter that might make me into a commercial proposition left me with a sense of dread.

'How would you feel about writing a history of the Goths?'

I heaved a sigh of relief. The sensation lasted about thirty seconds.

'I am honoured you should find me suitable,' I began, 'but....'

Castalius cut me short.

'The book is already written,' he reassured me.

'In which case...?'

'It is a little on the long side for most readers' tastes.'

I frowned.

'I know of only one such.'

'Cassiodorus,' Castalius confirmed with a nod. '*The History of the Goths.*'

'Exactly.'

'Would the work were as short as the title.'

'It is long?'

'It comes in twelve ample volumes.'

'Indeed?'

'Of the most turgid and bombastic drivel.'

'Exhaustive, then?'

'Exhausting, rather.'

I frowned. I knew little of Cassiodorus, but his reputation for learning was as great as his renown as a statesman.

'I fail to see...,' I began, before Castalius interrupted once again.

'I require a summary.'

'...how I might be qualified for such an exercise.'

The bookseller studied his fingernails, and leant a hip against a wall.

'You are a Goth. You are lettered. Who could be better qualified?'

I flushed. I was not aware my origins were so obvious.

'Your name, Jordanes,' he explained.

'Drawn from the river of the Holy Land.'

He stared at me, unconvinced. He was right, of course. It fooled most people most of the time. But not the bookseller. I tried a different tack.

'But my previous effort failed most dreadfully,' I said, casting an eye at the pile of books gathering dust in the corner.

'You don't write badly. All a question of finding a niche.'

'?'

'There are and have been any number of volumes on the history of Rome for as long as anyone can remember.'

'Yet…?'

'On the subject of the Goths, just Cassiodorus.'

'There is probably a very good reason for that.'

'And that would be?'

I glanced over my shoulder. Justinian's spy system had a certain reputation.

'The Emperor is not known to be fond of the subject,' I explained in a confidential voice.

In point of fact, he was known to be particularly touchy on the subject, since his attempts to recapture Italy from the Gothic kings had run into the sands. He was also known to be particularly harsh to those that defied his proscriptions.

Castalius shrugged.

'What he doesn't know can't hurt him.'

'And if he does know, it will hurt us,' I pointed out. 'Or me, to be more specific.'

Castalius gave a sly chuckle.

'Subscription only,' he said, glancing meaningfully at the door at the back of his premises. Where he concealed his more salacious manuscripts. What he called his 'closed stacks', no doubt. 'Besides, it doesn't have to bear your name,' he added.

'In which case…?'

'The bookseller bears all the legal responsibility.'

I was running out of excuses.

'How can you be sure there's a market for such a work?' I asked. 'From what you say about it, I can't imagine Cassiodorus' work sold like… what was it? …hog pasties on Palm Sunday?'

He sighed.

'Take my word for it. A man in my line has to keep his ear to the ground.' He made a rasping sound in his throat that could have been a chuckle. 'Usually if a subject is frowned on by the authorities, then a certain sector of the public, at least, develops an inexplicable and insatiable thirst for it.'

In which case, it could hardly fail to come to the ears of the Emperor. He had many that acted on behalf of his ears. He was also extraordinarily persuasive. I could not imagine that Castalius would withhold the name of his author for long if pressure were applied. I decided to put my foot down.

'Flattered as I am by your faith in my ability…,' I began.

Castalius eyed me with affected concern, then sighed.

'Instalments it'll have to be then,' he said with a shake of his head.

'Instalments,' I confirmed.

He looked across at his henchmen, who were looking amused.

'Hope our friends across the water understand the tenor of the agreement better this time,' he said, and shook his head again. 'Remember that poor bastard…. What was his name again?'

'Sebastianus, boss.'

'His body was returned by the courier...'

I shuddered.

'…in instalments,' Castalius continued. 'Ears first, wasn't it?'

'Then the digits, boss,' one of the heavies added.

'Then the middle picket,' said the other.

'A language breakdown, I suppose,' Castalius concluded thoughtfully.

'When would you require the completed work?' I asked.

*

And so the 'deal', as Castalius called it, was 'sealed'.

Thankfully, I was permitted to send the completed manuscript for approval by the normal means, rather than having it collected by the Bruttian brutalists. But my 'deadline' (again another unfortunate turn of phrase) was tight. I was to have the proof ready and in Castalius' hands by the spring of the following year.

'Strike while the iron's hot,' as he explained. 'The war can't last much longer. And when it ends, interest's bound to fall off.'

By the spring I assumed I would have taken up my duties in the see of Crotona. I also assumed, when that happened, I was going to have my hands full, servicing or, more likely, exorcising my flock. My commission, therefore, had to be carried out under the most extreme time pressure.

So you can imagine my frustration when I had absolutely no success locating a copy of the original that I was supposed to summarise. To wit, Castalius not only had no copy himself. He also denied any knowledge of copies extant in the city.

When he made this claim, I remember suppressing a snort of disbelief. But I returned crestfallen the next week. I had spent most of the intervening time scouring the libraries and booksellers of the city in vain.

When I protested that I had been set a labour at which Hercules might have blenched, Castalius grinned with his mouth.

'Not surprising, you know,' he said, 'given the text's been proscribed.'

I did not need to be reminded of how hazardous my task was. That it was also impossible simply added a further risk – this time of mutilation.

'To tell the truth,' he said, 'I lied. I know where to find a copy.'

I was unsure whether to embrace or punch him. Recalling the fate of Sebastianus, I decided on the former course of action, but was warded off by upraised palms.

'I wouldn't get too excited,' he said.

'Excited? *Relieved* would be more the word,' I replied. 'Just point me in the direction of the proud owner.'

'Proud author more like.'

My heart sank.

The last person likely to be ready to lend a copy of the text I had been commissioned to plagiarise was its creator.

*

After this major blow to my fortunes, I had two pieces of good luck.

Firstly, the autumn storms were of such ferocity that my departure for Italy was indefinitely delayed. So I still had time to locate and obtain a copy of the original. Secondly, the formidable Gunthigis Baza, my former employer, allowed me a stipendium pending the assumption of my duties and related income in Crotona. This was more than I had expected and I was duly grateful.

Baza had been responsible for my finding my way to Constantinople in the first place. After the plague had ravaged its way through the Eastern Empire, there had been a dearth of manpower in general, and clerks in particular. The scourge had, for reasons best known to the Almighty Himself, afflicted the monasteries especially heavily. These being the usual source of clerical functionaries and thus in serious deficit, I had been summoned from my military duties to the capital by the retired general in order to work as his amanuensis.

He had then compounded the offence by introducing me into Vigilius' dubious favour, so I suppose he owed me a favour. He had always been delighted by my ability to condense his ramblings into a pithy sentence or two, and had mentioned this skill in passing to the Pope. Vigilius had, in turn, bestowed on me the accursed blessing of writing a concise history of Rome.

'Never been done,' Vigilius pointed out. 'Plenty of multi-volume works. But nobody's ever been able to cram the whole chronicle into a single volume. Got to be a market for it.'

There might well have been, if Vigilius had not insisted on the history being written from an ecclesiastical angle. This approach made little sense when dealing with the many centuries preceding the birth of Our Lord, and significantly reduced the commercial appeal of the few that succeeded it.

Not that Vigilius had been bothered by this lack of success. On the contrary, he had been delighted to see his name inscribed as co-author, and had probably bought up the few copies that had actually been sold to present to his friends in the hope of impressing them. He had also rewarded me by appointing me bishop to an Italian backwater. This in turn required me to take training for orders, by making the occasional token appearance at a local monastery for the remainder of my stay in Constantinople.

And so, in a sense, Baza had got me into this predicament. And so, in a sense, it was only fair that he should allow me the leisure to get myself out of it.

My first task, of course, was to find where the venerable Cassiodorus lived. It was my understanding that, after the fall of Ravenna to Justinian's forces, he had been taken captive to Constantinople, along with other worthies of the Gothic regime. So, to begin with, I had visited some of the better-class prisons of the capital in my efforts to track him down. Even if he had been on the wrong side, he was a Roman patrician and was hardly likely to have been obliged to consort with common thieves and murderers.

My enquiries met with no success. But at the last penal institution, a debtor's prison for the impoverished nobility, the warden took pity on my obvious distress and pointed out that Cassiodorus now resided under what he called 'a very loose kind of house arrest'. Naturally enough in one of the more upmarket quarters of the city.

My next problem was how to gain access to his library without disturbing the owner. As I have pointed out, it was hardly likely that Cassiodorus would simply hand over his precious works to a plagiarist. It was even less likely if the works in question were proscribed, or at least out of favour with the authorities.

I would like to say the solution came to me in a vision from the Almighty. In fact, the truth was more mundane. One day, I was taking some refreshment in a tavern across the road from Cassiodorus' villa, gazing with mournful eyes at the white marble that lay tantalisingly out of reach behind the iron railings.

The inn was of a piece with the area. On my way there, I had walked along avenues lined with plane trees and past villas with grounds as large as the Hippodrome. The tavern itself was less extensive, but looked out onto the street from under a clean striped canopy and through pilasters either side of the portico.

When I had entered the inn, I couldn't find a free table. But I noticed that there were a number of seats unoccupied next to a solitary drinker who was also, ironically enough, gazing at the street with mournful eyes.

When I asked if I might sit there, he had answered with a nod and explained that he was waiting for company. But that company would be in the singular, so there were spare seats.

The man showed no further desire for conversation. So I took my place and joined him in drinking heavily diluted wine and studying the street outside. In the meantime, he tapped his fingers impatiently on the table-top.

Our mutual reveries were eventually interrupted by the entrance of a tall individual with a deep-red silk tunic and a deeper-red face.

As he sat, he pulled up his long sleeves and scowled at the world in general.

'Damned place we live in,' he said eventually. 'Can't tell whether you're being dunned or stalked.'

It turned out that, on his way to his lunch rendezvous, he had noticed that he was being followed by a 'shifty-looking chap' in a dirty tunic.

'Wasn't sure if he was a cutpurse or a bailiff,' he said. 'Well, you know the problems I've been having with the business, old chap. So I thought, what the Hell, I'd lead the sod a merry dance.'

He chuckled.

'Twice round the hippodrome, in fact. Problem was, I couldn't shake him off. Younger than me, and a good deal fitter, I dare say.'

He shook out an elaborate napkin that he produced from a pouch on his belt.

'In the end I decided to grasp the nettle and confronted the bastard.'

He gave an aggrieved sigh.

'Know what he did?'

His companion shook his head in ignorance.

'Produced the Imperial Seal,' came the answer in a loud whisper. Then a little louder, 'Bugger was one of you-know-who's spies.' The man pulled down the lower lid of his eye.

His friend looked worried.

'You in trouble?' he asked.

'Not a chance. 'Flavius Maxentius Quintus Gabianus,' I told him. 'Not Gabinus.' Sent him away with a flea in his ear.'

Hardly likely, I thought. Justinian's spies were notorious for possessing not only their patron's imprimatur but also his peevish self-regard.

The anecdote did give me an idea though.

As I paid for my wine, I asked the waiter if he knew Cassiodorus' maggiordomo.

'Gorgeous Giorgos?' he laughed. 'Why? You want a date?'

I gave a feeble laugh.

'However gorgeous he might be, my vows would forbid it.'

'Apologies, father,' the waiter said, flicking his cloth at some stain on the table. 'You don't look the part exactly.'

I glowed inside. Not that I was vain of my appearance. But it was good to know that my military background still showed.

'You hang around, he'll pop in in about an hour. Usually needs a drink after a long day with the pig's bladder.'

'?'

'Giorgie boy ain't the only one with an inflated opinion of himself.'

He refused my attempts to reward him for the information, suggesting I put the money in the alms box instead. Charity comes in many guises. I ordered another glass of wine and settled down to await the arrival of the Gorgeous One.

I figured it shouldn't be too difficult to spot him leaving his workplace, since I was sitting just opposite the gates of the mansion. And my obliging new friend had promised to give me the nod when he entered.

The new friend nodded. Gorgeous Giorgie entered, wearing a tunic trimmed with coloured braid and a flash of emerald green set into the seam under the armpits. Or rather I should say, he made an entrance. As if he owned the place and expected a line of servants competing for turns to serve him. I guessed he didn't get his name so much from his sexual leanings. Rather more from the airs he gave himself.

I caught his eye and pointed to my glass.

He cocked an eyebrow, whispered something to the maître d', and minced over. Leaning one hand against a pillar and running the other through his pomaded hair, he asked me in what way he could serve.

I wondered for a moment if I had got him right the first time. He acted like a catamite for hire. But I signalled for him to sit and for the waiter to bring two more beakers of wine over.

He didn't drink, just eyed me over the brim of the raised beaker.

'What do I have to do to earn this?' he asked.

'You're in service over there?' I said, pointing with my head.

'Wouldn't call it "service".'

'What would you call it?'

'I'm employed in a managerial and consultative capacity.'

My drink found its way into my lungs. When I had finished coughing the wine up, I asked him who his master was.

He gave me the answer that I already knew.

'The famous writer and academic?' I whistled. 'Your patron must have some library. Given his reputation.' I guessed he would prefer the term 'patron' to that of 'Master'.

'You have no idea.'

'Well, give me an idea then.'

He pointed along the ground floor of the villa.

'Lined with books,' he said.

'The whole floor's a library?'

'The whole floor.'

I didn't have to try too hard to look impressed. Even by patrician standards, that was quite a collection.

'Quite a responsibility,' I said.

He looked confused.

'Curating such a large number of manuscripts.'

The light came back to his eyes.

'You have no idea.'

This was becoming tedious. But it was at least clear he played no great part in the care of the library. I decided to get to the point.

'I am interested in making use of the collection.'

'It's not a lending library.'

'I'm aware of that.'

'You'd need to ask the patron, then, wouldn't you.'

'I'm also aware of that. Along with what the answer would be.'

He nodded slowly.

'So what's in it for me?'

I had thought about that. Money was a problem. Indeed my lack of it was the reason I was here in the first place.

'The gratitude of the Holy Mother Church,' I said.

Now both eyebrows rose.

I pulled out the commission Vigilius had blessed me with. For the Roman History. The Original Sin, as it were. Carefully folding the letter to conceal the name of the work appointed, I held the document out for him to read. Assuming he could, of course.

'The Bishop of Rome?'

'The very same,' I replied, hoping fervently the man was not of the Arian faith. 'He wishes me to compose a summary of your patron's *History of the Goths*.'

Giorgie shrugged. Clearly he had never heard of the work.

'What's he want that for? The bloody pagans should burn in Hell.'

My hopes sank. Clearly the man was a fanatic, even if his heart was in the right place. I had little sympathy for the heretics myself.

'He wishes to show them how misguided they are in their faith.'

It was the best I could manage on the spur of the moment.

'And how would you rewriting their history do that then?' he asked, not unreasonably.

'It's all a question of how you slant it,' I babbled, playing for time.

'Like it's all been downhill for them since they departed from the true faith?' he asked.

I wasn't sure they had ever been parties to the True Faith, as we now knew it. Even if the Arian doctrines had been orthodox when the first Goths adopted them. And even if I couldn't give a damn for the bones the zealots squabbled over.

But the answer suited my purposes.

'You've hit the nail on the head,' I said.

*

And I had solved my problem. For the moment at least.

In the interests of saving the souls of the barbarian heretics, or of consigning them to everlasting damnation, Giorgos started lending me the volumes of his master's Gothic *History*. Unbeknown to his master, of course. He was as certain as I was that the loans would not have met with approval. For the same reason, I was allowed access to the history only 'in instalments'. Giorgos argued, with some justification, that removing all twelve volumes at a stroke would have left a detectable gap on the shelves.

The going was tough at first. Whatever his merits as a statesman and Christian, Cassiodorus was not the most direct of writers. Every relevant fact he introduced, he illustrated with an analogy that stretched the bounds of credibility. This would be followed by a digression so long that the original point was forgotten.

King Ermanaric, for example, was, for no reason that I could make out, compared to the great Alexander of Macedon. Out of respect, I retained the association. But I did cut the succeeding passage, which went into Alexander's conquests in considerable detail and included parentheses on pearl fishing in the Orient and the sources of Imperial Purple dye. A snail, if you are interested. As Castalius had suggested, it was long on style and short on substance. It would have taxed the patience of a saint, and the Latin of a scholar, neither of which titles I could lay claim to.

After a while, I grew more expert in separating the wheat from the chaff and was able to pick up speed. The process was hardly inspiring. The earlier volumes examined the origins of the various tribes and consisted largely of lists of meaningless names and endless peregrinations.

Even trimmed of the padding, some of Cassiodorus' 'facts' were questionable. I had not studied the origins of my ancestors with anything like the rigour he would, no doubt, have claimed. What knowledge I had was passed down to me on the knee of my mother, who early in my infancy had been happy to discover that these stories would send me rapidly to sleep. But I remembered enough to realise that Cassiodorus' account departed radically in places from the household legends that constituted our history.

Still, I suppose in the absence of reliable sources, he might have felt safer relying on his own imagination. My role was not to judge the work but to summarise it as quickly as possible.

This proved not to be quickly enough. When I arrived for my final appointment for the final volume at the regular time (Cassiodorus liked to make himself visible at court during the Emperor's afternoon audiences), I found Giorgos packing books into crates.

'Too late,' he said, hammering a nail into the textual coffin.

I turned round in panic only to find that most of the shelves had already been plucked bare.

'I don't need long,' I insisted. 'You unpack it, I can more or less do the business on the spot.'

I had got that good at it.

He shook his head, a tight smile on his face.

'Already gone, that batch. Going to have to do some explaining as why this one's not with the rest,' he said, taking the penultimate volume from my hands.

'Gone where?'

'Some monastery. *Vivarium*,' he replied looking at the freight order.

'And where in the name of Saba would that be?'

He gave me a suspicious look.

'Wasn't he a Gothic saint? Arian, to boot.'

'And recognised as a martyr by the Holy Orthodox church,' I replied. 'To boot.'

There was no sense in complicating the issue. True, I had passed through the whole spectrum of belief myself. From pagan to Arian to Orthodox. But pointing this out would not have helped matters.

Giorgos continued to examine my face. Fortunately, it gave little away. By some fluke of my ancestry, I had the dark sallow features of a Greek or Italian rather than the florid fairness of a Goth.

'Land of the Brutti,' he said at length.

'Italy?'

'Deep south.'

'And what, in the name of... all that's holy, are they going to be doing there?'

He nodded his head at the cases that were scattered across the floor.

'Same as the rest of these. Donation to the monastery's library.'

Lucky library, I thought. It would end up being as well-endowed as any in Christendom.

'And what exactly has the monastery done to deserve such a display of largesse?' I asked.

Giorgos shrugged.

'I just do what I'm told.' He corrected himself. 'Asked.'

'And your patron himself?'

'Doing the rounds somewhere or other. Checking on his estates probably.'

'Free at last?'

'On his parole. *Furlough*, he called it. No longer confined to Constantinople, at least.'

Well, as long as he hadn't gone in the same direction as his books, there was still hope for me.

'Left you here then? Surplus to requirements?' I couldn't resist the dig.

He looked at me with puppy-eyes of aggrieved abandonment.

'You have no idea of the responsibility, the honour bestowed.'

I did, actually. Dog-eyes was left minding the house. As for me, I would be heading on the next ship to Brundisium. With a bit of luck, this fishpond of a monastery would not be too far from my new benefice.

*

Which it wasn't, of course. Not too far, that is.

And this was how I ended up having to write a history of my own people, whom I strove to despise, for a degenerate, whom I had little difficulty despising.

Not without some parting words of wisdom from the degenerate, it goes without saying. I made the mistake of dropping in to tell him I was leaving and why. I hoped in this way to forestall any visits from his Bruttian colleagues on my arrival in Italy.

As I took my leave, he put down the books he was holding and gave me an earnest look.

'You know, this is really a great opportunity I'm giving you here.'

I assumed he was referring to the possibility I might be able to retain all of my limbs in working order. So I returned his look with an earnestness all of my own.

'I know lots of struggling writers that'd give their eye teeth for such a chance.'

Interesting, I thought. Now we were on to dentistry as an incentive. It made a change from dismemberment.

'Source material you've got at your disposal, you should be writing a best-seller,' he explained.

Regardless of the fact that it wasn't in the least at my disposal. Which was why I had wasted the last few weeks tracking it down, and was now leaving the country to complete the task. Still, the thought was an attractive one.

'You mean, I get a cut?' I replied, regretting immediately my choice of words.

Castalius' mouth twitched at the edges and I heard a guffaw from the shadows. I turned and saw the two colossi playing *ludus* in the corner to the accompaniment of a jug of wine.

'What do take me for, Excellency?' the bookseller asked.

This was the first time I had been addressed by my new title. I felt a glow of gratification.

'Of course,' he continued, 'you'd have to make use of some of the tricks of the trade to spice up your material a little.'

I gave a sigh. I could see what was coming.

'I've already written most of it,' I replied.

'But it's Theo that the public are really going to go for.'

'How so?' I asked. The last volume of the *History* was apparently devoted to Theodoric the Ostrogoth, who despite his heretical beliefs and barbarian origins, had at the end of the last century usurped power in Italy. As far as I was aware, his name had not so far been tainted by scandal beyond that of his origins and beliefs. Indeed, Justinian's excuse for invading the country had been to restore his line, rather than expunge it. Theodoric's daughter and legitimate heir had met an untimely end in a bathtub, as I recalled. A double indecency, which had no doubt moved the Emperor to tears.

'Put it this way,' Castalius explained. 'Look on it as a win-win situation. Win One: The more incest, bestiality and virgin sacrifices there are, the more happy readers there are going to be. Butchering babies also goes down well, by the way.'

I fought an urge to comment on the marvels of the modern digestive system, and asked instead:

'And Win Two?'

'The more you blacken Theo's name, the less likely the Emperor is going to proscribe the work.'

'I thought that proscription was taken for granted,' I said. Indeed, I had thought it was designed as a spur to sales.

'Two kinds of proscription,' he replied. 'One: The wholesale extirpation of all known copies and the hanging, drawing and quartering of the poor bastards responsible.'

I gave a shudder.

'Two: The going-through-the-motions kind of proscription of immoral works that serve the Imperial purpose, and so are conveniently ignored.'

My scepticism must have been obvious. He gave me a quizzical look.

'The Ostrogoth King won't have been an angel you know,' he continued. 'Angels don't get to rule kingdoms.'

This was hardly perceptive. The East was at present ruled by a ruthless peasant with delusions of intellectual grandeur, and widower to a retired circus performer and courtesan. To put it politely. I had heard more salacious stories about Theodora's background. God bless and save her soul. Of course.

Again Castalius read my thoughts.

'The Right Royals prove my point, don't they?'

Another guffaw from the shadows and a pause for thought from the boss.

'If it's all too much for you, besmirching the reputation of a fellow Goth,' again the penumbral chuckle, 'a good mystery always sells well.'

'A mystery,' I repeated dumbly.

'A mystery. A puzzle. Something that can't be explained until a solution is discovered.'

'Like "Prior Discovered to be Behind Nun's Virgin Birth!"', I suggested. There were scandal sheets that specialised in this kind of poppycock. Or so I had heard.

Castalius grinned.

'Something along those lines would do perfectly,' he said.

*

Once again, I browsed through the open shelves of Vivarium's library in search of Cassiodorus' *History*. More in hope than expectation. I suspected that at least the final volume would be found, if anywhere, amongst what Basilius called the 'closed stacks'. I would have to take up the matter with the abbot if I found nothing here. Perhaps I could practise on Basilius some of the persuasive techniques I had picked up from Castalius.

For the moment, I contented myself with looking through the shelves again to see if I could find any texts that would help me on my way until I located the missing volume. My eye fastened on a set of volumes by Ennodius, included one called *A Panegyric on the Rule of the Blessed Theodoric*. I was surprised by the title. The little I knew of the late bishop suggested he was ultra-Orthodox and no lover of heretics, whether they be kings or not. But a brief leaf through the book was enough to convince me that his purpose had not been satiric. Indeed, a sense of irony was conspicuous by its absence. The eulogy was effusive to the point of boot-licking. Still, I decided it would serve the purpose.

Just as I was about to leave the library in the company of the blessed Ennodius and return to my cell, I noticed a copy of Ovid's *Meta-morphoses*. And again I was struck by the broad-mindedness of the Master of Vivarium. After all, the stories had found their way onto Justinian's Index of proscribed works.

When I first began to learn Classical Latin, his version of the myths had given me much guilty pleasure. Now I was not so sure I approved. But recalling Owen's orgiastic slumber, I flicked through the pages of the work again. I was immediately reassured. The text had been ruthlessly expurgated. Which, it must be admitted, had resulted in some absurdities. Apollo's pursuit of Daphne, for example, was not resolved by her transformation into a laurel bush, but rather by her converting him to a life of monasticism and sexual abstinence. I recalled the abbot was looking forward to new and better translators and smiled to myself.

Replacing the corrupt text, I picked up the Ennodius and headed back to my room, looking forward to seeing what information on Theodoric I could thresh free from the chaff of flattery.

My luck was out. Owen had woken up and made it obvious he was in need of company.

'Worried, I was,' he said, stretching his arms and yawning without raising himself from the floor. 'Honest, guv. Wondered where you'd got to.'

'I'm touched by your concern,' I replied. 'But I think I have learnt to look after myself.'

'Yeah, right. I'd forgotten you'd been in the goon squad.'

'I take it you mean the Imperial Auxiliary Forces.'

'Right, yeah. But now you're a gentleman and a scholar, entcha?'

'The life of a cleric is not incompatible with a military background, as far as I know,' I said, although I could not, for the life of me, think of any other examples.

Owen chuckled.

'A paradox. That's the word, innit?'

I frowned, having no idea what he was getting at. Not for the first time admittedly, although I was surprised he was familiar with the term.

'A contradiction in terms?'

'Military intelligence. Geddit?'

I smiled, in spite of myself. I should not have done. Thus encouraged, Owen continued:

'Thing is, I'm bored.'

'Perhaps it's time to better your mind.'

He gave a good-natured chuckle.

'Too late for that, innit.'

'It's never too late to improve yourself.'

'Mmm.' He thought it over. 'What're you up to, yourself.'

'What I came here for. Finishing my history.'

I had not explained the purpose of my mission before, having assumed he would not be interested.

'Interesting, izzit?'

'That remains to be seen.'

He gave me a knowing look.

'Not decided how to wrap it all up, then?'

'I've yet to find out how it finishes. But I'm dealing with the real world, not the imaginary one. So the ending is not my choice.'

'Seems to me there are as many real worlds as there are unreal ones. Depends who you talk to, dunnit?'

At this, he stretched out again and went back to sleep, obviously exhausted by the intellectual effort. He left me wondering whether my man was wiser than he appeared. It would not be difficult.

I studied him, more closely this time, as he slept. There was little evidence either way now that he had his eyes closed. At rest, he could have passed for a Goth. He was a little shorter than the average. But his arms and legs were solid muscle and sinew, and his hair was of the flaxen colour more common to the race than my own darker plumage.

A fine specimen, then. I expect he would have made a good soldier, if only he could have learnt to take orders. A failing of barbarians in general. Had they been able to follow a single and unified command, they would have overrun the Eastern Empire as well as the West by now.

I muttered a prayer of thanks for this racial flaw and a further prayer that the defect had clearly extended to the character of Theodoric himself.

Illumination the First
The Two Theodorics

AD 478,
ca. 70 years earlier

The young king of the Amal Goths stifled a sigh as Pitzias pressed him on the subject once again.

'The trust is sacred, General,' Theodoric explained once again.

Pitzias held out his arms in frustration.

'Trust must be mutual to be sacred, Lord,' he insisted. 'Besides,' he nodded towards the rear, where the Folk had encamped, 'your most sacred trust is to your own people.'

Theodoric took the point. Both of them.

Zeno was a slimy bastard, for sure, even for an Emperor. But a sure way of forfeiting what little trust he had invested in the Goth king, along with any hopes of advancement, would be for Theodoric to seek peace with the man he had been ordered to destroy. A man that bore the same name as himself.

On the other hand....

He looked across the river and up at the mountain where the Others had pitched their tents. The position was too far away to make out exactly how many they were. But the two armies, and their families, looked evenly matched. Even if the Amal came out victors, their strength would be much reduced. He turned to look behind him at his own people's camp. Wagon-rings round the camp fires. Squat figures hunched against the cold. The distant murmur of hushed conversation, like mosquitos round a pond.

How many of those would be innocent victims of his pledge to Zeno, Emperor of the East? And of the West by now, for all Theodoric knew.

He gave a shudder and pulled the furs closer round his neck. Then noticed a young woman suckling a baby. This child was the future. If there was a future.

Still, he had sworn an oath before the slimy bastard.

'I'm afraid...,' he began, before he was interrupted by the sound of war-whoops from the slopes on the other side of the river.

Not again.

Theodoric Strabo was galloping down the mountain with a small escort, hallooing as he rode. The sound was echoed by the warriors left behind, who raised their axes and swords above their heads as they shouted.

'The Squinter' had reached the floor of the valley now. Late spring and the river was in full melt-flood, the brown water wild-churning, and hurling claws over the walls of the narrow bridge. Every now and then, it threw a tree-trunk at the parapets as if trying to lever out what it couldn't dislodge by main force.

But the Romans certainly knew how to build. Centuries of this kind of treatment and the construction still stood firm.

Theodoric waited for what he knew would come next.

Sure enough, Strabo and his party crossed the bridge, then made for the line of outposts Theodoric had installed. Nothing so grand as a stockade. Just a series of sentries at random intervals, behind which the mass of the men and their families were camped.

Strabo had reached the far end of the line now and the whoops were giving way to intelligible words.

'Hungry, are you?' he shouted. 'So are we!'

'Cold, are you? We're freezing our fucking arses off up there!'

The group slowed to a canter so that the words would carry the better.

'Fight, would you?' He swung round in his saddle and held out an arm towards the other side of the river. 'Well, we're ready for you.'

Now the party came face to face with Theodoric and his officers. Always keeping out of spear-cast. Since the taunting sessions had started, Theodoric had thought of trying to outflank them and cut off their retreat. But Strabo was no fool. He was saddle-steady and his horse was swift.

This time Strabo stopped when he was level with the young king. Theodoric wondered if this was a prelude to a challenge to single combat. It would be an honourable solution to the impasse and one that he would be bound to accept, even if he knew he would lose. The other was battle-seasoned over many years; the young Amal king only sap-green.

But Strabo just fixed him with his eyes while he continued his harangue.

'Where's the sense? We're all Goths. Why should we be killing each other when we could make common cause?'

Theodoric could have sworn the Squinter winked at him. But the squint and the distance between them made it difficult to know for sure. What was easier to make out was the growling that could be heard from the ranks of wagons behind him.

'Good,' thought Theodoric. 'They're not taken in by this nonsense.'

But as the growling grew, it became clearer that it was aimed at him rather than Strabo.

The king shifted in his saddle and listened for murmurs of discontent closer to him.

Nothing.

His own commanders were staying loyal for now. But he wondered for how long. He glanced to his side. Pitzias was scowling at the marauder. Some of the others seemed less convinced. Theudis, his sword-bearer, was, as usual, smiling.

Strabo gazed at him one last time, then raised a spear and whooped again, then moved on along the rest of the line.

What would you call this? Theodoric wondered, as he watched the riders disappear back over the bridge. Some kind of mind-war? He'd never seen anything like it before, but was forced to admit it had its uses. And its effect.

For Strabo was right. The Amal had been camped here for a three days now. They couldn't go forward, and Theodoric dared not go back. The wind bitter-blew down the valley. And they were running short of both food and fuel in this barren country.

*

The night was quite moonless. Theodoric was left guessing what the movements of the enemy might be.

Nothing dramatic, in any case. The echoes would have carried across the valley. There were also ancient strictures against night-fight that had survived the conversion to Christianity. Not that any Goth had anything against fighting. But no Goth wished his soul to be lost to the darkness.

He blew into his hands to warm them and watched as the wind took his breath. It came from the North-East. That explained the bitterness of the cold and the clearness of the sky. In all likelihood, the next day would be bright and crisp too. Much good that would do them.

He took one last look up at the stars. Their light was the greater for the lack of moon, and had allowed him to check the line of sentries without the need for a torch.

Not for the first time, Theodoric wondered if each flicker-flash was the soul of a fallen warrior. He liked the thought. It made more sense than Christianity did, even if – officially – followed the adopted Arian

Christianity of his people. Star-souls would make the great vault of the sky into the canopy of Valhalla.

Cheered by the thought, he made for the wagon-ring that contained his own family and their campground. He threaded his way between the shafts of the carts and the tethered mules, coming closer to the fire that was the heart of each bivouac. As he leant to kiss her head, his mother looked up and gave him a worried smile. He had made no noise, but she always seemed to sense when he was near. She shifted her position slightly, shaping a gap for him to sit, then patted the blanket that lay on the ground for him to sit.

'The children?' he asked as he stooped.

Eusebia nodded towards the other side of the fire, where his sisters, Amalafrida and Amalasuentha, leaned and dozed over their young charges. The children's mother, Theodoric's consort, had died delivering the younger of the two girls, and his sisters had been glad to take over their care.

The king stretched out his legs to get his feet closer to the fire. The movement roused his younger brother. Theudimund shook a drowsy head and stared about him in confusion. Eventually he focused on Theodoric.

'Just you, then,' he said.

'Just me,' his brother agreed. 'And just Erelieva awake.'

His mother poked him in the ribs. She hated being called by her pagan name.

'And just as well somebody is,' she said. 'Fine sentry your brother turned out to be.'

Theudimund gave a sheepish look. His brother tousled his head.

'Just as well we've got other sentries posted then,' Theodoric said. 'More experienced ones.'

Theudimund's embarrassment gave way to shame.

'Sorry,' he mumbled.

'No worry,' his brother replied.

'Glad you think so,' Eusebia said.

Theodoric grunted. He knew what was coming. They'd been through this the previous night. And the night before that.

'The wall-eyed one's making a donkey out of you,' his mother began.

'He'll laugh the other side of his face when the Imperial troops turn up,' Theodoric said.

'You don't really believe they will.'

Theodoric grunted again. He didn't. Zeno had promised thousands of reinforcements at various stages of his journey here. Not a single troop had shown up.

'Strabo's not the only one.' Eusebia piled on the agony.

'Humph?'

'Everyone's taking you for a fool. Even your own folk.'

Theodoric shifted his arse on the blanket.

'Not that bad surely?'

'You're not around to hear what they're saying,' Eusebia said. 'Up there on your high horse with your fine generals.'

Theodoric looked over at his brother. The boy was still in his early teens and spent his days in camp, seeing to the needs of the women, the children, the aged.

'That bad?' Theodoric asked him.

'That bad,' Theudimund nodded.

'It's not just that he rides up almost to within a javelin cast and throws insults at you,' Eusebia said. 'It's that he's right.'

Another grunt.

'Why should we fight against each other? His people are of the Folk too. And the Folk know how to keep the word,' Eusebia persisted.

'You can't know that,' replied Theodoric quickly. 'I'd trust him as far as I could cast a javelin.'

'Well, that would solve the problem,' Eusebia pointed out.

Theodoric smiled. They had tried that the first time Strabo had come on his rounds. The man seemed to have an exact idea how far an arm could throw a spear.

'Fact is, Ma's got a point,' Theudimund said. 'The Emperor hasn't kept his side of the bargain.'

'And that releases you from your pledge,' Eusebia added.

Theodoric sighed. For 'that' didn't save him from losing face.

'It doesn't work so,' he said. 'Once it gets around that I'm not a man of my word, then the game's up with me. With us,' he added after a pause.

Eusebia gave him a scornful look.

'Nobody is to be trusted in these dark days. And everybody knows that. Your father....'

'Is dead,' Theodoric interrupted her.

'The Folk chose you only because you are his son. And they can unchoose you when they like.'

Theodoric looked up at her sharply.

'We can't just stay here forever,' she said, her tone now pleading. 'It's a question of whether we starve first, or freeze.'

'And so…?'

'You need to make a decision. Before your own people turn against you.'

Theodoric took a deep breath.

'Very well, then,' he said, flicking his cloak over his shoulder as he lay down. 'Tomorrow we attack.'

Eusebia, for want of alternatives, glared at her younger son.

Theudimund glared at the ground.

*

'We attack at first light?!' Pitzias echoed. He tugged at a greying beard-braid. Each braid was a battle fought and won. There were many braids. Theodoric rubbed his own beard. It was not even long enough to plait.

'The men are all drawn up and ready, I take it?' he asked the other general.

Mammo nodded, but also looked uncertain.

'Lord. And the wagons removed, along with the families, to the mouth of the pass,' he said.

'So we are all ready, then.' This time it was not a question.

'Ready to die,' Pitzias snorted.

He pointed towards the narrow stone bridge ahead of them, ghostly and barely visible in the starlight.

'There's no way we can get enough men across to form a shield-wall before the enemy is upon us. We'll be massacred to a man.'

Theodoric flushed. He understood the argument, but his mind was made up. There would be an end to the waiting. If the worst came to the worst, then the remnants of his army and people could join forces with Strabo. But he knew he would not be among them.

He turned to the shorter of the two generals, a bald man with eyes that rarely settled on anything or anyone for long. Theodoric did not trust hairless men. But he had no choice. He did not trust Strabo either.

'Count Mammo.'

'Lord?'

'I want you to take your men downriver.' Theodoric pointed in the direction intended.

'What nonsense is this? Pitzias demanded. 'If you detach such a large number from the main body, you reduce our chances even more.'

Theodoric gave him a weary look. He had not been able to sleep during the night.

'Count Mammo?'

Mammo dutifully looked downstream.

'Towards the mountain the Squinter's folk are camped out on?' he asked.

Theodoric nodded.

'Just so.'

'We scouted the area thoroughly,' Pitzias said. 'There's no trace of a ford down there. Not with the river in full spate. And I can guarantee that Strabo knows this as well as we do.'

'A diversionary tactic, Lord Pitzias. I'm sure you've heard of them. Even if he has scouted further downstream, this will be enough to sow a seed of doubt in his mind. There's bound to be a ford or bridge somewhere down there.'

Pitzias flushed crimson. He spoke as if he were being choked.

'If Mammo continues all the way to the Thracian coast, then I'm sure we'll be able to outflank the enemy. But by then the rest of us will be dead.'

Theodoric stiffened.

'Am I to take that as an incitement to mutiny, Pitzias?'

'You can take it as an invitation to stick it up your….'

Theudis interrupted.

'Theo. Look. Yonder!'

The first gleams of dawn had arrived and it was just possible to make out the blurred outline of a man down by the bridge. On a horse. With a white cloth tied to a lance.

'Strabo?' Theodoric wondered aloud.

'The very same, by the look of it,' Mammo said.

'If I may make so bold,' Pitzias said, his voice heavy with irony, 'I suggest you take up the invitation.'

Theodoric's face darkened.

'It can do no harm,' Mammo added in a milder voice.

'It could be a trick,' Theodoric said.

Pitzias tugged a braid and lifted his chin.

'He's a Goth. A white flag is as good as his word.'

'As the Emperor pointed out, his word is not worth so very much. That is, after all, why we are here,' Theodoric said.

Pitzias sighed and gave a shrug of his shoulders.

'Then we should prepare to die then.' He crossed himself and turned his horse to retreat to the line of warriors. Theodoric looked over at the figure of Strabo again. The warlord was holding the lance upright – one end planted in the ground, the flag fluttering from the other.

Mammo stood his ground, bowed his head.

'Lord,' he said. 'If *I* may make so bold….'

Theodoric turned towards him.

Mammo let the sleeve of his tunic fall loose. Suddenly a long thin knife appeared in his hand.

'It is tipped with belladonna, Majesty.'

Theodoric's eyebrows shot up. He had wondered why Mammo favoured the long flowing sleeves of a woman's robes.

'A precaution, solely,' Mammo smiled feebly, still not looking Theodoric in the eye. 'And perhaps, after all, preferable to a waste of life.'

Theodoric wondered whose life was being referred to.

'If I am to die, dear Count, I shall choose to die so with no stain on my name,' he said, turning his horse's head towards the bridge and giving spur.

The Count's words had acted as a goad on him too. He was, after all, King of the Amal. Mammo had served to remind him at least that that his first responsibility was to his own folk. The Emperor came in a distant second.

*

Theodoric brought his horse to a halt on his side of the bridge, as Strabo had done on his own. The Squinter walked his horse onto the middle and waited as the king did the same.

It was the first time Theodoric had got a good look at his namesake. When the horsebreath-mist cleared, he saw a man about his own size, but about ten years his senior. Or so he guessed. Strabo could have been older still given the lines on his face and the scars that crossed them. He wore a patchwork of leathers and furs: the furs were the colour of his hair, the leathers the texture of his skin. The cast in his eye wasn't so severe. The other eye seemed to transfix Theodoric like a bodkin through calf-hide.

Strabo leaned forward on his horse's mane, and tilted the pennanted lance towards the ground. He grinned.

'Cold, ain't it?' he said in Gothic.

Theodoric gave a shallow nod, and looked down at the horse's hooves, where water was lapping over the parapet and across.

'Question is,' Strabo continued, whether you're colder from riding over. Or me from having to wait half a bloody hour for you to come up and join me.'

Theodoric remained silent.

'Of course, I forgot. We haven't been introduced,' Strabo said.

'You know who I am,' Theodoric said in Greek.

'Remind me.' Strabo persisted in the Gothic.

'Theodoric, son of Theodemir. King of all the Amal.'

Strabo chuckled.

'You got balls, son. I'll give you that. Perhaps we could throw dice for the title.' He bowed his head and swept his arm across his body.

'Theodoric, son of Triarius. King of the rest of the Amal,' pointing to the rest behind his back. 'Well, most of them anyhow. There are a lot of us. Kings of the Amal, that is.'

Theodoric raised an eyebrow.

'Triarius? But I'd heard....'

'Well, you probably heard right. Norbert really. Cattle rustler and sheep-shagger extraordinary. When he wasn't shagging my ma, that is. I thought Triarius sounded posher.'

He grinned again.

'Won't tell anyone, will you?'

Theodoric shuffled in his saddle. Strabo was right. It was cold.

'*Quo usque tandem abutere patientia nostra*?' Theodoric quoted, cold-peevish.

'Latin, is it now? Quite the polyglot, aren't we?'

Strabo scratched his chin.

'Let me guess. Cicero, right?'

Theodoric nodded.

'To the effect that you're in a hurry to get down to business, right?'

Another nod.

'But you want to impress me first with what you picked up during your schooling in Constantinople.'

He held out his arms as if in surrender.

'I confess. I'm impressed.'

Theodoric nodded. But he was greatly taken aback that the roughneck opposite him had identified the Latin quote.

'It'd be even more impressive if you could speak Gothic as well,' Strabo continued.

Theodoric flushed.

'As you please,' he replied in that tongue.

'You see, you should never forget where you came from, son of Theodemir. Nor who you represent, Theuderiks.'

Theodoric turned a deeper red at the reminder of his Gothic name. And what it meant – leader of the people.

'Besides,' Strabo continued, 'you don't want to pick up bad habits.'

'Bad habits?'

'Greek habits.'

'Like schooling?' Theodoric asked with a sneer.

'Like breaking your word.'

Theodoric sat upright in his saddle.

'I was not aware I had done so.'

'Plenty of time to learn, sunshine. Just let Emperor Zeno the Magnificent keep bending your ear.'

'I'm not sure I get your drift.'

'What did he promise you for rubbing me out?'

Theodoric looked blank.

'For getting rid of me,' Strabo explained.

Theodoric gave a smug smile.

'He's already rewarded me with your previous position.'

'*Magister militum*, is it? Master of the Soldiers? *Strategos*? What title did he come up with this time?'

Strabo hawked and spat over the parapet.

Theodoric flushed red.

'All of the above?' Strabo asked again. 'And probably some land for your folk to farm? And then an annual handout to help you settle in nicely?'

The red of Theodoric's cheeks deepened.

Strabo spat into the river again.

'Fucker. Another quote for you. "Beware of Greeks bearing gifts."'

Theodoric had to swallow hard before he could speak.

'He promised you the same, I take it.'

'Many times. Latest, if I managed to get rid of you.'

The red in Theodoric's face turned to ash-grey as Strabo cocked his arm and produced a dagger from his sleeve.

Strabo grinned and tapped the knife against his wrist.

'You see what they don't understand, or what they've forgotten....'

'They?'

'The Romans. Or Greeks. Whatever they call themselves now.'

'Is what?'

'The value of keeping your word.'

Theodoric glanced back over his shoulder, and wondered briefly if he should have followed Mammo's advice and brought a concealed weapon of his own.

'To Zeno, you mean? To "rub *me* out"?'

Strabo chuckled.

'You don't quite get my drift. Again,' he said. Then he pulled the blade of the knife across his open palm and held it up for Theodoric to see.

'No poison, see. But a bond – soon as you do the same and we join as brothers.'

'Against Rome?'

'Against Zeno.'

Theodoric considered his options and what would happen if he refused. He held out his own hand palm up. The two Goths then joined hands in blood.

'"United we stand",' Strabo whispered in Theodoric's ear, as he raised their joined hands. They looked each at their own bands. A cheer and clash of swords went up all round the valley. 'Quote: Aesop.'

'And "Divided we fall",' Theodoric thought. He looked into Strabo's eyes as a confirmation of the new trust between them.

The cast in the other's eyes seemed more noticeable now. The one was fixed firmly on Theodoric's face, the other roamed into space behind him.

As Theodoric was riding back to his lines, he heard Strabo calling him one last time. He turned in his saddle to hear what the Squinter was saying.

'Another quote for you. *Fide nemini*.' He chuckled. 'Trust no-one, young Theo.'

Theodoric nodded.

'Except for me, that is,' Strabo added with a laugh.

Theodoric spurred his horse forward.

'Including you, I rather think,' he muttered.

Greek Hay

Whoso calm, serene, sedate,
Sets his foot on haughty fate;
Firm and steadfast, come what will,
Keeps his mien unconquered still;
Boethius

I closed the book, leaned back in my chair and heaved a sigh.

It was only to be expected, I supposed. Panegyrics are not designed to be read as histories. Rather they aim to please those to whom they are addressed, and, I suppose, to advance one's own position in the pecking order. By those lights, I expect it was successful. Ennodius, as far as I knew, had continued his climb up the ecclesiastical ladder. And if I had been Theodoric, I imagine I would have been mightily pleased. Not being Theodoric, however, I felt mildly nauseated.

I flicked open the volume again and glanced at the preface.

'The year of Our Lord 507.'

Still fairly early in Theodoric's 'reign', then. Otherwise you would never have known. There were plenty of battles mentioned, but no indication of when, and little of where they took place. More space was devoted to the virtues of the man who triumphed than the means by which he did so.

Similarly, Ennodius praised Theodoric for having brought peace, prosperity and justice back to Italy, but did not mention how. In any case, I suspected I should take these claims with a pinch of salt, given the nature of the exercise. A panegyric would hardly point out the defects of rule or ruler.

For example, Ennodius made no mention of the way that Theodoric dispensed with the services of Odovacar, the previous barbarian ruler of Italy. This was one of the many features of Theodoric's rule that had achieved notoriety, and thus passed into common folklore.

As for the style, it made Cassiodorus' history seem a model of frugality. At least Cassiodorus' verbal acrobatics showed some sign of imagination. Ennodius wrote as though he were filling in the spaces in a census.

To make something of this as a historical source I would need to pay the closest attention in order to find the grains of fact within the midden of verbiage. And to render the result a coherent and gripping narrative, I would need to perform an act of imagination equal to one of Cassiodorus' digressions into horticulture.

Still, the occasional crumb was interesting and instructive. I had no idea, for instance, that Theodoric was educated at Constantinople during his period of captivity there as boy-hostage. On the contrary, I had always assumed him to be 'agrammatus'. Nor was this just an ignorant guess on my part. Even today in the Eastern capital, the Gothic king remained a byword for boorish illiteracy. Anecdotes about him signing his name with a stamp or stencil still did the rounds in the marketplaces. I had even heard customers telling street traders their name was not Theodoric, when the vendor deliberately made a mistake in totting up the bill.

I wondered how the rumour started. That it was only a rumour, I was convinced. Ennodius clearly lacked the fantasy to have made it up. Still, the extent of Theodoric's education was moot. An ape can be taught to dance without achieving a sense of rhythm. And a parrot can be trained to speak without attaining conversational skills.

Withal, the sooner I located the missing volume the better. At least there was a certain perverse pleasure to be found in reading Cassiodorus' imaginative absurdities. This so-called panegyric was just plain self-serving vacuity. And as such, it could not be trusted.

*

But first there was matter of food. The rumbling of my stomach almost drowned out the sound of Owen's snores. As luck would have it, the bell rang for dinner at just the right moment. My gastric juices had started to ferment, triggered perhaps by the odours of something vaguely organic coming from the direction of the kitchen.

I kicked my servant awake and made for the hall. Somehow, despite my head-start, Owen contrived to reach the refectory before me.

At least he had the grace to make space for me by using his buttocks to shift the monk next to him farther along the bench. Even so I still wasn't sure if it was becoming of a master to dine in public with his servant. I looked around in vain for Basilius and better company. In the end, I took up the place he had created for me and sat opposite and next to a pair of monks who looked as though they would have been more at home in a barracks than in a monastic retreat. This made me feel better about any possible breach of protocol. When I myself had served in the army, I had never stood on ceremony but chosen, as the best officers always did, to eat with their men.

I nodded to the monk opposite me – a giant of a man with a high forehead and a lower half to his face that looked as if it had been compressed into too small a space. The jaw, the chin and the mouth seemed to form a single line.

He introduced himself as Brother Uldin, and the monk to my right as Brother Arminius. I turned to acknowledge the latter and found myself looking at another large man, the skin stretched so tight across his face and arms that it reflected the light from the oil lamps. Both barbarians then – Uldin a Hun obviously; Arminius, I would guess, some variety of German.

*

I had to admit I was hungry. But on the basis of our previous meals, I had not expected my palate to be tickled by the food on offer. Nonetheless, as a pair of monks came in bearing trays covered with dishes that contained what looked like the usual swill, my nose picked up an exotic aroma of herbs and spices. Cumin was there definitely. Perhaps sage too. But there was something else, deep and pungent, that triggered my gastric juices and filled me, inexplicably, with a sense of melancholy.

The sadness did not affect my appetite, however, and I wasted no time when a dish was set in front of me. My sense of smell had not deceived me. The stew was delicious. Apart from the spices, the ingredients were simple enough – the usual root vegetables that were staple during the winter, along with some scattering of cereal. Barley, I would guess. But the whole dish was transformed into a sensory experience by the subtle interaction of the spices.

It was difficult for me to restrain myself from shovelling the food down my throat as quickly as hands and mouth could operate. But I realised the moment was one to be savoured. Whoever had put this meal together had had nothing to do with the previous hogwash we had been served. So the Lord only knew when we would get something as good again.

Between mouthfuls, I closed my eyes and tried to extract the utmost flavour out of every mouthful before taking the next. When I opened them again, I noticed that a monk with long greying hair and beard had seated himself next to Brother Uldin, who was sucking the food into his mouth with a slurping sound.

The newcomer looked at me with interest and appreciation through what appeared to be the bottom of glass bottles – thick enough to make his eyes seem enormous. The glass was held in place by pieces of metal filament.

I nodded to him, and then at the food.

'Your creation?' I asked.

He nodded back.

'A work of art,' I said.

'We aim to please.'

I swirled my spoon round the bowl.

'Cumin, I am sure.'

He nodded.

'A touch of sage, I think?'

Another nod.

'But something more. A profound wistful flavour.'

The smile broadened.

'I have never heard it described that way before. You capture it well.'

'And I have never tasted it before. Of that I am sure.'

'*Faenum graecum*,' he explained.

Not that the explanation made me any the wiser. Greek hay, indeed? That hardly did justice to the sweet nutty flavour.

'A local herb, then?' I asked, thinking 'Greek'.

'A little farther east. It is common enough in my homeland.'

I raised an eyebrow.

'The Holy Land?' I suggested, thinking 'Hebrew'.

He inclined his head.

'I cultivate the plant here, in the garden of the monastery. In this you have the dried seeds. But the leaves also make an excellent herb and salad.'

I had never heard of nor come across a son of Moses that cooked for Christians before. I gave my plate a suspicious look.

'Brother Josephus,' he said by way of introduction. 'A convert of sorts, you could say.'

This place was taking on a more bizarre aspect by the minute.

I looked around quickly for more congenial company. Still no sign of the abbot. Owen perhaps sensed my unease. He gave me a grin, then spoke my thoughts.

'Boss not around then?' he asked his neighbours.

Brother Arminius laughed from somewhere deep in his belly. Uldin chuckled.

'I fancy that none of us have ever actually seen him,' Josephus explained, glancing round at the rest as if for confirmation.

I gazed blankly at him and wondered if I had wandered into an asylum for the insane. Surely all these monks had been here when Basilius ate with us last.

'I think Brother Isidorus has been here longest?' the Jew went on.

He nodded further down the table towards a squat hunchbacked figure who was studying his food as if trying to locate it. The monk next to him gave him a nudge.

'Did you ever see our sainted Master?' Josephus asked with the faintest trace of irony.

I gave a silent sigh of relief. They were talking about the invisible Master of the monastery.

As I was working this out, Isidorus was shaking his head. Then he returned to the study of his dinner.

'I think my manservant was referring to the Abbot and not the Master,' I explained.

'Speak for yourself,' Owen interjected. 'I know what I meant.'

I ignored him.

'Have any of you any idea where Father Basilius may be?'

Uldin gave a derisive snort and winked across at Arminius. The latter winked back and wiggled his buttocks on the bench so they nestled against mine. I pulled away with difficulty and found my own now in uncomfortably close proximity to those of my servant. He grinned, then gave me a wink himself.

Again it was Josephus that obliged by answering my question.

'Friday is the day for the Father Abbot's fasting and self-mortification,' he said.

'Mortification is it?' Uldin asked and made a crude gesture with his fist.

A peal of delighted laughter came from a figure on my side of the table whose identity was obscured by the bulk of Arminius. I leant forward and saw the young monk that had earlier been labouring to transcribe text in the *scriptorium*. He was mimicking Uldin's gesture.

'Don't get too excited, Anacreon,' Josephus said. '"Mortification". Not the other one.'

'Brother Anacreon does enjoy his little joke,' he went on, 'even if his sense of humour is somewhat on the youthful side.'

I turned to Uldin.

'In all the monastic establishments I have previously visited,' (all two of them, I reflected), 'obedience to and respect for the Father Superior is one of the dominant rules.'

The Hun snorted.

'In my rulebook, you have to earn respect,' he said.

Not a very Christian attitude, I thought.

Unexpectedly, Isidorus came to the abbot's defence.

'Indeed, as God's grace has to be earned. Through charity of mind.'

That was boldly done, even if the doctrine was a little heterodox. Isidorus was no physical match for Uldin if the Hun decided to take offence.

Fortunately, Arminius gave him a warning glance across the table. His friend shrugged and sank back into his seat.

I looked at the puckle-back with interest and wondered if he had been tainted by the teachings of Pelagius. But I was intrigued by the mystery of the missing Master.

'So none of you has actually met the Master of the Order,' I declared.

There was a mix of murmur and sidelong glances.

'Do you know what manner of man he is? I asked.

Again the room fell quiet. Arminius looked down at the plate in front of him. Uldin scowled and shuffled his feet. Josephus seemed amused. So did Owen. But then he seemed to have found the whole proceedings funny.

It was Uldin that broke the silence eventually. Inspired by the sight of his empty dish, no doubt.

'You see how we live?'

'On the charity of another?' I asked provocatively.

The Hun glared at me but was again quelled by a glance from Arminius.

'He provides for us. That is all we know, and all we need to know.'

'He gave all this over to the common good,' Isidorus agreed, gazing up at the ceiling, then round at the walls.

I followed his eyes but couldn't help feeling that it resembled nothing more than a converted stables.

'And more importantly to the contemplation of the Almighty,' Arminius added devoutly. To my amazement and disgust, I felt his hand brush my upper thigh. I looked over at him, but he seemed oblivious to the transgression.

'In the greatness of his heart and soul, he has provided us with shelter and food,' Uldin added, almost as if he were saying grace.

'And bloody good tucker it was – tonight at least,' interposed Owen suddenly with a wink at Josephus. I assumed my man was getting bored with the pious turn the talk had taken.

Everyone, it seemed, was conspiring to avoid answering my question. I decided to challenge them directly.

'So I am to take it that none of you know the Master. Do you even know his name?'

Most of the monks appeared to believe they would find the answer written on the table in front of them.

'The classic anonymous benefactor, then,' I concluded.

Anacreon gave an uncertain giggle. I supposed the words were beyond his vocabulary and he had decided to give them the benefit of his smutty doubt.

'Rather like the Christian God, wouldn't you say?' Josephus commented. He swirled the last of his bread round the edge of his plate to mop up the remains of the gravy, and with exaggerated care inserted it into his mouth.

I raised an eyebrow in question.

'Credited with all the qualities we aspire to, yet never manifesting himself in any very obvious manner.'

I raised the other eyebrow. As a convert, he clearly had much to learn. Including some respect for the Almighty. Not to mention the Master.

Uldin scowled first at the table in front of him, then at the apostate Jew.

'What the fuck are you getting at?' he demanded.

'Our Master might be God himself, for all we know,' Josephus explained.

The Hun had trouble digesting this. But he got the general idea. As for myself, I was dumbfounded. Was there an orthodox Christian to be found in the whole monastery? I wondered.

Before I could answer my own question, Uldin had overturned the table and grasped Josephus by the collar of his tunic.

Arminius reacted the quickest. He vaulted across the table and laid a restraining arm on his friend. Then leant over and whispered softly in his ear, as I have seen horse charmers do. Whatever he said, it worked. Uldin relaxed his hold on the Jew. Josephus straightened up and pulled down his sleeves. He had never stopped smiling during the whole episode. I wondered if he was deeply in love with death. If Arminius had not intervened, the burly barbarian would have crushed him like an insect.

Despite Arminius' attempt to mollify the Hun, the atmosphere was still charged with tension. The persistence of the smile on Josephus' face did not help. It rather served to reignite Uldin's fury.

But suddenly the attention of all was diverted by the entrance of new persona on the stage. At the far end of the table, a diminutive and very aged man was being helped into his place by a tall bearded figure. The smaller creature had all the appearance of an imbecile. He seemed to be incapable of motion on his own account, but allowed himself to be moulded into a suitable posture for eating by his assistant, all the time staring straight in front of him with a vacant smile upon his face.

He did not hold the attention of the other monks for long. But his presence seemed to dispel the tension, replacing it with a mixture of indulgence and contempt. Uldin exchanged a knowing smile with Arminius and relaxed his aggressive stance. Then both the Hun and German left the table for their cells. The others began to disperse too, leaving me alone with Owen, who was mopping up the leftovers from the abandoned bowls. And then there was the newcomer, of course, who I regarded with curiosity for a while before deciding eventually to return to my own room.

*

I was sitting at my desk, trying to decipher the sycophantic ramblings of Ennodius, when Owen walked in.

'Never a dull moment, eh?' he commented, throwing himself down on his mattress.

He was right, although I took less pleasure from the fact than he appeared to do. A choleric pagan. An atheistic Jew. A cretinous Greek.

And what looked like a heretical Italian. Or was he Greek too. He had a Greek name but not the accent.

'A madhouse,' I replied. 'Rather than a monastery.'

'I'm sure they're all right, really.'

'How do you come to that conclusion?' I was mystified.

'Well, no-one got killed. Hearts in the right place, then, ennit?'

I didn't answer immediately.

'More than can be said for their hands,' I grumbled eventually, thinking of Uldin's paws round the throat of Josephus.

Owen grinned.

'Arminius got you too then, diddy?'

I flushed. So that buttock-chafing and thigh-brushing was not accidental then.

'Why I moved across when you came along,' Owen added. 'Not that I minded, mind. Just wanted to spread the love a bit.'

He giggled and turned over on the mattress. Thereby signalling an end to the conversation. I turned back to my labours but could not focus my thoughts immediately.

And, to cap it all, a German sodomite, I added to my mental list of grievances.

Obviously Roman civilisation had managed to teach the Hun and the German nothing about restraining their appetites, whether for lust or for violence. I presumed they had both served in the military. But they had clearly learned little from the experience. It simply bore out my hypothesis. Barbarians were essentially uncivilisable. Theodoric's usage of Odovacar was another case in point.

They were all beyond redemption.

With a few striking exceptions, I added, again mentally. After a moment. And with all becoming modesty.

Illumination the Second
A Question of Trust

AD 493

Theodoric ran his eye down the line of dinner guests to his right. Up to a point, the tableau could have been lifted from any of a thousand banquets. The diners sat in a row with their respective cup-bearers behind them and their goblets and plates in front of them.

But there the resemblance to normality ended. Some of the guests had slumped forward onto the table top, blood pooling round their slashed necks, while their attendants wiped knives on the napkins that hung over their arms. Most irregular of all was the body that lay sprawled across the seat and the floor next to the Goth king. It appeared to be cleft from crown to pelvis.

A silence had fallen on the room – understandably enough, he supposed. It was eventually broken by Count Mammo, who emitted what sounded disturbingly like a squeal of delight.

The other leading Goths, although of necessity apprised in advance of the plan, looked on with barely concealed disgust. Again understandable, since most were splattered in blood from their fellow-diners.

The Romans that had been invited to attend, being seated at the far end, had largely escaped the bloodbath. Nonetheless, most wore expressions that conveyed emotions ranging from astonishment to terror. More than understandable. No doubt, most reckoned it would be their turn next.

With one exception.

Theodoric studied him again. The head and shoulders reminded Theodoric of busts he had seen of Julius Caesar – the high brow and even higher fringe, the aquiline nose and prominent cheekbones. This classical throwback had the temerity to look straight at the Goth king with undisguised contempt.

Theodoric could match that contempt and double it. And that contempt shared the same object. He too was filled with loathing – self-loathing. He tried to console himself with the thought that such a feeling would pass. It had been necessary, he told himself again. Though, doubtless, the carcases would have disagreed.

The silence had become unbearable. Theodoric felt compelled to break it. Nothing came to mind but for one thought that he couldn't shake off, no matter how tasteless it might be. He said it anyway – anything to break the oppressive quiet.

'The man can't have had a bone in him.'

He looked around the room hopefully. Again it was only Mammo that found the comment funny. As an icebreaker, Theodoric thought wryly, it left something to be desired.

The shaking began slowly at first, working its way from his guts and coursing its way through his torso and into his limbs. Before it reached his fingers, he grasped his sword more tightly and wiped it clean with his other hand before planting it back in its sheath.

He had to get out before the tremors became visible.

'Mammo,' he growled, 'get this place cleaned up.'

He strode towards the door with all the calm he could muster.

'And tell Count Tulum to meet me in my quarters in half an hour. With his charge.'

He sincerely hoped he could pull himself together in the interval.

*

Once back in his rooms, he made for the private latrine and, kneeling by the edge of the opening, he retched violently. There was not much to show for the effort. The slaughter had begun shortly after the meal had commenced and Theodoric had been unable to eat anything much before the mayhem. Still the spasms continued, racking his body with pain and draining him of strength, if little else.

'Trust no-one,' his namesake had said. Even if Strabo hadn't given the advice, Theodoric would not have trusted Odovacar any more than the German had trusted him. Best to get your revenge in first, then.

The convulsions eased for a moment and Theodoric leaned back against the wall, his legs sprawled out in front of him. He should be getting ready to receive Tulum, but felt he had unfinished business in the latrine. Sweat ran down his brow and coated the inside of his tunic.

He chuckled as Strabo came to mind again. The bastard had followed his own advice. In that he had been consistent, if nothing else. No sooner had the two kings made common cause than Strabo found himself courted once again by Zeno with money and position. Thus the roles had been reversed and the younger Theodoric had found himself outlawed once again.

He felt his stomach cramp again and braced himself for the next convulsion. Nothing more came of it than a hiccup and a taste of bile in his mouth. A good sign, he supposed. A turn for the better. He spat towards the opening of the latrine.

He supposed he should have felt bitter. Like the bile. But you had to hand it to them – the two devious bastards. Strabo was a slippery fuck. But Zeno was in a class of his own. Clearly the barbarians still had much to learn from Roman civilisation.

Some minutes had passed since the last spasm. He decided to risk standing up. A little giddy still. He turned to the wall and rested his forehead against the cool tile. As he did so, he heard the faintest of sounds. There, one sill of the sill of the open window, a tiny bird. Theodoric screwed up his eyes to make it out against the bright light behind.

A king's wren, with its golden crest for a crown.

The Goth king smiled. Another good sign. The bird performed a shallow dip, a curtsey almost, and then flew out again.

Theodoric made his way to the basin on the other side of the room, and looked at himself in the polished copper that hung above.

He might be a barbarian himself. But he had also learnt something, he thought, turning his mind back to the slaughter in the banqueting hall.

'Know thyself', he said aloud. He splashed water on his face. Then wiped it more thoroughly with a cloth to remove the furrows traced by the passage of sweat.

'And trust no-one'. He repeated the mantra, then added, 'not even your favourite horse.'

He laughed aloud, feeling his spirits returning.

Strabo had omitted his beloved grey from the maxim and had paid dearly. During manoeuvres, it had thrown him onto a rack of standing spears. The Squinter had died impaled on his own weapons.

Predictably enough, Zeno had once more called on the younger Theodoric to 'protect the Empire'. In effect, this took the form of a bribe designed to divert his marauding into other channels. And so the dance had begun again. When the subsidies dried up, Theo would turn his attentions back to harassing the Imperial territories, and would make feints towards Constantinople itself in the event that Zeno was late in responding.

None of this had been satisfying in the long run. Because in the long run, what Theodoric wanted most of all was land for his people – within the *limes* of the Empire. Each time, this had been the main element of the agreement with Zeno, and, each time, Zeno had reneged on this promise before all others.

In the end, Theodoric's patience had exhausted itself and he had marched to the very gates of Constantinople to press his case. The result of the negotiations marked a breach with precedent. Zeno had commissioned the Goth to deal with the usurper of the Western Empire, no doubt reasoning that this would at least remove Theodoric and his army to a safer distance. Theodoric had been aware of the motivation. But the idea suited him as well as it suited the Emperor. He would be able to distance his people from the whims of Zeno and aimed to carve out a little territory for himself.

'And here we all are, then,' Theodoric said, grimacing at the mirror. He dipped a finger into a bowl and rubbed the soap up and down his teeth and gums. Tasted like shit, but might disguise the hog-breath. He spat and drew himself upright again. Swept back his hair and practised a statesmanlike pose or two. In profile, then full face.

Feeling a little more like his usual self, Theodoric allowed himself a moment of fleeting sympathy for the bisected corpse in the hall. Really, Odovacar had done little to incur the Eastern Emperor's displeasure. The last in a long line of barbarian generals to wield the true power behind the Western throne, Odovacar had simply dispensed with the formalities, shunted the last 'Emperor' aside to God knows where, and assumed the reins himself. As far as Theodoric knew, he had ruled the West wisely. And with great good sense, he had submitted himself to the authority of the East in all matters, showing all due respect to its Emperor.

The idea of respect being due to Zeno, the scheming invertebrate, was enough to bring on a fit of laughter that almost managed to undo Theodoric's recovery. Much good it had done Odovacar, in any case. The poor bastard. He wet his face again and smoothed down his hair with damp hands, then took a deep draught of water. He checked his appearance in the mirror. A change of clothes would also be a good idea, he decided as he observed the traces of vomit that had congealed on the front of his tunic. He'd be unable to remove the stain.

After five years of warfare, including three years in which the capital, Ravenna, had resisted all attempts to take it, Odovacar had finally agreed to terms. The two of them, barbarians both, would rule the West jointly. A banquet within the walls of the capital would seal the deal.

It had sealed Odovacar's fate instead.

Theodoric shrugged to himself as he peeled off his clothes. Zeno would never have agreed, of course. But the abortive deal had had something going for it. The slippery sod would never have been able to withstand the combined armies of the Folk and the Western Empire.

He inspected himself in the full-length bronze in the corner of his sleeping quarters. A black tunic. Sombre and sober. And totally puke-free. Just the job.

But Strabo's words remained with him. He could be sure that, if he had waited longer, it would have been his body that lay in pieces rather than the German usurper's.

Poor bastard. Too bad. To the victor, the spoils.

He dug deep inside the chest. He was sure he had it there somewhere. Finally he found what he was looking for. He pulled out the gold chain. His father's badge of office.

Theodoric rarely wore such ornaments. 'Trinkets', he called them. But he had people to impress. He polished the metal against his robe and drew the chain over his head. Studied himself in the glass once again. Lowered his chin slightly and looked down his nose. That should do it. Now he was ready for them.

But when he walked back into the atrium, it was not 'them' he found. The imperious expression he had assumed became one of pure delight. He strode over and clasped his friend's shoulders.

'Theudis!' he exclaimed. 'When did you get back?'

Equal delight was written on the fresh face of Theudis. Not for the first time, Theodoric felt he could be looking at his own reflection when he looked at his sword-bearer. Save that Theudis seemed unmarked by battle, age or anxiety. He even wore his long hair in the same way as the king – combed forwards over the forehead and ears.

'This very moment,' Theudis replied. 'I've left them rubbing down my horse in the stables.'

Theodoric was amazed. Although by now, he thought, he should be used to it. His friend could survive hours of pitched battle and still emerge looking as though he were ready to attend a ball. Not that he required him to fight so very often. His skills were more in the diplomatic line than the military.

The king suddenly frowned face in puzzlement and inspected Theudis' face.

'I do believe you're even growing a moustache!' he said. 'Soon they won't be able to tell us apart.'

'A homage, purely,' Theudis said with a trace of embarrassment.

'Perhaps I can persuade you to act as my stand-in during occasions of state.'

The sword-bearer's confusion grew.

'I would not presume…,' he began.

'No, perhaps not such a good idea,' Theodoric added thoughtfully, 'bound to be people out there thirsting for my blood.'

The side of Theudis' mouth twitched. He raised his hand to his mouth to smother what appeared to be a ticklish cough.

'You will be glad to hear that everyone is in place and everything is going to plan,' he said. 'I left Pitzias in the thick of it.'

'Best place for him,' Theodoric thought. 'He'd hardly have approved of what we've been up to here.'

'Excellent,' he said aloud. 'Though I thought you might have stayed until the job was done.'

Theudis' face suddenly looked years older. He tugged at an imaginary beard.

'*You just leave it to me,*' he said in a gruff voice. '*It's a bloody business. You'll just get in the way and get your hands dirty. That'd never do.*'

Theodoric laughed and clapped his friend's shoulder.

'Pitzias to a tee. How'd you do it?'

This was one of the things he liked best about Theudis. There were few people that made him laugh. And he supposed he would have even less occasion for mirth in the future.

'I just listen carefully,' Theudis replied. And use my imagination when necessary, he added to himself. Pitzias did not even know he had left.

'So by dawn, all resistance should be at an end, I guess,' the king said.

'I heard there was little resistance here.' Theudis grinned. 'Like a hot knife through butter.'

Theodoric shook his head. 'A bloody business indeed. But necessary. And let's hope that's the end of it.'

Theudis coughed again, this time the cough of a diplomat. Theodoric looked up at him.

'I sense a 'but'…,' Theodoric said.

'Tufa managed to get away.'

'Hell's teeth,' Theodoric said. 'How did he catch wind of….'

Theudis shrugged.

'The man has six senses, obviously.'

'And nine lives,' Theodoric added.

Of all Odovacar's lieutenants, Tufa was the most formidable. And the least trustworthy. Strabo's maxim might have been designed with him in mind. Tufa had already changed sides twice – once to Theodoric's forces when his own were threatened with destruction, and once back to Odovacar's when the danger had passed and Theodoric had entrusted him with an army of his own. He had taken the army with him, of course.

The king laid a hand on Theudis' forearm.

'How thoughtless of me,' he said. 'Here you are probably dead tired and hungry, and I haven't even offered you refreshment.'

Theudis grinned.

'I thought you'd never ask.'

Theodoric turned to a page and ordered food and drink to be brought. When the servant returned, he was followed closely by a lank-haired carbuncular man in a grimy sheepskin waistcoat. He in turn was followed by three Romans.

'You come with a formidable retinue, Tulum,' Theudis commented with a smile.

Tulum glanced at him and snorted, then turned to Theodoric.

'A thousand pardons, Liege. They insisted on an audience. At least this pair of jokers did.' He pointed to the two just behind him, who were jostling for position. The one was short and sharp-featured; the other large and round.

'T'other, you said you wanted to speak with.'

Tulum flicked a thumb towards the final member of the retinue – the Julius Caesar lookalike.

'What's more, I've got a bloody bishop screaming blue murder in the courtyard. So if it's all the same to you, I'll dump these characters on you and get back to nursing him.'

'John,' thought Theodoric. Ravenna's bishop had every right to feel aggrieved. He'd negotiated the deal between Odovacar and the Folk. But he posed no threat. He could be dealt with later.

In the meantime, he turned his attention to the trio that Tulum had 'dumped' on him. As the general pointed out, he had summoned Liberius. Theodoric was unsure of the identity of the two frontrunners, although he recalled seeing them at the bloody banquet.

It was the larger of the two senators that succeeded in presenting himself first.

'Lord...,' he began.

'Lord Festus, if I am not mistaken?'

'Faustus, Lord.'

His companion sniggered.

'So be it. Whatever your name, in future it will be much to your advantage if you address me as Highness. Or something to that effect.'

Faustus swallowed hard.

'Observing the finer points has been proved to extend longevity. Considerably,' Theodoric continued.

Faustus flushed purple, and tried desperately to control a fit of trembling. His companion meanwhile took the opportunity to push himself forward.

'Most esteemed and serene...,' he began.

Theudis turned to wink at Theodoric.

'No need to overdo it, eh?'

'Lord Festus, now, I take it? *Highness* is sufficient.'

Both Festus and Faustus bowed, each vying with the other in their desire to demonstrate the depth of their submission.

'How exactly may I be of service to the revered Senators?' Theodoric asked.

'Majesty...,' Festus began, only to find a huge forearm creased with cellulite obstructing his mouth and forcing him back.

'Highness,' Faustus emphasised the favoured honorific, 'what my esteemed colleague, and indeed, if I may be so presumptuous to speak on its behalf, the entire concourse of the distinguished assembly of which we are but two insignificant members....'

Faustus paused to recover his breath. He had also lost track of his syntax. His esteemed colleague took up the baton.

'More to the point, Excellency, we wish to know in which way *we* might be of service to *you*,' he declared.

Theodoric glanced at Theudis who was just about managing to keep a straight face. As Festus and Faustus burbled on, competing in servility and confusing honorifics, he looked over at the figure to their rear. This was the individual whose apparent distaste for Theodoric had engaged the king's respect. One Liberius, apparently – and one of Odovacar's must trusted public servants.

He certainly carried himself well. Theodoric had learnt that the man was of no great patrician lineage. But he bore himself with greater dignity than the two ultra-aristocratic senators that accompanied him.

Liberius suddenly became aware he was being studied. From staring into space, he glanced with disapproval in the king's direction, although Theodoric could not work out whether the look was a comment upon himself or upon the senators. Or, for that matter, upon the farcical scene they all found themselves involved in. After a moment, however, the Roman appeared to lose interest and reverted to his study of the infinite space beyond the walls of the room.

Theodoric turned his attention back to the senators, who were each trying to make themselves heard above the other.

'Enough,' he said. 'You will conduct yourself with all seeming dignity in the presence of your lord and master.'

Liberius made no attempt to disguise a snort.

'Serene Highness…,' Faustus ventured after a pause. 'If I might make so bold, Majesty. A word in confidence perhaps.'

Theodoric inclined his head and Faustus came closer.

'A word to the wise, if I do not appear too forward. My esteemed colleague,' he nodded towards Festus, as if there could be any doubt of his meaning, 'is not altogether to be trusted.'

He smiled grotesquely at the king.

'He means well, I'm sure, has been a devoted servant of the state for many years. But he suffers from an incurable disorder.'

Theodoric cocked his head to the side and studied the object of their attention. The man was, perhaps, afflicted with a certain atrophy of his limbs, but it did not seem to impair his movement. Indeed at the moment he was hopping from one foot to the other with impatience.

'The senator has an insatiable appetite for power,' Faustus explained with a wise nod of the head. 'And has few scruples as to how he achieves it.'

Theodoric suppressed a sigh.

'Well, thank you for the warning. I will do my best to bear that in mind.'

He nodded his head again, this time to signify the private audience was at an end, and Faustus stepped back, his eyes still on the king and his finger tapping the side of his nose.

'Highness!' Festus protested.

'You wish to give me some more invaluable advice?' Theodoric suggested.

'You divine my wishes exactly, Majesty.'

'Approach, then.'

Festus held his hand up to his mouth and spoke through it. The king wondered if Faustus were an expert at reading lips.

'My worthy associate has many amiable qualities, but I feel it my duty to warn you....'

'We speak of Count Faustus, I take it?'

'Your powers of perception deprive me of breath.'

Unfortunately, I suspect that will not prevent your speaking further, Theodoric thought to himself.

'... he is prey to unnatural and uncontrollable lusts.'

Theodoric lifted an eyebrow. He could well believe that. He had already noticed that the senator's lips were sensuous and his gut ample. He glanced over in Faustus' direction for confirmation. Faustus was rolling his eyes significantly at him, as if to suggest that his colleague were to be humoured rather than believed.

'We have no mandate nor intention to intrude upon the private lives of our subjects,' Theodoric replied at length.

'Well said, Majesty. But when the private itself obtrudes upon the public? What then?'

'Then that is a matter of public concern, of course.' Theodoric suddenly felt very tired.

'We speak of peculation, Lord. I can guarantee that each bauble on the senatorial robe over there has corresponded to a loss of revenue to the public purse.'

'Quite clearly, I shall have to keep an eye on our good friend,' Theodoric agreed, 'that he should not fall too great a victim to his own weakness.'

Festus gave an earnest nod.

'You understand me too well, Lord.'

Festus withdrew to a level with Faustus and gave his colleague a look of triumph.

'I cannot thank the two of you enough,' Theodoric said. 'I have learnt much already that will prove useful to me in my new and unsought-for station.'

The two senators regarded each other with companionable satisfaction.

'I look forward to educating myself in the art of statecraft more fully with the benefit of your counsel.'

Preferably in epistolary form from exotic locations. I see a great future for you both as envoys to remote parts, Theodoric decided to himself.

'For now, please assure your esteemed senatorial colleagues of my greatest respect and undying affection. And reassure them that their past loyalties will be forgotten as long as present loyalties remain constant.'

'Highness,' the august representatives intoned in perfect harmony, as they withdrew to the doorway, the crowns of their heads towards Theodoric and their faces towards the floor.

'Lord Liberius.' The third official had turned to join the senators in departure. 'Hold up a moment.'

Liberius turned. He looked confused.

'Those other clowns came seeking an audience,' Theodoric said. 'You, I summoned.'

Liberius inclined his head slightly.

'Otherwise, I would not have come.'

Theodoric smiled.

'So I guessed.'

'You wish to speak with me, then?' Liberius appeared wholly indifferent to the prospect.

'In confidence,' Theodoric said. He dismissed Theudis with a smile of apology.

'A word to the truly wise, perhaps,' he said. He tapped the side of his nose.

Liberius responded with the ghost of a smile but remained silent.

'You served Lord Odovacar well,' Theodoric persisted.

'I served Rome better, I hope.'

'By which I take it you served the one in order to serve the other.'

'You may take it that way.'

'I would beg to be served in the same way.'

Liberius raised an eyebrow, either in question or scepticism.

'You do not appear accustomed to beg,' he said.

'Indeed, I am most fastidious in my choice of benefactors.'

Again a ghost of a smile.

'And what would you require of this benefactor?' Liberius asked.

'Integrity. Wisdom.'

'You ask much. Such commodities are in short supply – in these times, and in this place.'

'You managed to find sufficiency for my predecessor, from what I have heard.'

Liberius nodded.

'He did not require much.'

'I fancy, then, I will require more. You may find your resources and resourcefulness stretched.'

Liberius drew himself upright.

'Forgive me for asking. But what exactly are *you* asking?'

'In the first instance, I have a victorious army to satisfy.'

Liberius sighed.

'The problem has become a familiar one for Italy.'

'I have also a new set of people to propitiate.'

Again the eyebrow.

'That compounds the problem significantly.'

'Irresolvably?' Theodoric asked.

A frown.

'There is a clear conflict of interest in the accounts to be settled,' Liberius pointed out.

It was the king's turn to nod.

'*Prima facie*, it could be argued that those conquered were Odovacar's barbarians, rather than the Roman population,' Liberius continued.

'The transfer of all such titles has been set in motion.'

'Ah.'

'It will not be sufficient to balance the account. My people are many.'

'Ah.'

Liberius thought for a moment.

'The usual emoluments take the form of land or money. I imagine your followers would be equally if not more satisfied with the latter as with the former.'

It was Theodoric's turn to think.

'Those in our army that are not of my people, certainly. Some of our own too, perhaps. Those without families, at least.'

'Would it not be possible then to transfer title, on condition that the former owners continued to manage the estates in question? Against suitable financial compensation, of course.'

Theodoric frowned. Eventually his brow cleared.

'The former owners would become tenants, you mean?'

Liberius nodded.

'And would, no doubt, appreciate the protection of their landlords.'

The king laughed out loud.

'The reports of you were not mistaken,' he said.

Liberius raised a supercilious *supercilium*.

'Was that all?' he asked.

'No "Lord", then?' Theodoric asked, still amused.

'None that I would acknowledge.'

'But one that you would serve?' Theodoric asked. 'If, in doing so, you were serving Rome?'

Liberius turned his long neck to stare at Theodoric – in the eyes for the first time.

'In what capacity?'

'Praetorian Prefect.'

Theodoric had the satisfaction of seeing the Roman struck dumb for a moment by surprise.

'You are aware of my lack of years?' he asked.

'As you, no doubt, are aware of mine.'

This time Liberius allowed himself the luxury of two raised eyebrows.

'Prefect,' he repeated. 'With responsibility for…?'

'Romans. And, more specifically, what shall we call it? The land issue.'

Liberius paused a moment, then bowed his head, more in agreement than deference.

'Meanwhile, the Goths will retain their own laws, the Romans theirs,' Theodoric continued.

'I will strive to be worthy.'

'…of my trust?' Theodoric asked.

'…of my fellow Romans.'

The two men exchanged something resembling a smile.

The Closed Stacks

Who truth pursues, who from false ways
His heedful steps would keep,
By inward light must search within
In meditation deep
Boethius

I gave up on Ennodius' blather when I found my head swimming, my eyes blurring and my mind reading the same never-ending sentence thrice without it once making sense.

The gasbag could not compete with my limited attention span, not to mention my man's sleep-talk. Sad to say, Owen's night-ramblings were not so much the low burbling of a mental infant. Rather, they took the form of a highly dramatic monologue in an alien language. They also came with a full set of muscular spasms, grinding of the hips and thrusts of the arms. I supposed he was re-enacting the fornicating and fighting highlights of his life to date. I wished him much joy of it. But the spectacle did little to help my powers of concentration. Nor did it allow sleep on my own part.

So I took the oil lamp from my reading desk and decided to explore the monastery. The place was full of mysteries. A further inspection, unescorted, might bring me closer to solving them. And if anyone discovered me during my night prowl, then I could, following the lead of my servant, claim to be afflicted by sleep-walking.

But as I went through the door, a gust of wind caught the flame of the lamp. I wondered where the wind could have come from. As I had left the refectory I had noticed a brother securing all the doors of the building. He had not been among the diners, so I studied him with care. He was stocky with high shoulders and little neck, and had such an expression of bland innocence on his face that at first I took him for not much more than a youth or yet another cretin. But at one point he noticed that he was the object of my attention and turned towards me with a smile that revealed crow's feet round the mouth and eyes. The smile would have been engaging if it had not also revealed teeth filed to a point.

He flourished long thin fingers in acknowledgement of my presence. I wondered briefly if he had been a lyrist in a previous life. In this one, he had presumably been charged with safeguarding the monastery from night predators – human or otherwise.

As he had continued his rounds, I examined the doorway he had been securing. This was clearly not an original feature. The door itself was about five thumbs thick and composed of planks that were reinforced by studs and stout iron crosspieces. The locking unit itself was monumental; the key that the monk had used was as large as his hand. As if all that were not enough, he had finally lowered a couple of cross-beams so that they rested in place across the door and nested in hooks or latches on each side. With a final flick, he had drawn a large curtain across, as if to give the whole a less martial aspect.

The opening had been rendered proof against virtually everything except fire, I guessed at the time. It also seemed pretty much draught-proof, since what little air made it through was absorbed by the thick heavy drapery. True enough, the cell Owen and I occupied exhaled currents of air from the very bricks and mortar. But the gust that had caused my lamp to sputter had come along the corridor rather than from the room. What is more I could still feel the air moving the loose sleeves I wore. It was not winter-cold. It was warm.

I decided to investigate the source of this weird sirocco. So shielding the flame of the lamp with my hand, I headed into the storm, as it were.

Sure enough, as I walked through the passages towards the garden, I detected a faint gleam of light. And coming closer, I discovered a door that had not been fully closed. It was from here that the faint glow and the warm air were flowing. As carefully as I could, I opened the door further. It made not a sound. Even by the light of my lamp it was clear that the hinges had been recently oiled.

I have to confess, I was more than a little apprehensive. My impression of Vivarium so far was that it resembled more a prison for the criminally insane than a place of prayer and contemplation. For all I knew, I was about to uncover devil-worship with all the trimmings, including unspeakable, bestial rites.

I had served in the Eastern army for some years, – seen much suffering and caused much grief. And I like to think that I do not lack courage. But I have always had a fear of the dark and of the unknown, and my period of service had done little to remove this phobia. The combination of the two here brought my heart into my mouth and caused my stomach to flutter. I attempted to shield the light of my lamp, fearing more that it would give me away than that it would be blown out. Then I stepped forward cautiously into the void.

And nearly broke my neck.

Only at the last moment did I realise that I was standing at the top of a flight of steps, and pulled myself back from falling to the bottom. I put my hand against the wall to steady myself, and pulled it back again sharply. A red-hot pipe. As I nursed my hand, I suddenly realised where I was. This had to be the cellar that housed the original hypocaust system for the whole villa complex.

The answer to the one question immediately raised another. For neither in our cell, nor in the living or eating quarters of the monastery had I noted any evidence of central heating. If the hypocaust was functioning, it was doing so within a very limited space. But why have the system operating at all, if no-one benefited? And as far as I could see, the only area where the system was engaged must have been directly under the garden. Was this how the Jew grew his exotic spices? If so, it would be a preposterous indulgence.

As I perched a few steps down, another odour, added to the more expected blend of rust and dust, struck my nostrils. A whiff of ammonia. I drew a deep breath. More than a whiff, I decided with a grimace. A stench, rather. Just then, I sensed rather than saw a shadow approach from below. I hardly dared look. Suddenly I felt something curl itself round my calf and shin. Again I teetered on the brink. But summoning up the courage to look down, I saw a familiar form wind and slink its way past me and out of the still-open door above.

I gave a shudder. Partly, I was disgusted with myself. But I had never liked cats. I took them for repositories of ancient mystic lore. To be honest, they appeared to know too much about me too, as if they were able to cut through the veils of my own self-deceptions.

Well, at least the creature explained the ammoniac stink.

I pulled myself together with a shake, and in an attempt to persuade myself that I had nothing to fear, walked down the remaining steps with a bold air. Self-deception again, you will note.

The place was deathly quiet, apart from the constant hum of hot air along the pipes. At the far end of the cellar I could make out an intense glow of light, the source of which was still hidden from me. I shuddered again as I imagined that this was probably what Hell was like, and shuddered more violently when I imagined that it might indeed be the Devil's portal that I had stumbled upon. The impression was heightened as my nose now picked up the tart heaviness of bitumen in the air.

I lifted my own feeble lamp and positioned it in front of my face, as if it might provide some protection from the forces of darkness if my presence was detected. But as I did so, through the eerily mingled shadows from the two competing sources of light, I saw that the apparently bare walls were in fact lined with shelves. And on the shelves were rows upon rows of books. Large and small. Ancient and modern, on all species of parchment. I even noticed some pieces of beech and birch bark, presumably inscribed with the runes of the people of the North. I had come across these before on my travels, but never seen them in a library before.

For that was where I surely was. It could still be in Hell, of course. But the shelves were some consolation. If it was here I was to spend eternity, then I should at least have plenty to occupy my mind.

Less fancifully, I realised I had chanced upon the closed stacks that Basilius had referred to. Perhaps here I might find what I was looking for?

But first I would have to deal with the matter of the light at the end of the cellar, and more daunting perhaps, the custodian of that light, and presumably of the library.

In the meantime, my attention was drawn back to the shadows. For they appeared to quiver against the backdrop of the screen provided by the book-lined wall. Diaphanous waves rippled from shade to half-shade, wisps curled round each other, then merged into the ceiling amongst the pipes and cobwebs. To me, it was wondrous and I was entranced. The light and dark seemed to achieve a life of their own, and interweaved with each other, so that it became difficult to decide what was twilight and what was night. A dance of the spirits, I fancied, and felt something ancient stream through my bones, linking me to my own childhood and the souls of my ancestors.

So absorbed was I in the magical play that I did not notice the sudden increase in intensity of light. Instead I assimilated it into the choreography that my mind was directing. So I nearly jumped out of my felt boots when I sensed the presence of someone or something directly behind me.

I swung round, ready to defend myself.

It was the Jew. He was holding a pitch torch in his left hand, dispersing the shadow play on the wall and casting his own face into another shadow.

Through his lenses his own eyes showed as narrow gleaming slits, – yellow like the eyes of a goat. With his right hand, he stroked his billy-beard.

'Welcome to the nether regions,' he said in a sonorous voice. Then, disarmingly, he chuckled.

'I'm sorry if I gave you a start.' He tilted his head and ran his eyes over me. 'A disposition of the nerves, perhaps. I have noticed it before in those that have served on extended campaigns.'

I tried to pull myself together and grasped my forearm to stifle the tremors. I was loth to agree with his diagnosis. But I too had noticed the 'disposition' many times since I quit the army. I was eager to change the subject.

'The closed stacks, I presume.'

'Indeed.'

'And by what right and means do you claim access?' I demanded, wishing to assert myself after being startled.

He smiled his irritating, superior smile.

'The right is the pursuit of knowledge, which is open to all that search for it.'

He had an answer to everything, a habit that didn't endear him to me any the more.

'The means are a little less commendable, I fear,' he continued.

'Aha!' I said, rather obviously.

'I persuaded Brother Paulinus to manufacture me a copy of the keys.'

'Subterfuge, then.'

'In a good cause.'

'And the abbot?'

'I suspect the good fellow is aware of what goes on, but he seeks to avoid conflict.'

'So turns a blind eye,' I deduced.

A further nod. A further irritating smile.

'I pretend I do not enter, and he pretends to believe me.'

Something was still puzzling me.

'Paulinus? Was he one of the monks at dinner?'

'He was otherwise engaged.'

I recalled the doorkeeper.

'Stocky and neckless? Long delicate fingers?'

'You have him to a tee. You have perhaps missed your vocation.'

'How so?'

'You would have made an excellent *vigilus*. Or a census-taker, perhaps.'

I determined there would at some stage be a reckoning between myself and this disrespectful Jew. For now I contented myself with establishing the identity of this latest brother.

'He was securing the doors?'

'He is equally adept at unsecuring them.'

'A locksmith, then.'

'Something of that sort.'

So! Another degenerate monk. Either Basilius was a master evangelist, or he was planning to raid the Imperial Palace and make off with the Treasury. With the help of a hand-picked gang of master-criminals and general-purpose riff-raff.

I gave a disapproving snort and turned away from the Jew. My eyes were drawn to the walls of the cellar again. More of these now became visible in the greater light cast by Josephus' torch.

I was so astounded by what I saw I had to support myself against the closest shelves. The hypocaust cellar extended as far as the eye could see away from the monastery, stretching, I guessed, as far as the Master's house. And the lines of books stretched equally into the distance, covering every wall and every cavity.

I looked back at Josephus. I expect my mouth was hanging loose.

His smile was now accompanied by an eyebrow raised in question.

'It's… enormous,' I declared with pathetic understatement.

'To my knowledge, the largest of its kind.'

'The kind being…?'

He tried to restrain the smile becoming a full-blown grin, by puckering the sides of his mouth.

'How shall we put it? The most extensive collection of profane literature?' he continued. 'The most prodigious private collection of forbidden texts? The most impressive monument to the occult?'

He held up the torch and brandished it round the shelves.

'Or simply the grandest conceivable insult to the narrow-mindedness of our Great Leader.'

'Justinian?'

I had little love for the man myself, but valued my health and well-being too greatly to share the opinion with strangers.

'The bigoted pedant-in-chief himself,' Josephus confirmed.

I was secretly impressed and my heart warmed a little to the Hebrew.

'The Master must be a brave man indeed,' was all I said.

He shrugged.

'So it would appear.'

'You seem sceptical.'

'The library is well-concealed, underground, located in the rectum of the universe, and known to but few initiates.'

I could not help but smile.

'Safe from prying eyes and marauding barbarians, then.'

'We have as much to fear from the Imperial troops as from the Goths.'

'Mmm....' I was doubtful on that score. For all his faults, Justinian was no Vandal. While barbarians could be relied upon to be barbaric. It was in their nature. But I decided not to press the point.

'And preserved from the ravages of damp by the hypocaust,' I suggested.

'And from the ravages of vermin by the most excellent cat.'

'I met him on my way in. And his way out.'

'He enjoys a night on the tiles occasionally. And deserves it.'

I decided that was enough badinage for the present. Besides, feline foreplay was not a subject befitting my dignity as a prelate. So I quickly adopted a sterner expression.

'You realise, given my title, that it is incumbent on me...,' I started pompously.

'Please feel free to browse. Given my lack of title, I am hardly in a position to stop you.'

He bowed a little too graciously, and made his way back to where he had come from.

I waited till he had disappeared into an alcove, where presumably he had a desk and his reading material. Then ran my lamp and my eyes along the titles in front of me. They seemed designed to offend all orthodox sensibilities, ranging from the simply pornographic to the obscurely heretical. My intellectual curiosity struggled with my eternal soul. I was unsure whether I should be scandalised or fascinated. In the end I settled for an outraged expression that concealed a gratified mind.

Hermes Trismegistus, for goodness sake! Flanked by all the so-called Gnostic Gospels I had ever heard of and many more that I had never heard of. Indeed the unfamiliar heterodox texts far outnumbered those I had previous knowledge of. Sometimes it was the titles that made me aware of their true nature. On other occasions I was obliged to skim the contents to confirm their blasphemous tendencies.

As I explored further, I tutted my disapproval and browsed freely. The collection not only contained occult deviations from and bizarre blends of the sectarian and schismatic. Here there were whole shelves, whole sections devoted to the frankly idolatrous. Weighty tomes propounding the 'virtues' and expounding the 'truths' of Manichee and Mithras, Zeus and Zoroaster, Orpheus and Osiris. To be honest, I had never heard of most of these. I was more at home with the ancient pantheons of my own people. Needless to say, these were also represented here in early Gothic script on birch bark. So it was not only the Northmen that had used this medium.

There were even treatises, written in Latin, on the belief systems of the Far Orient. Veda and Buddha, Tengri and a certain Master Kong. This last, as far as I could make out, lived many centuries ago in the Land of the Chin, and dispensed advice on conduct and duty that would have passed muster in any Christian manual for parents.

In covering this catalogue of defunct philosophy and misguided theology, I had made little progress along the lines of shelves. I soon realised that a complete inventory would take me considerably longer than I wished to be immured in this bizarre establishment. So I decided to skip to the end. Just to satisfy my curiosity, you understand.

The texts on the last shelves could well have been supplied by my old friend, Castilius. Or they might well have been the leftovers from an earlier incarnation of the cellar, if, as I supposed, the monastery had been previously used for orgiastic parties. This section, devoted to 'erotica', was located on the far wall of the cellar, next to another exit that could only lead directly up to the House of the Master.

The usual suspects were on display, Sappho of Lesbos and Straton of Sardis, Catullus, Ovid and Petronius. More interesting, from an academic point of view of course, were the less familiar texts, again from the Indies and beyond.

The first of them I picked out because I was curious about the binding. While the covers were of vellum, the leaves inside were of a fine and tightly compacted material that I had not come across before. I stroked my fingers across the surface of the exotic script with almost sensory pleasure. A pleasure that increased as I became aware of the delightful illuminations that accompanied the text. The usual earth colours were broken up by malachites and cinnabars of an unusual pitch, along with the purples that Cassiodorus never tires of reminding us are made from the secretions of a species of snail. But what most struck my eye was a blue of an intensity I had never seen before.

So dazzled was I by the colours that it took me some moments to absorb what was being depicted. To put this as politely as possible, the pictures represented human beings, ranging in number from one to several, engaged in carnal activities. As soon as I realised this, I slammed the book shut. But my curiosity got the better of me. Some of the positions assumed had seemed to me so fantastic as to be physically impossible. A second brief inspection of the turbaned gentlemen and ear-ringed ladies assured me that this was indeed the case. Unless the denizens of the Indies trained their offspring to contort their bodies from the earliest age, that is.

I closed the book more gently, but this time with an air of finality. My browsing had satisfied my mind and frustrated my body. I decided I needed to return to the Jew and grill him further.

I found him in the niche he had vanished into. He had dowsed the torch or it had dowsed itself. Instead he was reading by the light of a foul-smelling oil-lamp inserted into a glass tube. A curious invention. It seemed to diffuse the light very effectively and I wondered briefly what he was using for fuel. As I approached, he looked up. The effect was unnerving. Instead of his usual full-circle bottle bottoms, he was now wearing half-glass lenses. Above the glass, his eyes appeared normal size, below they appeared more than twice as large. Moreover, the surface of the lenses were uneven so they reflected the light in various directions as if stars were shining from the Jew's eyes.

Once I had recovered, I begged pardon for interrupting, and since I was about to ask a service, politely asked what he was studying.

He held up the cover, on which the title was presumably written. But it was in an unfamiliar script.

'Hebrew?' I asked.

'Aramaic.'

'Forgive my ignorance.'

'The Gospel of Mary,' he explained without looking at the title.

'Non-canonical, then. A Gnostic text?'

'If you choose to call it that.'

I did not choose to call it anything. I had never heard of it. But it seemed a reasonable guess.

'Purporting to be written by the Holy Mother?' I asked.

'Claiming to be the dictated transcription of the words of the Magdalene.'

I felt my jaw dropping and forced it back into position.

'She was illiterate,' Josephus added, as if that explained everything.

'She was also reputed to be... a woman of easy virtue,' I pointed out.

'A patristic smear, I expect.'

'The Fathers are not in the habit of smearing.'

He smiled.

'I admit they are very good at it,' he said.

I did not want to antagonise him at this point. So I asked him what exactly had engaged his interest in the text.

He appeared to roll the question around in his mouth before answering.

'She was married to Christ, you know. According to this and other of the texts here.'

'Blasphemy!' The words popped out before I could stop them.

'Can Messiahs get married, I wonder?' he asked rhetorically. 'Wouldn't that make him less than a God?'

I refused to answer.

'And perhaps more admirable for all that,' he added.

I was forced to admit that it was an interesting idea. But most definitely heretical.

'You realise you could be excommunicated for less?' I pointed out.

For once he did not smile. Instead he looked thoughtful.

'Oh dear,' he replied at length. 'That was not my intention at all. Not by a long chalk. I am most sorry if I gave that impression.'

I beamed at him. Perhaps I had saved my first soul. My hopes were soon dashed.

'Brave men are so much more admirable than gods, don't you think? If Christ was truly divine, ergo immortal, the crucifixion would have been cheating, surely.'

He looked up at me expectantly.

'An interesting thought,' I agreed.

It was indeed. And not one that I intended to entertain for long. I had my soul's own immortality to consider. And once again I felt it being dragged off towards the nether regions.

He seemed satisfied with the response, equivocal as it was. Removing his finger from the place he had been keeping, he inserted a straw and closed the book. Then leaned back in his seat and stretched his arms.

'Unfortunately, neither my body nor my eyes are up to prolonged study anymore.'

He removed his bottle bottoms.

'Even with the help of the prosthetic *oculi*,' he added, and rose from his seat.

'A word before you go,' I said.

'As many as you wish. My larynx and ears are still in perfect working order.'

'You appear to be well acquainted with the contents of this library.'

'I flatter myself that I am. Was there a manuscript you were particularly searching for?'

'I have been trying to track down the last volumes of Cassiodorus' *Gothic History*.'

'You are a historian!' he replied. This time his smile was genuinely inclusive. 'A man after my own heart.'

'I expect my interests are rather narrower than yours. That is to say I have a commission to fulfil.'

'There is no shame in being paid for your work. I myself would relish the opportunity.'

'Perhaps I could put a word in…,' I replied not entirely altruistically. If all else failed, I might try to persuade Castilius to engage someone more qualified and enthusiastic.

'It would be a brave publisher that would defy the Emperor to employ a Jew,' he responded. 'As I have found to my cost.'

'Your meaning?'

'I had renounced the faith of my fathers, and was serving the Empire in high public office, even if I say so myself. But the Emperor in his wisdom decided that the 'murderers of Christ' could not be trusted with administering a Christian state.'

I had the grace to blush.

'As for the volumes you are looking for…,' he continued.

My heart sank with his tone.

'Not here?' I suggested.

'More likely to be upstairs, if anywhere, I'd have thought,' he said. 'In the authorised library. Not that I recall seeing them there. And I suppose that was the first place you looked.'

'It was just a shot in the dark,' I sighed. Presumably news that Justinian had added the History to his Index of forbidden works had not yet reached here.

'Let me know if you do find them. I would be interested in reading them. Theodoric was also a brave man.'

I repressed the impulse to contradict, suspecting that the Jew's good offices might be worth preserving for some time longer.

He looked over at me again as he slid his 'oculi' into a sharkskin case.

'The Master is always adding to his collection, you know. Books arrive regularly here from the most unusual sources.'

That I could well imagine, given some of the manuscripts I had turned up in the cellar.

'I'll keep my eyes open then,' I said.

'In the meantime, you might want to read round the subject a little. Cassiodorus is not the sole nor the most reliable source. Besides being a pain in the posterior to plough through.'

That piqued my interest.

'The alternative chronicles are over there.'

He pointed towards the pornographic end of the library, close to the alternative exit.

'Contemporary History, second stack from the end on the right.'

He made as if to go, then paused and turned back to me. Reaching into the pocket of his habit, he pulled out a large key.

'Can I ask you to lock up when you leave? For appearance's sake?'
I nodded.

'Thank you. But won't you need….?'

'I have a spare,' he said with another sharing smile. I thought he was beginning to take me into his confidence. I still wasn't sure I felt the same about him.

'So does Paulinus,' he continued. 'When he unlocks at dawn, and stokes up the furnace, he'll check it's all secure. In case it slips your mind.'

I did not want to appear too eager. So I waited until I heard the door swing to. Then with indecent haste I made for the zone he had indicated. It was a surprisingly small section and a quick glance was enough to satisfy me that Cassiodorus' history was not there. I would have to wait and hope that a new delivery would bring the collection. I cast around for other texts that might be of use in the meanwhile.

Ulfilas was there. He had been responsible, if that is the right word, for converting the Gothic nation to the heresy that was commonly called Arianism. His history was written in Gothic, which was not a problem for me, but it predated by some years the reign of Theodoric, which was. I supposed in any case that Cassiodorus had availed himself of the text as a source for his earlier volumes.

There was little on Justinian's reign either. Less surprising, given that it was still ongoing, and I could not imagine anyone brave enough to publish a critical account of the Divine One. I was about to pass further along the shelves when a small volume with no markings on its cover caught my eye. Out of curiosity I pulled it out and flicked through to the title page. This read *Anekdota* by Procopius of Caesarea. I had heard vaguely of a functionary of the famous General Belisarius who was called that. I assume his star had risen with that of his employer. But why a biography of the Emperor written by such a high-ranking official should find itself in this salacious company, I could not guess. I turned a few pages to get an idea of the tenor of the work and was soon reduced to sniggering like a schoolboy opening the oriental sex manual I had previously discovered. Why the text might be proscribed or secretly circulated, I now knew. Why he should feel compelled to write such a manuscript at the risk of his livelihood and his life, I had no idea.

I slipped the book into the belt-pouch of my tunic to explore more fully later, and was raising my ageing body from its aching knees when my eyes fell on a further book, tucked away amongst the histories of other barbarian tribes.

This time my jaw dropped all the way. I had heard the name of Boethius many times, not least from the mouths of the brothers with whom I had served my 'novitiate'. The man was considered as close to sainthood as you can get without Papal certification. Why his celebrated *Consolations of Philosophy* should find itself in this den of bibliographical iniquity was wholly beyond me. I flicked through the pages to ascertain whether the covers actually disguised a graphic account of how to engage in carnal relations with household pets. But all I found were reflections in verse and prose on the nature of existence in general, and Boethius' desperate plight in particular.

The only deviation from the norm that I could find was the addition of annotations written in a kind of shorthand Latin, both at the sides of the original text and at the bottom of the pages. Indeed, in some places, whole passages had been struck out with bold diagonal lines; in others a more selective form of editing had taken place, with sentences or phrases blocked out.

Why anyone should wish to desecrate such a highly-regarded and pious text was again beyond my ken. But even if I had to read between the lines, the book should provide rich pickings on the most unsavoury aspect of the reign of Theodoric the Tyrant. Poor Boethius was, after all, practically a martyr. His final thoughts might even offer me some 'Consolations' for the unsavoury pickle I was in – in this 'rectum of the universe', as the Jew had called it. I dropped it into my pouch to join its most improper bedfellow.

These should at least make for more lively reading than the odious Ennodius. For a moment, I almost felt sorry, or at least embarrassed, for Theodoric. He would have had to sit for hours at a formal oration of the bombastic drivel. But then, I reminded myself he was a barbarian and a Goth. And our ancestors revelled in being regaled at banquet with their triumphs and courage in battle. I am sure he lapped it all up. If he understood it, that is.

Illumination the Third
Death Conquers All

AD 507

Theodoric came awake with a start. He had been vaguely aware of being shoved on the shoulder. His first reaction was to reach for his sword. But then he remembered where he was and why he was there. The steady drone of Ennodius' voice reminded him.

He glanced to his side. Augofleda gave him a wink. He smiled back. She was no Aphrodite, he had to admit. But she had proved to be much more than that. A wise counsellor, a cherished companion, and a fierce bedmate. His own smile was answered with a lift of the head and a roll of the eyes in the direction of the tedious deacon.

For a moment, he wondered if anyone else had caught him napping. His eyes roved over the dignitaries, both Roman and Goth, sitting closest to him. He noticed with some satisfaction that he was not the only one that had found the occasion an ordeal. Pitzias' head was slumped forward and a trail of drool hung like gossamer from one side of his mouth. Everyone else's attention was dutifully focused on the rhapsodies of the cleric.

With one exception, he noted. Theudis was looking straight at him. Having caught his eye, his friend nodded towards Pitzias. Then nodded towards the King and grinned. So he had been caught out! He could expect some ribbing later from his friend. Hopefully over a drink or two.

That was part of the problem. It was not so much that he begrudged listening to compliments. After all, his own people had a similar custom. But in the Gothic case, the praises were delivered by a skilful *skald* and the eulogies were shared by the whole band of warriors. Last, but not least, the stories would be accompanied by food and drink. In significant quantities. At night. Not in the screech-scorch of the midday sun.

His stomach rumbled and his gullet rasped. He shifted to a more upright position and feigned full attention. This was not easy. Even if Ennodius' speech had been full of wit and invention, its single-note delivery would have cured sleeplessness. But instead it was sheer bombastic drivel. And only by an effort of the will was Theodoric able to ward off the winter-slumber of the bear.

He leaned forward in his seat in an effort to locate the sun from beneath the awning overhanging the royal enclosure. It must be late afternoon by now, and surely the priest would not go on beyond nightfall. Unfortunately the sun was at their back. But by looking at the length of the shadows cast by the troops flanking the pavilion, Theodoric reckoned it was still early afternoon.

That was bad enough, for Ennodius had started boring them mid-morning. Theodoric sneaked a look behind him. There were attendants ready to meet his every need. And he was hot, dusty and thirsty. But a panegyric was a mark of respect, and deserved to be met with equal respect. Even if he was under no illusions as to the true reason behind the speech. As Theodoric would have put it in his soldiering days, Ennodius was trying to cover his own Roman butt, while licking the king's Gothic one. He had heard rumours that the deacon was calling in favours to put his name forward for a bishopric.

The king lifted his royal arse very slightly to remove the folds of his sodden robe from between his buttocks and to relieve the circulation.

Well, he decided, before Ennodius found himself seated on a cathedra, he would have to make his speeches a lot shorter.

Theodoric decided to focus his attention on the panegyric – for a moment or two, at least. If he could figure out how far in his own illustrious history Ennodius had come, then he should be able to figure out how much more he would have to sit through.

He caught something about the Goths retreating. To the far side of the river. Theodoric frowned. That did not sound good. It sounded as if his men were craven fools.

Ah, but then our hero comes to the rescue. Undaunted, the invincible warrior-king rouses his troops from their torpor. Leading by example, he spurs his horse into the ranks of the enemy, laying them waste with his trusty blade.

Not much of a clue there, then. It reminded him of no battle he had ever fought in. Not surprisingly, he supposed, since he very much doubted that Ennodius had ever fought in one himself.

Who was the enemy? Perhaps that would give an idea of where we were in the timescale.

The Gepid host lay scattered on the ground, 'carrion for crows'. Mmm. That was a bit better. Sounded like a *skald*-like formula, at least.

Just a couple of years ago, then? Excellent! Must be nearly finished.

That awkward misunderstanding with the Emperor over territorial jurisdiction. Just when old wounds were healing. Pitzias should never have pursued the Gepids into Eastern territory.

But if Pitzias was leading the army, then it can't have been....

'...to do battle with the usurper....'

Theodoric sank back in his chair and sighed.

Odovacar, then. The story hadn't even reached bloody Italy yet. He was still being waylaid by bandits on his way to fight the poor bloody German. So we've still got years of civil war, not to mention all the marvellous deeds he had performed since taking the throne.

There were limits. He beckoned to one of the cup-bearers.

As he drank the diluted wine, he grimaced. He'd never acquired a taste for it. But try getting decent beer here....

The dispute with Emperor Anastasius, he recalled, had been a major diplomatic blunder, and he had hauled Pitzias over the coals for it when he returned from the campaign against the Gepids. Zeno's successor to what was left of the Roman Empire had been a completely different kettle of fish from the eel-like Isaurian. Anastasius was a man of his word, in short. And had been reluctant to recognise Theodoric in any capacity whatsoever. It had taken years of arse-licking from Festus and Faustus, in the capacity of envoys, to get Anastasius to accept the Gothic king as a vaguely defined governor of Italy.

Theodoric smiled to himself. At least and at last, he had found a use for the two toadies. Both before and after Pitzias' incursion. But even now, the rift with the Emperor had barely been healed. He had to watch his step every inch of the way – every edict, every law that concerned the Roman Italians had to be referred to Constantinople for approval.

'King of Goth and Roman alike!' Ennodius roared with unusual animation. And his roar was echoed by some sections of the audience. Even Pitzias woke up. Tulum meanwhile was on his feet jabbing the air.

No! That was the whole bloody point he had been making to himself. Theodoric himself stood up and the equivocal roar subsided to an uncertain murmur.

The King wagged his finger at the deacon.

'King of the Goths. Protector of the Romans.'

This time the clamour of the crowd was wholehearted. Ennodius flushed and appeared uncertain of how to continue. The commotion was so great that he was unable to.

Bowing his head to the King of the Goths and Protector of his own folk, and gathering up the considerable remainder of his speech, he slunk back into the throng until he was lost to view.

Theodoric sat down and grinned broadly to himself, then to Augofleda. Mission accomplished. He would, of course, be obliged to read the rest of the panegyric at some time in the future. It would not take him long, he was sure.

It would also give him more time to devise a suitable reward for the panegyric – one that would meet with public and personal approval but be enough to dissuade future forays into arse-cramp-inducing stupor. At the time, he had felt the award of a quaestorship to Cassiodorus for his own hymn of praise had been be too generous. It had certainly resulted in further effusions on the part of the pompous official at every possible turn.

But fair was fair. At least Cassiodorus knew how to keep you awake, varying pitch and speed, so that every time Theodoric had been about to nod off, a horn-like bray would summon him back to full attention. There was a lot wrong with Cassiodorus' verbal composition, but little to be faulted with his vocal chords. Besides, some of his more outlandish flights were positively amusing.

So he got his quaestorship after all. Not many people made the king laugh. A more material gift would have to suffice with Ennodius. Something that the deacon could display with pride, but that gave no promise of advancement.

He would have to think about it. He had little talent for tactful gift-giving.

*

The Goth king adjusted his robes as he sat on the throne. Then nodded to the attendant to admit the petitioners.

He wriggled on the seat. If he had been allowed any say in the design, he would have made it more comfortable. But the loyal and excessively capable Liberius had insisted. The purpose of the throne was to inspire awe, not induce relaxation.

His feeling of physical discomfort was matched by a sense of mental unease. He had been playing the part for more than ten years now. But still felt awkward in the presence of ultra-civilised Romans. As if their very cultivation were a tacit commentary on his own background. No matter that he had had an education in knowledge and manners from the best. He was always aware of his lack of, what should he call it? Pedigree, *they* called it.

Added to that, his own careful preparations for the audience had been interrupted and thrown into disarray in the most pleasant way. He had just finished an extensive toilet. This had included being bathed, scraped and perfumed, then robed in his finest. He was seeking approval from the hard-to-please glass in his chambers, when Augofleda had entered. She had primped and preened him with her stubby-soft fingers, adjusted the folds of his robe, oiled an unruly lock of hair into submission. Then found fault with the way the tunic hung around his lap. Then found the reason for this. Then lifted his tunic and her own and done her best to rectify the matter.

Nervously now, he took a furtive sniff of his armpits, leant forward slightly to check any giveaway odours from lower down. Then gathered the folds of his gown over his lap, as the memory of the romp with his wife aroused him once again. Rumours of a tumescent king at court were all his detractors needed. Put a monkey on the throne and see what you get. The king of the jungle. Bestial instincts running amok.

And the feeling of inadequacy was aggravated by the knowledge that the first and chief petitioner to be heard was generally considered one of the most learned and cultured of Romans, and of a line that could be traced back to the Republic.

Never mind that he himself considered Cassiodorus more than slightly ridiculous. The man always sounded as if he'd listened to too many panegyrics of himself and taken them too literally. Not that Theodoric held it against him. He enjoyed the man's company. He enjoyed the humour, intentional or not. On the few occasions that Theodoric was unable to restrain his hilarity, the fellow took it in good part, and joined him in laughing as if it was the best joke ever told. He had a glint in his eye that seemed to justify the idea that the humour was shared. Or perhaps he just had a self-love that rebuffed all attempts to undermine it.

Theodoric breathed deeply and sighed long. He missed the good-fellow belly-laughs of the wassail hall. In court he still wasn't sure what passed for a joke. Laughter here seemed to be restricted to the polite chuckle, the snide snigger and the raised eyebrow of appreciation at artfully constructed expressions. There was little that was shared about it. No doubt his lack of understanding of Roman wit was also due to his lack of pedigree. Perhaps his descendants would master the technique. All he could do was to imitate slavishly and soullessly.

Sound seeped through the doorway. Theodoric pulled himself upright from the slouch he had assumed in search of a more comfortable position. He glared at the doorway. It was framed by swirling columns that seemed to depict serpents devouring brightly-coloured birds, and was definitely not to his taste. Perhaps he could get Liberius to suggest something more acceptable that didn't breach protocol.

The doors swung open to admit two attendants who swung round with the doors, happily concealing the garish portico in the process.

As the servants took up their positions, two figures entered – one familiar, the other not.

The first was in himself of unremarkable appearance. Of middling height and no more than slightly overweight, with coarse almost plebeian features, Cassiodorus could disappear in a crowd when he chose to. Here in this elevated setting, the man seemed to inflate in size, so that his magisterial toga with its purple stripe looked suddenly too small for him. He advanced towards the throne with a curious mixture of confidence and deference, all the while with his left hand trailing behind him as if he were holding the second figure on a leash.

Theodoric's attention now switched to the follower, who was still partly hidden by the billowing robes of the quaestor. From what he could make out, the fellow seemed to be of an age with Cassiodorus, but carried himself more modestly. On his face he wore an abstracted expression, and on his body, a simple unadorned tunic. He approached the throne with his hands clasped in front of him and his eyes elsewhere, almost as if he were bored by the proceedings.

Inevitably, it was Cassiodorus that spoke first.

'Glorious Majesty! Illustrious benefactor! Father-ostrich to we poor Roman hatchlings!' He swept the sleeves of his toga towards the ground and bowed his head. Then half-lifted it to judge the effect. As he did so, he gave a knowing smile, as if challenging the king to take his nonsense seriously.

That was it, thought Theodoric. That was what he did all the time. Spouted like a geyser, then undermined his own performance. As if he were subverting either his own eloquence or the authority it was expended upon. Theodoric waved his hand as if to curtail the courtesies and encourage the quaestor to get to the point. To no avail.

'The father ostrich, whose love for his own race is so great that he happily surrenders his independence, assumes the mothers' role and cares for all the offspring of his harem, suckling them from his own bosom.'

The king had seen ostriches but had no idea of their habits.

'Is this another of your flights of fancy, Cassiodorus?'

'Regarding yourself or the lifestyle of the ostrich, Lord?'

'Well, both actually. I find the spirit of self-sacrifice on the part of the male ostrich somewhat hard to believe. Not to mention his ability to breastfeed his young.'

'And yet it is attested to by no lesser authorities than Herodotus and Pliny.'

Theodoric groaned. He was familiar with neither author, even if he had heard of both.

'Well then, it must be true,' he conceded. 'But the analogy is false. I may indulge you Romans, but you are hardly of my own race or progeny.'

'The male ostrich is also famed for his tenderness towards orphans, sire.'

'QED, I suppose.'

'You put the matter in a nutshell, Sire.'

'To business then, perhaps? To what do I owe the pleasure?'

'Ah, indeed. What pleasure is service? The service you do us all by shining so brightly on us for so long. The service I hope to do you by introducing you to my latest pet project.'

'Project, Cassiodorus?'

'Allow me to present the young Boethius.'

The quaestor stood aside for the king to get his first full view of the protégé.

'He looks no younger than you, Cassiodorus.'

'Young in experience, Lord. In experience. A deficiency that I would urge you to fill. As the spring rains bring refreshment and fulfilment to the parched river beds and dry valleys of Arabia.'

This was accompanied by a nod that broached no contradiction of the fact, although Theodoric had always assumed that it was summer that brought the rain to the desert.

'And what does 'young' Boethius have to say for himself? In what capacity might he best serve us?' he asked instead.

Young Boethius seemed to have lost what little interest he had shown in the proceedings. Cassiodorus had to prod him to get a response.

'I have many interests and equally many areas of expertise.'

'Perhaps his Lordship would care to set a task of his own choosing,' Cassiodorus suggested, with a furtive scowl at his client.

Theodoric was also beginning to get irritated. He wondered whether the fellow's reticence was due to shyness or arrogance. Or was it simply indifference?

'Very well. We were recently privileged to listen to a sublime summation of Our Career to Date. By the Inestimable Ennodius.'

Cassiodorus's lips puckered, as if he were enjoying a private joke.

Theodoric waited for a reaction from Boethius, although it was a while before the protégé realised this.

'I too was present,' he admitted eventually.

Theodoric nodded.

'I wish to express my appreciation in a manner befitting the artisan and his handiwork.'

Boethius stared back at him. His face gave nothing away. In fact the only variation in expression it seemed capable of were 'present' and 'absent'.

'If you will allow…,' he began.

Cassiodorus stepped forward, his hands clasped in supplication.

'Forgive, Lord. My client is unfamiliar with court protocol. I can assure you, he means nothing….'

Theodoric leaned forward to address Boethius in confidence.

'Your patron intends that it is conventional to address me with the customary respect. That is, affixing an appropriate honorific.'

Boethius looked blankly back at him.

'Like Lord, or Sire,' Cassiodorus advised.

Boethius let his gaze fall to the ground, then raised it again.

'I may have something 'befitting', *Sire*,' the protégé stressed the honorific. 'It will require you to accompany me to my workshop.'

Cassiodorus stepped forward, his hands out once again.

'Lord, a thousand apologies….' He whipped round to address Boethius. 'A king summons. He does not answer summons.'

Boethius shrugged.

'He is not my king. In any case, he may choose to refuse. It was hardly a summons.'

Theodoric chuckled.

'He has a point, Cassiodorus. In any case, I don't get out enough these days.'

He called for his cape to be brought and slung it round his shoulders, pulling the hood up around his face. Not from fear of assassination. The land was at peace and the people content, as far as he could judge. He simply wanted to be able to pass through the streets without being recognised. To see how people occupied themselves and hear what they talked about.

So it wasn't just getting out into the open air that attracted him. He did that on a daily basis when he tended his garden. It was more the diversion from court business. And a chance to see how his subjects lived. Most of all, perhaps, a workshop sounded fascinating.

The rest of the petitioners could wait.

*

'Fascinating' was an understatement.

They had approached through a garden devoted to exotic flowers and herbs and entered a modest one-storey mansion on the outskirts of Ravenna. Most of the area was devoted to the workshop, although Theodoric wondered if 'laboratory' were not a better word.

True, some of the implements and devices he recognised from his frequent visits to smithies within and without the Empire. There, occupying the far corner, was a blazing furnace, tended by a servant covered and masked in leather. In front of it, the obligatory anvil, hammer and tongs.

But elsewhere, the instruments were more mysterious. The room was flanked with wooden work surfaces, occasionally topped with marble slabs – more often with crucibles, mortars, pestles, stands and what looked like stills of some kind. Behind the work benches, there were serried ranks of shelves, on which rested glass jars containing powders of various textures and colours.

Throughout the room, an acrid smell hung in the air and seemed to condense on the king's hair and skin as he lowered his hood.

'Extraordinary, don't you think, Cassiodorus?' Theodoric said, rubbing his hands with delight.

Cassiodorus gave an uncomfortable nod. For once, he seemed lost for words.

'You live here alone?' Theodoric asked Boethius, looking round for signs of or space for domestic life.

'I sleep on the floor of the workshop while I am here.'

'Your family?'

'In Rome. Where I am also to be found when the senate is in session.'

The king gave him a questioning look.

'I can find what I need more readily here,' Boethius explained. 'And my wife does not appreciate the smell.'

'Much how I imagined an alchemist's workshop to look,' the king said. 'And stink.'

Cassiodorus began to look even queasier. Boethius, meanwhile stood with his head cocked on one side, gazing at Theodoric.

'You wished to see the suggested commission? Or are you waiting for a guided tour?'

'A guided tour indeed?' Theodoric chuckled again. He was beginning to find the fellow's gall a refreshing change from the gloze of courtiers and suitors. 'Later perhaps. For now, you are right to remind us of the purpose of our visit.'

Boethius gave a curt nod, and retrieved a box from a storage closet.

'Something along these lines, perhaps,' he said, pulling out the artefact in question and placing it on the work surface.

The king's eyes opened wide as he regarded the object. It was beautifully wrought, in every detail and shade faithful to the original. But...

'A peacock?' he asked. 'It is exquisite. But to your knowledge, is Ennodius an enthusiast of birdlife?'

'To my knowledge, you asked for a gift befitting the artisan and his handiwork. Not something that he would necessarily appreciate.'

Theodoric brought a hand up to his mouth to conceal a smile.

Meanwhile, Boethius pumped the head of the peacock up and down. It began to strut and scream along the bench, until the mechanism wound down. Then it slowed to a stop.

A worried frown appeared on the face of Boethius' worried patron. The king laughed delightedly. Cassiodorus' face cleared.

'A remarkable creature, the Argus,' he began. 'I have it on the best authority that it uses the eyes of its tail to hypnotise the female into quiescence.'

Theodoric ignored him. Again struggling to suppress a smile, he asked:

'And in what way would you say this artefact befitted the panegyrist?'

Boethius bowed his head.

'That is for yourself to deduce, not for me to dictate,' he replied, adding 'Lord' as a postscript.

The king bent over and prodded the device.

'It certainly keeps in motion, and voice, for a remarkably long time,' he said. 'I have never seen anything like it. May I?'

Boethius nodded, and Theodoric picked it up. He examined it briefly, then shook his head.

'Please explain. How does it work?'

'It is a spring-driven automaton. When I charge its head, there is a gear that transfers that vertical motion into a circular motion that in turn coils a spring. Further gears transfer the motion of the uncoiling spring to the legs and tail, and to a bellows that feeds air through a reed. Hence the accompanying sound.'

Theodoric exchanged a look with Cassiodorus. The quaestor was nodding approvingly, as if he had taught Boethius all he knew.

'I can't honestly say I understand much of that,' said Theodoric. 'But I am deeply impressed. Did you invent it *ab nihilo*?'

'I can claim no such honour. The Greeks had such automata. I have simply been reviving the science with the help of some research.'

'This, I have never heard of. Fascinating, don't you think, Cassiodorus?'

Cassiodorus gave a sceptical nod.

'Heron of Alexandria was reputed to have created machines powered by steam that were capable....'

Theodoric interrupted him.

'And do you follow any other trades besides the creation of such automata?' he asked.

Boethius gave him a look bordering on contempt.

'I do not consider 'trade' a fitting occupation for a patrician. This is a hobby merely. A bagatelle.'

Theodoric again found himself struggling to keep his face straight when confronted with such disrespect.

'Well, what other interests do you have, if that is a more fitting way of expressing it?'

Boethius wafted his hand in the air.

'Everything is of interest, if you have the curiosity. And the intellect, of course.'

Theodoric appealed to his patron in frustration.

'Perhaps you could inform His Majesty which other projects you are currently concerned with,' Cassiodorus urged.

'A treatise on music, based on Nicomachus of Gerasa's famous theory and Ptolemy's *Harmonica*, a commentary on and translation of Porphyry's *Isagoge*, a discussion of Aristotle's Categories.' He recited the list in a monotone and single breath. '*Inter alia.*'

A regal eyebrow shot up.

'You favour the neo-Platonists then?' he asked.

Almost for the first time, Boethius looked at the king directly.

'I find their ideas interesting. And challenging. And your royal self?'

That was a new twist on the honorific, and hardly a respectful one. Still Theodoric persevered.

'I find their ideas interesting and challenging.'

The edges of Boethius' mouth almost twitched into a smile.

'You may realise that my own faith is very much influenced by the teachings of Plotinus and his disciples,' Theodoric continued.

Boethius nodded slowly.

'Of course, you people are followers of Arius.'

The king nodded in turn.

'We have that privilege, although the faith is regarded as a heresy now by the Orthodox, of course.'

Boethius snorted.

''Orthodox' is a shorthand for 'ignorant'.'

'How so?' asked the king, shocked despite the apparent show of support.

'It means the search for knowledge, for truth has stopped. All things that attain stasis become infected, and decay.'

'And how would one ever find the truth then?' Theodoric asked, genuinely interested now.

'The truth is a process not a product. The finding is in the seeking.'

Theodoric cast a glance at Cassiodorus to see what he made of all this. The quaestor still seemed to be lost for words and responded only with a weak smile of commiseration.

'The journey rather than the arrival, so to speak,' the king mused aloud.

Boethius looked at him again, this time with some surprise and interest.

'Such is the tenor of much Eastern writing on the subject,' he said.

'I find this an intriguing idea,' Theodoric declared. He heard a barely audible sigh of relief from Cassiodorus. 'And would like to discuss it further with you.'

Boethius gave a gracious nod.

'For now, I would like to return to more practical matters,' Theodoric added.

'As His Lordship wishes,' Boethius replied.

'You have, amongst your many other talents, shown a particular gift for conceiving and creating fitting tokens of appreciation.'

Another nod, a little more doubtful this time.

'I have the most agreeable duty of gratifying two important allies in a similar fashion.'

Boethius gave a hesitant cough.

'The art of endowing appropriate favours requires a degree of research,' he said.

'Of what nature?'

'The nature of the recipient and the nature of the subtext.'

'Subtext?'

'The tacit message you wish to convey with the bestowal of the gift.'

Theodoric chuckled with delight.

'For example?' he asked.

'Do you wish to warn the ally, to threaten him, to please him, to placate him, or to put him firmly in his place?'

Theodoric laughed out loud now and studied the face of the young man before him. He had still not cracked a smile. The king wondered whether he had a sense of humour.

'The first recipient is my brother-in-law, Clovis King of the Franks and ruler of Northern Gaul.'

'The husband of your sister or the brother of your wife?'

Theodoric was momentarily thrown off-course. Considering the young man was such a polymath he was surprisingly ignorant of current affairs.

'The brother of my beloved queen.'

'The beloved brother of your beloved queen?'

'He aspires to the rest of Gaul. This would entail the removal of the existing ruler, an ally and a fellow-Goth. This in turn would place him in uneasy proximity with our own borders.'

'A threat then.'

'A potential threat, yes.'

'I mean the gift should convey a threat.'

'I have no desire to provoke him. Not at present.'

'You wish rather to soothe his savage barbarian brow, to quench his appetite for territory, to introduce him to more refined pursuits.'

Cassiodorus once again glanced nervously at the present barbarian king. Then once again looked away with relief, as the king continued to appear highly amused.

'I could not have put it better myself,' he said.

'I have in mind a harpist,' Boethius said.

Theodoric looked suddenly doubtful.

'I fear he already has a court minstrel and bard.'

'One, I guess, that celebrates the martial and incites to warfare.'

'That is the custom.'

'I have a musician of a different quality in mind, a fellow I know well.'

'And his quality?'

'He would reduce the stoutest soul to tears.'

Again Theodoric could not hold back. He guffawed loudly and violently. He seriously doubted whether a harpist would be enough to restrain the thirst for dominion of the Frankish king. There would be a time of reckoning there, when he himself would have to snuff out that ambition. But the idea of the degenerate thug weeping his heart out was hilarious, and definitely worth the outlay.

'I take that as a mark of approval,' Boethius said with a smile, more of self-satisfaction than amusement. 'And will make the arrangements. Now if that was all....'

He made as if to usher them out.

'Hold up one moment,' Theodoric said.

Boethius gave an audible sigh.

'There was something else?'

'I mentioned two allies.'

'Now that you remind me.'

'You will wish to know the name of the second.'

'I imagine I have little choice in the matter.'

Again Theodoric marvelled at the effrontery of the man. Now he had accustomed himself to it, he wondered how he could make use of one that had so little respect for the conventions. In his apparently indifferent integrity, he reminded the king of Liberius. But he was clearly more various in his areas of expertise. Theodoric decided he was intrigued by the insolent bastard, when he had got over being insulted and exasperated by him.

'You have heard of Gundobad?'

'I have, but forget in which context. With such a loutish name, I assume he is another barbarian.'

Theodoric forbore to ask him what he thought of his own Gothic name.

'King of the Burgundians. And another important, if dubious ally.'

'Dubious?'

'He breaks his word with the regularity of the watch calling the hours.'

'And you would prefer him not to, I take it.'

'That is too much to hope for. I would have him only delay breaking it for a while.'

'This has something to do with the problem you have with your brother-in-law perhaps.'

'There are elements in common. Gundobad is my son-in-law.'

'You seem to have exercised poor judgement in your marital alliances.'

Theodoric bridled again.

'This goes by the name of diplomacy,' he said.

'And it sounds as if you lack some expertise in this field.'

Theodoric almost rose to strike the insolent devil down, but thought twice about it.

'I shall seek out your advice in future,' he said at length. 'For now, in further answer to your question, I fear Gundobad will, despite my efforts and his pledges, ally with the Frankish king against the Visigothic kingdom.'

'Also I presume, a relative of yours.'

'Alaric is also my son-in-law.'

'So the subtext is placation again?'

'I do not fear Gundobad. He has all Clovis' ambition but none of his intelligence.'

'So a bribe and a warning.'

'You put it in a nutshell.'

'As you did.'

Theodoric looked at him, totally bewildered.

'*The barbarian king breaks his treaties with all the regularity of a timepiece.* To paraphrase your words.'

The king was none the wiser.

'Item,' Boethius continued, 'One sundial. What comes around goes around. As the sun completes its course daily, so do our broken promises return to bite us in the rear.'

'Excellent,' the king said, smiling.

'Item, second timepiece – one water clock.'

'Same message writ larger because repeated?'

'And an exhortation to patience.'

'A product of your own workshop again.'

Boethius nodded.

'I fancy the chiming of the clock's hour can be signalled by a *caput mortuum*.'

'A skull?'

'*Mors vincit omnia*. Death conquers all.'

'As opposed to love being all-conquering, I take it.'

Boethius raised an eyebrow and nodded.

'Catullus?' asked Theodoric.

'Virgil actually, sire,' interjected Cassiodorus, suddenly coming to life. ''Let us then yield to love', being the continuation. An interesting development of the bucolic with its invention of a mythical Arcadia, although Catullus….'

''Let thou then yield to death' would rather be the 'subtext' here I guess,' Theodoric broke in.

Boethius was regarding the interaction between his patron and the king with something approaching amusement now.

He gave another curt nod.

'You wish to approve the result before dispatch?' he asked.

'I wish to witness the construction of the project,' the king replied. 'I also look forward to discussing Plotinus with you.'

Boethius glanced at Cassiodorus again. And yet again Theodoric had difficulty reading the expression on Boethius' face. It could have been interpreted as a request for the patron's approval. But going by the corresponding expression on Cassiodorus' face, it had clearly been taken as a gesture of the client's triumph.

A Matter of Interpretation

Guilt's deserved punishment
Falleth on the innocent;
Boethius

I awoke with a crash and a start. Owen stood over me grinning. I had not even been aware I slept. Or conscious of where I was, for that matter.

It came back to me. The cellar had become too warm for comfort. And in any case, I had no desire to be discovered *in flagrante* by Paulinus when he came to stoke up the boilers at dawn. So I had taken myself back to my cell along with my booty, and continued to read by the light of the lamp. The cold and Boethius would keep me awake, I figured.

I figured wrong. For some reason Ennodius drove sleep away, while Boethius brought it on. I could only think that the deacon impelled me to think of anything but his own words, while the philosopher soothed me with his own thoughts. Or simply I had been deprived of sleep so long that even the amiable Boethius could not keep me awake.

'I'd be obliged if you would contrive to make less of a racket at this time in the morning,' I told Owen, in an effort to wipe the grin from his face.

'It's nine o'clock, and you've missed Prime,' he replied, swinging the shutters wide-open so that the piercing light of a fine winter's day might blind me and thus prove his point. 'But if you hurry, you might make it for Terce.'

His eyes turned to the floor.

'Besides. You woke yourself.'

I followed his gaze until my own eyes rested on the ground and the bookstand that lay shattered upon it. I must have pushed it off the table as I slumped forward in sleep.

'Shame about the furniture,' Owen continued relentlessly. 'Nice bit of wood that.'

I glared at him.

'Wasn't here when I went to bed.' He switched his eyes to the table and chair. 'Neither were those.'

I had, in fact, decided I had had enough of standing at the lectern when reading and exchanged it for the furniture in question after returning to my room. As I made clear to my servant. Though why I felt obliged to provide him with an explanation was beyond me.

'Borrowed?' he repeated.

I nodded.

'Nicked, more like.'

'Nicked?'

'Stolen, Purloined. Removed from the purlieu of their rightful owner.'

The man had become a walking thesaurus.

'Borrowed,' I insisted. 'Temporarily removed from the custody of its rightful owner and to be restored to same in due course.'

'With said owner's permission, of course.'

My lips remained tight-closed.

'In the middle of the night,' Owen persisted.

I turned my face away.

'I will, of course, inform the custodian of my action as soon as our paths cross.'

Owen grinned again.

'Perk of the job, innit. A bishop's got more clout than an abbot.'

The interrogation by a menial and his rapid shifts between the formal and the vernacular were doing nothing to settle my newly-awoken brain. The man, but for the twists of fortune and birth, would have cut a pretty figure in the legal profession.

'Any case,' he continued, 'you'd have a bit of a job restoring that to its rightful owner.'

I gazed forlornly at the broken stand.

'I don't suppose…,' I began.

'Union rules, mate. I don't do joiner's work and he don't do mine.'

I gathered up the fragments and inspected them. There was a clear split down the middle of the stand, while the book slope was splintered into shards.

I wondered if for a small consideration Owen might take the blame. After all, he had no face to maintain.

'Perhaps you might….'

'Not on your nelly, Nelly.'

I took that as a refusal. But 'Nelly'? What had she to do with it?

Owen looked thoughtful.

'Simplest course would be to pay for a new one.'

I squirmed in my seat and ran my hands over the shattered object. I was on a meagre allowance until I took up my post. What little money I had left would see me back to Crotona and no further. At the monastery I was reliant on the hospitality they owed to travellers.

A thought came to me, and I rushed to my bed in a panic.

Thrusting my hand under the mattress, I retrieved my purse and gave a sigh of relief as I tested its weight.

Now Owen's look was reproachful.

'A den of thieves,' I said. 'I have it on good authority.'

'Not a very Christian attitude, your bishship,' he replied.

I resisted the urge to hurl Boethius at him, and settled for Procopius instead. He caught it in mid-flight. My man was proving as adept at *trigon* as he was at splitting legal hairs.

I determined to test him further and hopefully put him in his place.

I lifted the *Consolations* from the table where it had landed following the collapse of the stand, then hefted it in my hand.

Owen immediately took up a parody of a catcher's stance.

'Let me throw a question in your direction. Instead of a book, that is,' I said.

He maintained the stance.

'Ready when you are, guv.'

'Boethius asks why evil men prosper, and good men fall into ruin.'

In truth, I had no more than browsed the book, and found little to advance my understanding of the events of the time. The passages of verse I found delightful. But I had difficulty following the argument. Perhaps because I've never had much of a grounding in philosophy. These days it was only taught insofar as it lent support to theological truths.

I was also a little wary of the tenor of the book. I had read only a small part of it, but had seen no mention of God or Christ, despite its popularity in Christian circles.

The central question, variations of which ran through the sections I had browsed, was one that had troubled philosophers and theologians alike, and one that had troubled me throughout my training for ordination. And it was also the one that I now challenged Owen to answer. I was interested to see what the voice of the people would make of it.

Owen looked surprised.

'Well, they don't necessarily, do they?' he said.

Now it was my turn to look surprised.

'I mean, generally speaking, you're as likely to find an honest man doing well for himself as a wicked one,' he continued.

I felt my hackles rise again. How did he manage it? First principle in casuistry – deny the truth of the propositional premise.

'Well, generally speaking, why do evil men prosper at all?' I demanded, as if he owed me an explanation for the general state of affairs.

He gave me an earnest look.

'I'll level with you, guv. In my line of business, I don't come across too many prosperous men.'

'But you must have served some.'

'And they were very good to me, they were.'

I sighed, and decided to try a different tack.

'Well, what about the wicked? Shouldn't they be punished for their transgressions? I mean, look at the so-called brothers in this place.'

'Mmm. I wouldn't say they're actually prospering here, would you? Besides most of the bad lots I've come across, have pretty much come to a bad end.'

He nodded to himself.

'A very bad end, in some cases.'

Then he looked at me squarely.

'Besides, if you don't mind a word to the wise. You ask me, you shouldn't be so ready to rush to judgement. If you look into it more closely, you'll find that some of the *so-called* brothers here have been punished out of all proportion to their *so-called* crimes. Even the toga-lifter.'

'Toga-lifter?'

'Polite word for a sodomite.'

'Ah.'

I believe I might have blushed a little. No doubt the rank and file used such terms. But not in front of the officers. Probably because quite a few of the senior, that is Roman, officers would have fit the description. The rest of us, I imagine, preferred to think such phenomena did not exist – at least not in the lower ranks. And if they did, then the men would sort matters out amongst themselves.

I suddenly felt exhausted. And ignorant of so much. Game, set and *trigon* to the amateur. He was out of my league, outclassing me in forensic law, philosophy and theology in one fell sweep. Not to mention being considerably closer to the brim in Christian charity. If he hadn't made me feel so inadequate, I would have clasped him in my arms. As it was, I had to restrain myself from clasping him round the throat.

And the only way I could manage that was to head for the open air.

*

The light through the window had not deceived.

As I stepped out into the gardens at the rear of the monastery, the brutal beauty of the mountain winter hit me with full force. Indeed, the sun was shining so fiercely that it blinded me for a moment. But as my eyes adjusted, I began to make out the majesty of the skyline, one that reminded me of the campaigns in the Caucasus. On the one hand, the stark contours of the mountain crags, fleeced with a fine coating of snow; on the other, the restless sea, appearing as a bed of shifting, inverted cloud. And cradled in the lap of the mountains and seeming to spring from the earth itself, the squat buildings of the monastery, constructed from the surrounding tufa, and still overlaid in places with crumbling slabs of marble.

Suddenly elated by the change in weather and the stunning vistas, I turned my mind back to the conversation with Owen and began to look on the bright side. Both here at Vivarium and then at Crotona, he might actually prove to be a fount of common-sense, and keep my head on my shoulders. *Vox populi*, indeed. Speaking truth to power, they called it. I wondered if Boethius had tried to do that with Theodoric. I wondered if that had caused his downfall.

A bell rang somewhere to my left. When I had toured the gardens with the abbot, I had been so impressed by the magnificence of the Master's house that I had failed to notice a smaller building tucked in between the main complex and the Residence. Now I could not fail to see it, for the monks and the abbot were, in ones and twos, coming out of the portico. The end of Terce, I assumed. I had not attended the Monastic Hours since my arrival. I had taken clerical rather than monastic orders, and felt no obligation to fall in with the others.

But two things caught my attention. Firstly, the full complement of monks was not much greater than the few that had attended meals in the refectory with me. Secondly, the building itself bore more resemblance to a minor pagan temple than the churches I had seen in the Eastern capital and beyond. It was rectangular in form with a shallow pitched roof, and although the gaps between them had been filled in, it was still possible to discern the columns and capitals that must have formed the original frontage. No doubt, if I inspected more closely, I would find statues of priapic figures cavorting round the nave and satyrs flaunting themselves in the apse.

My attention was suddenly drawn back to the monks themselves. Arminius was arguing fiercely with the abbot, waving his hands about in barbarian fashion and at one point grasping hold of Basilius' arm. It looked as if his protests were on the point of becoming more violent until Uldin laid a restraining hand on the shoulder of his friend.

It seemed that not all was peace, love and harmony here. And that the lack of respect for the abbot I had previously noted sometimes took forms other than the merely verbal. Out of idle curiosity, I checked the reactions of the other monks. Anacreon, the cretin, was close behind the leading trio. He appeared to be enjoying the entertainment. Further back, the heterodox Italo-Greek, Isidorus was it? looked a picture of abstracted piety. Head down and arms folded over his breviary, he seemed totally unaware of what was going on around him. Meanwhile, the doorkeeper, stoker and retired lock-picker, Paulinus was standing by the entrance of the church, as if waiting for someone else to come out prior to locking up.

Josephus, presumably, although I wondered whether the man would condescend to attend the hours.

Not Josephus.

I had forgotten about the aged dwarf that had been escorted in to dinner on previous nights. Now he had two brawny attendants assisting him as he hobbled down the steps of the church-cum-temple. As before, it was not entirely clear whether they were there to protect or guard.

Another mystery perhaps. Although it was one that did not touch closely upon my commission, the identity and status of the man aroused my curiosity.

As Paulinus closed and secured the door, his robes were suddenly whipped up about his calves. A moment later, the gust reached me. The wind had changed about and now blew from the mountains of the north. I gathered my own robes about me and headed for the shelter of the main building.

*

Despite the bracing wind, I felt I had not yet recovered my self-respect enough to face my man. So I headed to the one place I was sure he wouldn't be.

As I entered the library, I found I wasn't alone in seeking refuge there. Josephus had presumably hidden here to avoid Terce. Or perhaps he claimed a higher duty by reading some uplifting tract. Augustine, perhaps. Or Jerome.

After nodding a greeting to him, I lowered my head to read the title on the back of the volume perched on his bookstand. Then my head snapped back and I stared at him in surprise.

'*Various Epistles of Cassiodorus*?' I asked. I had never heard of such a publication. Nor had I come across it when browsing either the open or the closed stacks.

Josephus also looked surprised. He swung the stand round slightly and read the title himself. Did the man not realise what he was reading?

'So it would appear. Is the volume of interest to you?' he asked.

If it had anything to do with the reign of Theodoric, then it might well be of service.

'Of what do the letters speak?' I asked.

'I have absolutely no idea,' was the reply.

I looked at the book again. It was lying at an angle and open approximately halfway through.

Josephus read the question in my eyes.

'I selected it at random a few days ago,' he said, as if that explained it all. 'Please take it, if you feel it might be of interest to you.'

He picked up the substantial volume, closed it and handed it over, leaving a sheaf of loose parchment perched on the stand. As I took the book into my hands, I peered round at the writing on the front of what it had concealed. I was none the wiser. The script was unknown to me. Oriental erotica, perhaps. Though that did not square with my image of the Jew.

'Hebrew?' I guessed.

'Chaldean. An astrological guide.'

'Necromancy, in other words.'

'The words are yours. The interest all mine.'

He walked over to the bookshelves, paused to read a few titles, and selected out a title that presumably met with his approval. Then he walked back to his stand, opened the book at random and placed it behind the Chaldean manuscript.

I sneaked another look. Ambrose's *Exposition of the Psalms*.

Josephus smiled at me.

'Probably give me a better excuse for missing Terce,' he said.

I heaved a sigh. The man was incorrigible. As his present or future bishop I supposed I should remonstrate with him, even if I was sure my words would be wasted.

I was saved the effort by the entry of Basilius upon the scene.

It clearly cost him even more of an effort than it would have cost me to reprimand the Jew. He had screwed his face up into a tormented caricature and wrung his hands together, perhaps to stop them shaking.

'It grieves me greatly...,' he began.

Josephus looked up over his half-bottle-bottoms, all innocence.

'Pray share your thoughts with us, dear abbot,' he said.

'This is not the first time I have been obliged to remind you of the rules of the order and of your continuing presence within the monastery walls,' Basilius said, speaking it seemed as much to me as to the Jew. 'I regret having to do it in the presence of his Lord Bishop.'

'Good Lord!' Josephus replied. 'Did Terce ring already? I must have been so carried away by the words of the Blessed Ambrose that I missed the summons.'

The abbot looked down at the forbidding book propped up by the stand and flushed.

'Words of wisdom, indeed, Father,' Josephus continued and proceeded to quote. ''What is more pleasing than a psalm? It is a shield when we are afraid, a vision of serenity, a promise of peace and harmony.''

Poor Basilius blanched and looked as though he wanted to sink into the earth.

'A lesson to us all, I'm sure,' he managed to squeeze out eventually, though his voice was a hoarse whisper.

I took the abbot aside.

'We all find our own roads to salvation,' I said by way of consolation.

His expression was that of a dog that thanks its master for stopping beating it.

'Your flock seems particularly refractory today,' I added sympathetically. While I tried to think of some similar platitude to conclude with, along the lines of a good shepherd allowing his charges some latitude or some such nonsense, Basilius looked at me with panic-stricken eyes.

'I hope you don't think….,' he began.

I don't know what he thought I thought, because he never finished the sentence. Perhaps he thought I thought that Arminius had acted like a rejected lover. If that was the case, I tried to put his mind at rest.

'Our friend here does not seem to be the only one reluctant to observe the Hours. Brother Arminius looked less than enthusiastic.'

He drew himself upright.

'The offices are a form of penance as well as monastic duty.'

I nodded slowly.

'And they have much to repent, I suppose.' I was curious, after all, how and why this motley crew had decided to take orders at this place and this time.

'We all have sins to atone for, Lord Bishop,' he said with an absent air. Almost as if he were talking to himself.

'There was one of the brothers in particular that I was interested in,' I said. 'I wondered what specifically he might have to repent.'

'If I may enlighten you without breaking the seal of the confessional,' Basilius replied, recovering his dignity a little.

Needless to say, I hadn't figured the confessional into the equation. Indeed, not everyone practised private confession. But given the nature of his flock, public confession might prove too time-consuming, not to mention embarrassing.

'An aged man, always accompanied by one or more escorts,' I said.

He gave me an odd look and drew himself up straight.

'I cannot help you there,' he said.

'Then perhaps I will have to approach him directly.' There was something about the abbot's sudden assertiveness that annoyed me.

'As you say, he is always accompanied by escorts. These will doubtless interpose themselves.'

'But not in the confessional, I take it.'

A look of panic flitted across his eyes again.

'As his immediate superior, I am his sole confessor.'

'And as your not-so-immediate superior, I can override that privilege,' I pointed out.

His arms hung by his side, but I could see that he was clenching his fists. I wondered if it was from frustration, or out of a desire to punch me.

If the latter, he restrained the impulse. He turned on his heels and left the library.

I looked across the room at Josephus, wondering how much of our conversation he had picked up.

'That went well,' he said. 'I wish you much joy of it.'

A certain satisfaction, yes.

It struck me with increasing force that the abbot held the key to the many mysteries abounding in this place. But trying to get information out of him was like trying to squeeze sap from a stone. Yet the effort brought a pang of guilt too. Apart from the feeling that I had abused my authority, I felt sorry for the man. It was possible that, by his own lights, he felt he was doing his best for the abbey and for its occupants. But only by unlocking these secrets could I judge whether his benevolence was sincere.

In the meantime, Josephus' comment suggested he was also privy to facts that were still hidden from me.

'How so?' I demanded. 'You think I might experience difficulty?'

'You may find you need an interpreter for your interview with the fellow.'

'Meaning he is not of these parts?'

'I am not sure of his country of origin,' the Jew replied. 'But he speaks in an idiom that even the Chaldean necromancers would have trouble deciphering.'

I grunted in reply. That remained to be seen. If the fellow proved to be beyond my capabilities, then I could enlist the help of Owen in the first instance. He seemed to be capable of making himself understood in most circumstances, so presumably the reverse was true too. If all else failed, I could once again abuse my authority and enlist the help of my fellow-confessor, the abbot himself.

Meanwhile I would check through the collection of letters that Josephus had used to camouflage his studies of the occult.

I opened the front cover and glanced through the preface, which seemed an exercise in false modesty. Of the kind that expresses a reluctance to publish, but under pressure from friends and in the interests of the public, he feels an obligation to make the extent of his own selfless service known to the world at large.

Stuff and nonsense.

I let the book drop, and rubbed my arm. The volume was heavy and my arms were no longer young. I needed a stand and looked around for the library for one that I could use as a support. There was none visible apart from the one Josephus was using.

I looked over at him. He was looking at me.

'There appears to be a sudden shortage,' he said.

I agreed.

'I regret to say that the monks are in the habit of removing them from their rightful place. Goodness knows what they do with them. Few are even able to read.' He shrugged. 'Firewood, I expect.'

I think I had the grace to blush.

'I have to count myself as one of the offenders.'

The Jew grinned.

'As the good abbot pointed out, none of us are wholly innocent.' He cocked his head on one side. 'May I enquire, then, why you do not simply fetch the stand from your room?'

I explained the accident.

'I'm sure it happens to the best of us,' he said. 'I'll have a word with Brother Isidorus.'

Then he returned to his study of the Oriental night-sky.

'And how would that help?' I demanded.

Josephus peered over the top of his documents.

'The man is an absolute genius with wood and stone. Even made the frame for these.' He pointed to his lenses. 'Ever visited the baptistery in Asculum Picenum?'

I shook my head.

'The exquisite carving over the porticos? His work. He'd have gone far if it hadn't been for you know who.'

He tapped the side of his nose.

Nosetaps or no nosetaps, I had no idea who he was talking about.

'A victim of the Codex,' Josephus explained in a stage whisper.

Right, I thought. Justinian had outlawed not only Jews and pagans from public office. He had also clamped down on heretics. And the meek brother had expressed Pelagian sentiments. Church work would be out of the question, then. And there would be little other outlets for the talents of a gifted stone and wood-carver.

'Poor chap was a nervous wreck when he first arrived,' Josephus recalled. 'Better now. Though not entirely recovered.'

He smiled tightly at me.

'I'll have a word,' he said.

I thanked him.

He rose and stretched.

'I think I need a break. The Chaldean form of Aramaic is unfamiliar to me, and a strain on the eyes and the brain.'

He closed the Ambrose with its less orthodox cargo and laid it on the desk. Then he pushed his stand in my direction.

I nodded my embarrassed thanks and returned my attention to my own volume.

The rest of the book was devoted to the letters themselves – correspondence with both high and low – pleading, exhorting, commanding, on behalf of his master, King Theodoric. The preface had insisted that the style was adapted throughout to the station of the addressee. But I would never have noticed. As usual, he appeared too much in love with his own voice to forgo the most outlandish flights of fancy and erudition.

As far as my own purposes were concerned, there was little I could use. It was clear that Theodoric ran a tight ship of state and managed to delegate well to trusted servants. There was confirmation of facts that I was already aware of. And there were details that were altogether too trivial for inclusion in a summary of the kind I was engaged in. Elsewhere some of the letters hinted at their importance, but without an explanatory context, I could make no sense of this significance.

Before putting aside the text entirely, however, I decided to skim through one last time. I wondered whether the paths of Boethius and Cassiodorus had ever crossed, and if so, what Cassiodorus had made of the philosopher. To my surprise, the only mention I could find were letters addressed to Boethius by Cassiodorus on behalf of the king, commissioning him (in the most flatulent and patronising language) to send gifts to the Kings of the Franks and Burgundians.

I turned to the front of the book. The given date of publication was 542AD, years after the deaths of both Theodoric and Boethius. Yet there was no further reference to the philosopher, despite his years of public service. And it was astonishing that there was no mention of his trial. The latter at least, I should have thought, would have generated a good deal of government correspondence.

I slammed the book closed in frustration. It was as if I was being thwarted at every turn from fulfilling my own commission.

Josephus looked over. He had resumed his study of the arcana without the aid of his book support. An eyebrow was raised in my direction over the top of his bottle-bottoms.

'You claimed to have been employed in 'high public office', if I remember rightly,' I said.

He nodded.

'Can you be more specific?'

'The *Cursus Publicus*.'

Now it was the turn of my eyebrow. The office was prestigious and important, not only for internal communications but also, as I understood it, the disbursement of funds to the provinces.

'And did you ever have dealings with Cassiodorus during your time there?'

He coughed. Or it may have been the closest he could come to an outright laugh. Then he pulled at one side of his moustache.

'My public office was not that high,' he replied eventually.

'But Cassiodorus would have been your ultimate chief?'

'With many other chiefs, intervening between us. Besides as Master of the Offices, he was effectively everyone's chief.'

'So you knew nothing of him.'

'I did not say that. It was difficult to know nothing of the first minister to the monarchy.'

'So what did you know of him?'

He shrugged.

'He was convivial, as far as that went. He always had a '*salve*' and a '*vale*' for those he wanted something from.'

Perhaps he did have the gift of talking to people from different levels of society then, I reflected. When he wasn't trying too hard to impress.

'And your general impression?' I asked.

Another shrug.

'He was good at getting what he wanted.'

Another thought struck me.

'He succeeded Boethius as Master, is that not so?'

Another nod. He looked at me with half-closed eyes.

'Your general impression of *him*, then?'

'On the basis of even less evidence. Boethius was considerably less involved with those that worked for him.'

'His reputation then?'

'Something of a prig, I would say.'

'You thought him self-righteous, sanctimonious even?'

'I did not say that. You asked for his reputation. He could equally well have been a man of honour for all I knew. Refusing to lower himself to subterfuge and flattery to get things done.'

Well, this was getting nowhere fast, I thought.

'We did have one thing in common, though,' the Jew added.

'To wit?'

'An interest in the occult. Or so it is rumoured.' He gave a chuckle, and returned to his reading.

*

I tried to curl my body into the smallest amount of space in the corner of the mercy seat. At least that was what Isidorus had called it as he restored the bookstand to me in pristine condition after lunch. When I complimented him on the quality of the workmanship, he simply shrugged, and talked about charity as stepping stones towards heaven. The Pelagian speaking again, I assumed.

When I asked him what other good works he had managed to add to his account here in the abbey, he replied that he had been charged with the design of the confessional and its 'mercy seat'.

And quite exquisite they both were – delicately carved in an abstract pattern that recalled the pagan Greek meanders, and scrolls that recalled the capitals of similar provenance. Quite compact too, so much so that there was no room for me to stretch out, even if I had wanted to. A superb compromise between the functional and the aesthetic, you might say. With the exception of the wind-proofing, or lack of, which was causing me to shrink into the angles of my otherwise ample seat.

There were curtains draped across the top of the stable door into the confession box and between the two compartments it contained. These did little to lighten my mood as I waited for my first penitent, since the draught caused them to flap across my face at regular intervals, forcing me further into the confines of my prison.

I pulled the drape to the side slightly to see if the penitent was on his way yet. Basilius had said that the scheduled time was just after *nones*. *Nones* had been and gone for the past half hour and there was still no sign. I moved my eyes away from the entrance of the chapel and looked around the rest of the interior, just in case he was waiting for *me* to show up. The rest of the bleak interior did little to lighten my spirits. The walls had been whitewashed, presumably out of decency to disguise what lay beneath. The only decorative relief was afforded by Isidorus' subtly ornate custom-made divine thunderbox.

I was just about to give up hope when I caught the sound of distant footsteps. Then a protracted creak as the chapel door was pulled open. I hastily drew the external curtain back and adjusted the dividing curtain so that it would not be immediately obvious that I had taken the place of his usual confessor. As I did so, I heard the sound of whispers. Much as expected, he had his escort with him.

The curtain moved a little again as the penitent took his seat on the other side.

'Forgiveness, please,' came the disembodied voice.

That went without saying, I thought. It seemed to be a prerequisite for taking orders here.

There was a pause, and I realised that something was expected of me in reply. Unfortunately, I had no idea what. The practice of private confession was by no means uniformly accepted, and I had had no training in the forms.

I mumbled something indistinct in Latin.

The screen between us was ripped open.

'Where is he?'

A wizened crab-apple of a face confronted me. But despite the ripples that surrounded each feature, the snub nose, moist lips and rheumy eyes remained well-defined. I stared back at him and realised that he was peering into space. The eyes were covered with a film of pale-blue and he must have been nearly sightless.

'The Father Abbot is indisposed,' I explained. 'As his superior, I felt obliged to fulfil his usual pastoral duties.'

'And who is he?' he asked, to my confusion.

'Father Basilius, of course,' I said. 'Your usual confessor.'

'He,' he insisted and pointed at me.

'My name is Jordanes, Bishop of Crotona.'

I felt that this was going to be either a very short or a very long confession, if the penitent had command of only one pronoun. I hoped for the former. If he confessed regularly then he had no long-outstanding sins to get off his chest. As for more recent ones, it was difficult to see what a half-blind geriatric in a monastery could get up to, that would take so very long to account for and absolve. Then we could proceed to the questions I had about his identity and his reasons for being here under escort, or guard.

'Your sins, I reminded him.'

'We made weewee in our pants this night,' he said. He giggled and rubbed his hands.

My heart sank. The man had obviously entered his second childhood. If there had ever been an intervening period of intellectual maturity, that is.

'Continue,' I sighed.

'And this morning.'

I wrinkled my nose. This afternoon too by the smell of it.

'*Te absolvo in nomine padre etcetera*,' I said, wishing to bring the proceedings to an end. The smell was becoming overwhelming in the confined space.

I started to make the sign of the cross, then a thought occurred to me.

'I need a name to address you by,' I said.

His eyes looked blankly at me.

'Why?'

'So God knows who to forgive.' Of course.

'This must not be said,' he replied, a finger on his lip.

'It will be between you, me and God,' I explained.

'Not to be said,' he repeated, and this time drew his finger across his throat.

Clearly he was not totally demented.

'Well, why are you here, then?'

A grin this time.

'Not to be said.'

I sighed once again, and this time completed the cross.

Out of frustration, I threw away a final question, the sarcasm in my voice scathing and no doubt totally lost on this cretin.

'And in your days at the Academy I don't suppose you ever came across the famous statesman and philosopher, Boethius, did you?'

A tear formed in the corner of the rheumy eye.

'Uncle Manlius was very good to us,' he said.

Well, that was that then. The man was a total moron. It was quite obvious that if I wanted to research the history of the man-with-no-name further, I should have to take it up with Basilius again.

The penitent left the box and re-joined his carers.

Then it struck me. Father Basilius himself lacked a confessor. None of the monks would be qualified for the position. And the poor chap looked like he had a load to get off his chest. A good confession would have a huge amount of therapeutic value, I was sure.

And I knew just the man for the job. It would fill in the idle hours as I waited to fulfil my main commission.

I smiled to myself, rubbed my hands together and followed the idiot out.

Illumination the Fourth
The Consolations of Philosophy

AD 524

'I Anicius Manlius Severinus Boethius, being of sound mind…'

That begs a question. If the world has not lost its faculty of reason, then I must have done so.

'…do bequeath all my worldly goods…'

I would rather leave a good name. But there is little possibility of that when I have been found guilty of treason. Inter alia.

A pointless exercise, perhaps – the writing of a will. If I die intestate, then my property will in any case revert to my eldest son, to whom I, being of (questionably) sound mind, would in any case bequeath it. Unless it be forfeit to the state, that being the traditional penalty for my supposed crime.

Why doth guilt's deserved punishment fall on the innocent?

A rhetorical question, perhaps.

But the King is not Roman, so he may choose not to apply the traditional penalty.

He may still choose to extirpate my line, another traditional Roman practice. But Theodoric, withal, is a Goth. And a just ruler.

Was a just ruler.

For the most part.

Perhaps a Goth blood mulct, then? A ransom, so to speak. A King's ransom.

*

He does not come to me. If only to curse me and mine.

I could then explain the nature of the plot against me. Or what I understand of it. He has always listened before. Is a good listener.

Then he would surely pardon me.

'Pardon'.

The word presumes a crime and forgives it. It does not absolve the perpetrator of guilt. And I am not guilty. Not of that, at least.

127

So I would have to refuse. To do anything less would be a stain on my honour. My name is all I have left, even if it is left only to myself. He still does not come. He has not been once to visit me. Did not even attend the show-trial. But then, neither did I. They did not even allow me to defend myself.

And I, more fool I, had always thought him a reasonable man. Had come to respect him. Love him, even. If I am capable of love. If love can exist in a world such as this.

I am sure he loves me.

Loved me.

How then, when all is cast into doubt, can I be sure that his love for me once existed? Even if now it appears to have been withdrawn?

Reason, Boethius. Reason it out.

Reason the First:

Since our paths first crossed, he bestowed preferment upon me above all others. To the extent that I reached the highest office in the land, preceding and exceeding everyone in rank and favour.

Reason the Second:

He bestowed preferment on my line, raising my sons jointly to the rank of consul. Unprecedented, both on the grounds of number and of youth. And the happiest day of my life.

'In adverse fortune the worst sting of misery is to have been happy.'

A happy thought?

Reason the Third:

Not a reason.

I recall the hours we spent together in my workshop, enquiring into nature either by reasoning or by experiment. We shared our curiosity, our spirit of enquiry.

And they accused me of necromancy? Then the King was my partner in the so-called black arts.

Perhaps that is why he keeps his distance.

Aristotle called the discipline 'Physics'. And like Aristotle, we did not limit ourselves to the study of subhuman nature, but spent many happy and fruitful hours examining, debating human nature. Both in general, and more specifically the motives and characters of our allies, and our enemies.

If loving friendship may be defined by shared interests and intimacy, then we were loving friends.

Surely.

But how, other than grace and favour, intimacy and shared interests, did he prove himself worthy of my affection?

Response:

He showed himself to be honourable. Above all else, honourable. Fair in his dealings with both Roman and Goth. And, despite his barbarian temperament, he learnt how to bridle that passion in the interests of the common weal.

Or so I thought.

Though proud, he was not too proud to ask for advice. For indeed, his judgement was uncertain. To his credit, he was aware of this. To his detriment, he often chose unwisely in his counsellors and his officers.

Exemplum:

The case of Theudis. Why the King should have entrusted him with the role of regent to the infant Visigoth King of Spain is beyond me. Already the scoundrel is giving every sign of usurping the throne for himself. It would seem that Man by his very nature inclines towards treachery and ambition.

An all-devouring greed
Yawns with ever-widening need.

Indeed.

Theudis' appointment was recommended by my own patron, as he likes to call himself. Another case in point. Cassiodorus was and remains a plodding functionary in all but his own loud opinion.

Him whom good fortune has made a friend, ill fortune will make an enemy.

Perhaps.

Withal, I have spent the years of my service in admiration of a flawed man doing his best to rule honestly and well, and have done my best to correct the mistakes of his other advisers.

And for the most part succeeded.

*

Or perhaps the King himself changed. Degenerated, as barbarians are reputed to do.

Perhaps he became unhinged by the death of Eutharic, his chosen heir. Husband to the King's daughter. Father to his grandson Athalaric. No doubt, the King had hoped to leave the dynasty and his dreams secure.

Now it hangs by a thread. An infant in the arms of a woman, neither recognised as legitimate heirs by the Emperor of the East.

And thus 'unhinged by grief and despair' the good King became a tyrant?

Why, then, shouldst thou feel affright
At the tyrant's weakling might?
Dread him not, nor fear no harm,
And thou shall his rage disarm;
If only….

It is more likely that his mind was poisoned by the same traitors that poisoned my name and my honour.

*

A gaoler enters bringing me food. That is what he calls it.

He is broad as a barn and tall as a tower, and has to stoop and squeeze to get through the narrow door.

I have two gaolers. Like everything else in Italy, there is an 'equal' divide between the Roman and the Gothic. Equality before the law, but two respective law codes. Equality of opportunity but within respective spheres. And here, equality of responsibility for my safe-keeping. Touching, is it not?

The other gaoler, then, is Roman. He brings me smiles with my food, and allows my meals to be brought from home. For a suitable fee, of course. He also smiles as he listens to my questions and entreaties, and promises to convey them to the appropriate authority. Then he brings me no answers, only more honeyed words, empty assurances.

The Goth promises nothing. Instead, he takes delight in spitting into my food before my eyes. After he has tasted it to demonstrate it is not poisoned. His sputum can do little to impair the taste, so I take it in good part. I smile. He smiles back.

I prefer my Goth carer.

*

The responsibility for my betrayal, if I should call it that, was also shared. Gothic treachery was more than matched by Roman perfidy.

*

The Goth gaoler watches me eat, then announces I have a visitor. It can only be Symmachus. My oldest friend. My true patron. Adoptive father, father-in-law and godfather to my sons. Apart from my gaolers, he is the only person I see.

For the King himself does not come. Perhaps they keep him away from me. Have forbidden him to visit? Forbidden a King?

I have forbidden my wife and children to visit me here. Partly out of shame. Mostly out of fear. They may be tainted by association with me. Even Symmachus says he is being followed. And watched. He may not be able to gain entry again.

My other 'friends' have deserted me.

To be fair, I have never consciously solicited friendship. I have rarely felt the need for it. When others seek my love, I am immediately put on my guard. Most usually, they wish for my patronage. What they request most often conflicts with my own sense of honour and virtue. When I dismiss their suits, the word goes round that I am haughty, priggish, sanctimonious even.

There is perhaps some truth in the charge.

Symmachus makes the same point. Once again he stresses how ill-advised I was to take upon myself the supposed guilt of Albinus. I admit my words were poorly chosen. I had intended only a standard rhetorical trope. To wit, 'I find it quite incredible that this man should be guilty of what you say; if this be true, you may as well assume that I am equally guilty'.

Unfortunately, either as a matter of convenience or as a genuine instance of literal-mindedness, the inference was that I was, in fact, equally guilty. That I was, in fact, the ring-leader of the so-called conspiracy.

I can imagine Cyprian's expression of triumph as he read out my testimony, then brandished the letter before the court and announced that I had thus admitted what the letter claimed. I had been tricked. Cyprian had not told me that my 'signature' was appended to the letter, along with Albinus' own. I had thus 'confessed' what they had already 'proved'.

The letter was forged, of course. Forged well, I assume, if 'my signature' was anything to go by. I was later allowed to read that part of the letter for myself. And that part only.

'And my suit?' I ask Symmachus, as casually as I can manage.

My friend looks down. Perhaps he has been distracted by the rats that scurry through the rotting straw spread across the earth floor. They search for scraps from my unlovely meal. But no. He is, again, simply unable to meet my eyes.

The lack of light casts all into shadow.

'The King continues to refuse to see me,' he says. 'Refuses to see anyone, for that matter.'

Now he looks at me.

'They say he falls into a rage at the very mention of your name.'

'They?'

'I have solicited the help of your successor as Master of the Offices.'

My other 'patron'. He, at least, survived the taint. He would survive the Second Flood.

'To what end?' I demand.

'His new position allows him access to the King at Ticinum.'

He pauses and studies the floor. It is far from here to Ticinum.

'He has managed to obtain pardons for Albinus and other of the accused senators.' Another pause. 'He has offered to do the same for you.'

I wonder for a moment if I have done the man an injustice, but then say, 'I would prefer not to solicit his help.'

Symmachus looks up now. His eyes are moist.

'The King listens to him....'

'He takes too much pleasure in imagining himself me to be his client.' Now I pause. 'As if I were his subject.'

'He has shown himself generous.'

Meaning the King, of course. I meant the Master of the Offices.

I let the misconstruction be.

'When it suits him,' I add as a qualifier.

'Then I am afraid all hope is out.'

'Perhaps the Emperor himself...,' I begin.

My friend allows himself a wry smile.

'That would simply compound the assumed felony,' he says.

My Roman guard minces in, stands and simpers a moment. Asks if there is anything we need.

'Justice,' I think.

'Wine,' I say.

He minces out again, but Symmachus' voice drops to a whisper.

'They claim you demanded *libertas* for the Romans.'

'I demanded no more than the safety and independence of the Senate,' I reply.

'They say ....'

The guard returns with what he claims is the best Falernian. Even though I liberally reward him, it is obvious from the quality that he takes a commission from the vintner.

Symmachus follows him out with his eyes and waits until the cell door closes before continuing.

'They say your call for liberty was in the letter.'

'The forgery, you mean.'

'Forgery or not, any appeal to the Emperor would simply be taken as confirmation of the authenticity of the letter and thus of your guilt.'

'The assumption being that liberty from Goth rule can only be granted by the East?' I ask. Although I know the answer.

Symmachus dips his head almost apologetically, as if it were his fault somehow.

I feel a knot tighten in my stomach and imagine one round my neck.

If true liberty were to be had, it would be more likely to come with the old and improbable Goth dream of a fusion of races than from the pseudo-intellectual tin-pot tyrant that effectively rules the East. I know this now.

I snort. My friend looks even more downcast. If that is possible.

'The letter was addressed to Justinian, after all,' he explains.

'The forged letter,' I point out patiently.

A pause. Symmachus does not think as quickly as he used to.

'If the letter was forged...,' he begins.

I look up sharply, then relent. I forget how frail he has become, my true patron.

'Given the letter was forged, – the question remains,' he says.

'Who forged it,' I finish for him. 'Cyprian, perhaps?'

'He claims the letter was passed to him by another.'

'But fails to mention by whom, I suppose.'

The state prosecutor is too astute to name names. He is also too smart to forge evidence himself.

Symmachus seems to collapse into himself.

'I can't think of anyone who...,' he begins.

I can, I think to myself. Someone that was not averse to feathering his own nest and had the effrontery to claim it was standard practice to accept bribes.

'Lubricators of state affairs', he called them.

'High office has always been a corrupter of the soul,' I say to my old friend in an effort to comfort and shield him from the brute reality.

'By their perversion to badness, they have lost their true human nature,' I think to myself.

It was their choice. No use blaming 'high office'.

Symmachus' tears run freely now. I place my hand on his shoulder to console him. As if it is he that is in need of consolation.

*

'Consolation' indeed. Where was I now…? My magnum opus. Also in a more accurate sense, my last will and testament. And if the judgement follows its course, then my last opportunity to reason my way to an understanding of the gross injustices inherent in human existence.

Perhaps I should rather say 'in my existence'. But I like to think that my case is not unique, and that I may therefore draw some broader lesson from my experience that may be of service to others. Or a consolation at least.

For as I wait on time, my text is a consolation to me.

In the absence of a pardon.

After all, whom am I trying to deceive? Of course I would accept a pardon.

What kind of Stoic does that make me then?

A fair-weather Stoic, I suppose. It is, after all, not difficult to exercise philosophical detachment when one's affairs are prospering.

However, *'good fortune deceives, but bad fortune teaches.'*

Or so I will claim in my manuscript.

Symmachus has repeatedly urged me to accept the 'one true and merciful god', as he puts it. And *'thy love the good must have, the bad thy pity claim.'* When all is said and done (his words again), I have made my contribution to a greater understanding of the faith. By means of my theological treatises, I suppose.

I had no wish to disillusion him, least of all at this time of tribulation. But these were never more than an intellectual exercise, an infantile and self-regarding pastime. For what were my intentions? Simply to demonstrate that I could dance as well on the head of a needle as any of those who made a living and a name at such pedantry.

Vanity. Sheer vanity.

Though if my desire for self-preservation were greater, and my desire to preserve my good name less, I could always claim a death-bed, or rather death-cell conversion. In the hope of 'forgiveness' or 'redemption', as they call it. A sort of wager that I could never lose. But a death of that kind would be a denial of my life, which I feel must have had some significance. If only to myself. And if my legacy is to be my name solely, then it is best that I leave one that is unsullied by duplicity.

What consolation can I find, then?

The souls of men certainly die not with them.

Or do they? As the case may be.

Perhaps acceptance. A quiescence that will allow me to slip gently back into the oblivion of Nature. A change of state merely.

For change is surely the natural order of things. And unless I embrace the shifts of Nature, I will never be able to accept the present and coming change in my own condition.

But we have alienated ourselves from the natural cycle, and I am no exception. For what else is civilisation? No less than the attempt to arrest that change. To call a halt to time, to history. Another vanity. For all reverts, like the salmon, to its source. The only course for me now is to bear up. Show true Stoicism when it is called for most.

One law only standeth fast:

Things created may not last.

That sounds right. Short and to the point.

In the meantime, where was I up to in my text, this Socratic dialogue by which I desperately search for synthesis?

Let me see…

Yes. I have summoned up Mistress Philosophy to answer my own charges – that she has betrayed one of her faithful followers. Myself, of course. In response, she has promised to prove her worth and cure my 'wound'. To wit, why the wicked prosper and we virtuous philosophers fall.

Yes. And so I call on the example of Plato, who claimed that all would be well with the common weal if only it were blessed with a Philosopher King. For it was thus I chose to enter public service to guide the Goth and teach him to rule in the desired manner.

I should have known better. Plato himself failed to distinguish philosophers from tyrants. Or are philosophers as corruptible as the rest of mankind?

Mmm. I should take this up later perhaps. But here I think I will simply emphasise my own good intentions in the face of the moral torpor of others. Cunigast, for example. And Triguilla, most definitely.

And thus to the accusations levelled at me. The hatred of Cyprian, the Prosecutor. The perfidy and perjury of the informers that witnessed against me. All of whom had grudges, all of whom had rightly suffered justice at my hands. (Should not that fact have been taken into consideration?)

Opilio, there was. And his partner in crime, Gaudentius. Then most treacherously of all, Basilius. And what credit did these have as witnesses? Basilius. I ask you. On my advice, he was arraigned for his debts and dismissed from royal service for corruption. The King, in this at least, showed good judgement.

The King, alas.

Ah, if only he would come.

The Revised Version

Herein is revealed that of which thou didst erstwhile profess thyself ignorant.
Boethius

'Basilius?!'

I must have shouted this, although I had not meant to wake Owen from another interminable slumber.

And I must have shouted it with some force, because he jumped to his feet. His hand fumbled for the knife that he usually wore at his waist. Not finding it there, he cast his eyes about him wildly until he found me looking back at him.

HIs confusion diluted the sense of discovery that had thrilled through me. A sense of discovery, along with a sense of something less pleasant. Owen's discovery of no-one more threatening than myself in turn dispelled his alarm.

'Where's the fire?' he asked, recovering his composure at the same time as his absurdity.

'No fire,' I replied, 'but plenty of smoke.'

He thought for a moment as if groping in the darkness of his consciousness.

'The abbot?' he asked.

A good question.

I had decided to plough my way through Boethius' *Consolations* in the hope of finding clues to the mystery of his downfall. Or, failing that, clues to why an apparently pagan book should be so popular amongst Christians. Or failing both, some Consolations for my exile to the 'rectum of the world'. Owen also described Vivarium in a similar manner. But used different words.

I had not got far into the book before I reached Boethius' account of his indictment and trial. It did little to enlighten me. It simply compounded the mystery of his crime and punishment. But the manuscript did mention some of those who testified against him – 'informers', he called them.

One of those was called Basilius.

Owen shook his head.

137

'Baz's all right. Anyway, I know a grass when I see one. He'd not even turn in his worst enemy.'

I really wished he wouldn't do this. It was guaranteed to annoy me and was probably intended to. And it was bad enough having an insubordinate subordinate without having this secretive omniscience thrown in.

He looked up at me as if he was waiting for me to throw the obvious next question in his direction – how exactly he knew this. I decided to keep the bone to myself and the dog waiting. For the time being, at least.

'The man may have a shady past,' I said instead.

'Not what you've done that's the matter,' he insisted. 'But what you do about it afterwards.'

That struck even closer to home. I gave a shudder as I recalled my own multifarious misdeeds. But Owen hadn't finished.

'I thought that's what your religion was all about.'

'What exactly?' I asked, genuinely puzzled.

'Letting bygones be bygones. Making good what you done wrong.'

I must have blushed. He at least had the grace to look away, before going out to feed the horses. Then another thought struck me.

'Your religion,' he had said. Which begged the question of what his religion was. If he had any. Which in turn begged another question. What had I ever done to deserve such an unholy servant? Courtesy of the Holy Father, to boot.

Left on my own, without distractions, I turned my mind back to the problem in hand. Boethius must have been writing the book just before he was executed – somewhere around 525, I would guess. Our abbot was now, probably in his mid-fifties. Which would have put him in his twenties when Boethius was tried. The time frame fit.

What's more, Basilius was obviously, judging by the way he acted and spoke, a patrician. Indeed it would have been out of order, I supposed, for a pleb's testimony to condemn a patrician like Boethius.

On the other hand, Basilius was a fairly common name and it would be an astounding coincidence if I had ended up at an abbey run by someone that was central to the history I was summarising. Having said that, the monastery itself, its inmates and the whole set-up were strange enough to make such a coincidence look fairly run-of-the-mill.

The simplest course would be to bring the matter up with the abbot himself. Gently, of course.

Until I did, I was left to my own devices as I tried to work out what had really happened. I turned back to *Consolations* and re-read the passage in question.

Basilius was, along with a certain Opilio and Gaudentius, one of three informers mentioned by Boethius. I wondered what they had informed about, since the main evidence of Boethius' treason appeared to have been provided by some letters, presented by the prosecution at the trial and purporting to have been in Boethius' own hand. This would surely have been enough to condemn him.

But the case was secured, Boethius implies, by the testimony of these three. What would they have been testifying to? Treasonous words spoken elsewhere by the accused? In which case, they must have been in Boethius' confidence. After all, it was hardly likely that anyone would broadcast such a crime in the local tavern.

Then there were the letters themselves. Boethius, it goes without saying, claimed they were forged. But what was in them that was considered so incriminating? All the author says is that they called for the 'freedom of Rome'. Not, I would have thought, such a serious crime unless it was specified that the freedom in question was to be from the Gothic yoke.

And who would he have addressed the letters to? His fellow senators? That might explain how Basilius *et al* were able to inform against him. But then why would he write letters? It would have been much safer and more sensible to sound out individual senators by word of mouth and in private.

In any case, Boethius presents Basilius and his accomplices as people in whom he would be pretty unlikely to confide. So presumably the word was passed on to them by others. For Boethius explains he had made enemies of these very men because he had brought actions against them for fraud and corruption. They would thus have a grudge to settle. Furthermore, Boethius claims that the informer's denunciations were made on the very day they were to be banished as punishment for these crimes. So they had every reason to perjure themselves, as a means of delaying their sentences, discrediting their accuser and avenging themselves on him.

Another reason for challenging the abbot on the subject. If he turned out to be the Basilius in question, of course.

But the question remained. If the so-called forged letters were not addressed to the Senate, who would they have been sent to?

This was really frustrating. If only Boethius had been a little more explicit. As it stood, I knew he was accused of treason on the basis of the letters and the oral testimony of the informers. But it was impossible to work out exactly what form the treason took.

By now my head was going round. But I had the bit between my teeth. This was a real mystery, and as such, considerably more interesting than the rest of my assignment put together.

Out of frustration, I turned to the copy of Procopius's *Gothic Wars* I had 'borrowed' from the underground library. Not that I held out much hope. It was fairly unlikely he would mention events that took place more than a decade before his Wars started.

But it didn't take long before I came across the name of Boethius in Procopius' background to the conflict. Even more surprising was the fact that he referred to both Theodoric and the philosopher in the most positive terms.

The king, he wrote, had 'made himself an object of terror to all his enemies, and also left to his subjects a keen sense of bereavement at his loss.' And this from the secretary to Count Belisarius! His master, after all, had spent much of his career fighting the Goths in Italy at the instigation of Justinian.

Boethius, meanwhile, was of 'noble and ancient pedigree', was 'mindful of justice' and was 'prodigal in providing relief to the needy'. Further to this favourable review, Procopius went on to say that Boethius had been accused of 'fomenting a revolution'. Treason, indeed – whatever one thought of Theodoric. According to Procopius, however, a guilty verdict was returned only because the informers had 'poisoned the ear of the Gothic king'.

I wondered why he had gone so far out of his way to whitewash Boethius. Again my interest was piqued. He cannot have been privy to or present at the action he describes. Perhaps he himself had read the *Consolations* and been charmed into believing Boethius' own account.

In my own experience, a condemned man would proclaim his innocence with his dying breath. Many a time in the past, I had listened with incredulity to court-martialled prisoners denying crimes that had been witnessed by multitudes, including myself. It seemed that human beings would sacrifice all honour in the vain attempt to preserve their lives.

But the question still bothered me. Who would the letters, forged or not, have been addressed to?

I turned back to *Consolations* yet again. I still didn't know what to make of all the annotations. If I tried to decipher them, would they provide me with an answer?

I decided to see if I could find any common thread. I turned page after page making a note of each change and comment.

After a while, I had to lean back in my seat and take a deep breath. I had assumed that the annotations were the work of a scholar who was intending to publish a new edition of the work, along with learned footnotes.

Instead the margin was peppered with words like 'bosh', 'piffle', 'nonsense'. I wondered if the editor had been a witness to the events that Boethius was describing, and so felt entitled or obliged to contradict the author. However, as I read further into the more philosophical sections of the book, the remarks persisted.

For example, when Boethius pointed out that 'more often than removing wickedness, high office brings it to light,' the marginalia read 'poppycock!'

This was not helpful. Even when the notes were less childish, they shed little light – either on the text, or the puzzle I was trying to solve. Sometimes they purported to correct a grammatical or orthographical error – although even with my fairly basic grasp of Latin, some of the corrections seemed debatable. On other occasions, they took exception to the simplicity of the style.

But it was, of course, the historical background that was most likely to help. And I could find few changes that might help with this. The deletions might have been more revealing. But by their very nature they were designed to conceal.

One erasure I found particularly mystifying. Shortly after the description of his trial and sentencing, Boethius complains, that he has been 'banished from all life's blessings, stripped of honours, stained in repute, punished... [deletion].' Over the deletion was written 'for my services.' This appeared to be of a nature different from the other corrections. It was difficult to attribute this to a stylistic quibble. Yet I could imagine nothing that might substitute for the amendment that might conceivably be considered inaccurate. Or incriminating for that matter.

Unless it was a belated confession – 'punished for my crimes' perhaps. As it was, the correction made little sense. Why would one be punished for one's services? And services to whom exactly?

I turned the page and held it up to the light, then wiped the edges of the deletion with spit in an effort to remove the covering ink. To no avail. All I achieved was a blinding headache and a smudged piece of vellum.

At this stage I slammed the book shut and was tempted to sling it across the room. After all, what was I doing delving into a mystery that the past that had for ever closed itself to me? My frustration was aggravated by a sense that I was wasting my time gratifying my own curiosity when I would be more profitably engaged in writing the summary of the damned history itself. 'Profit' in both the commercial and the physical sense. For I stood to gain not only financially by the completion of the project. I would also gain by retaining my members in the order and arrangement that God had created them.

The feeling passed soon enough. I recalled that I could make no further headway with the history until the final volume of Cassiodorus' epic arrived. So I might as well fill the intervening hours with something related to that enterprise, however loosely it might be connected.

If only I could look at the course of events from a different angle. With fresh eyes, you might say. But by now, I was so deep into the history that I could hardly think straight.

Owen, then? He had the virtue, if I could call it that, of cutting through to the pith of problems. But then I decided I could do without having my self-esteem withered by his scorn once again. In any case, I would probably obtain a more informed response from someone that was familiar with the history.

Basilius was out of the question for the moment. He may well have been complicit. Josephus would have to do. Even if I still didn't trust him completely, at least he had no selfish interest in the case. He might even remember the trial.

*

I found him in the scriptorium. He was in the company of Anacreon, who was alternating between writing letters, dipping his pen, then picking his nose with it.

A vicious east wind blew from the window on the sea side, stirring the tunic of Anacreon, who otherwise seemed oblivious to the cold. Josephus meanwhile was sitting with a fleece round his shoulders and had managed to pull his reading desk into a sheltered corner.

I blew into my hands and stamped my feet. To attract his attention as much as any protection against the cold.

He looked up from his book. This was invitation enough. I made my way towards him, then glanced down at what he was reading. As usual I could make sense neither of the letters nor the mathematical formulae that accompanied them.

'Chaldean?' I ventured.

'Hebrew,' he replied. 'Kabbalah. Numerology. Or necromancy if you prefer.'

At least I think that is what he said. Most of it meant nothing to me.

So I nodded wisely.

'A progression from the Chaldean esoterica, then,' I said.

He looked amused.

'You might say that. You wish to be initiated perhaps.'

I shuddered.

'I would be grateful for your views on a certain subject.'

'Numerology?'

'History. Recent history.'

He shrugged and pushed his book aside.

I looked across at Anacreon.

'The lad is harmless enough,' Josephus said. 'He barely understands his own name.'

I nodded and sat down on the opposite side of the desk.

'You are persisting with your study of the reign of Theodoric, I take it,' he continued.

I started at the comment, and wondered if this ability to read thoughts, or perhaps to predict the future, was related to his own studies of the occult.

My confusion must have been evident.

'You have sounded me out already on Cassiodorus' history and epistles,' he explained with a sigh. 'It did not take the Chaldeans or the Kabbalists, or anything more than common sense to work that out.'

I gave a curt nod of acknowledgement.

'As I recall, you were in public service at the time of Boethius' trial,' I began.

'I had that privilege.'

'So you would have been in Rome at that time.'

'You will recall I was employed in the *cursus publicus*.'

I gave a nod of encouragement this time.

'The administration of the Imperial road network and its messengers were distributed amongst different centres throughout the Empire.'

I gave a sigh.

'And at this time, you were no doubt on a posting close to the Persian border.'

He grinned with cracked yellowing teeth.

'Gaul, in point of fact.'

It had been a long shot. But he might still be a competent judge of the evidence I had gathered.

'News of the trial travelled as fast as the official post along the *cursus*,' he added cheerfully. 'However.'

It was my turn to grin.

'Hearsay only,' he said. 'No doubt, inadmissible as evidence. But it gave me an opinion.'

'Which was?'

'The whole business was what my good friend Paulinus would call a 'stitch-up.''

'?'

'Boethius was framed.'

'You mean he was innocent?'

'As the newly fallen snow.'

'But all the informers?'

'Bitter envious men that would be only too ready to accept a bribe.'

'You knew them?'

'By reputation only.'

'What about the letters?'

'Counterfeit. Clearly.'

I slumped back in my chair.

'That is what Boethius claims in his book.'

'I have not had that pleasure. But the man was, for all his faults, not a liar. Quite the reverse. He was the epitome of self-righteous honesty.'

He paused.

'Indeed he could be most irritating.' A grin. 'Hearsay again.'

'From?'

'Friends who were less honest.'

Well then, I thought. I had looked for a new angle on the case. But I wasn't sure how much closer this had brought me to understanding what had actually happened.

I rose and turned to go. Then a thought struck me.

'And the incriminating letters?'

Josephus cocked his head on one side.

'Forgeries. As I said.'

'But who do you reckon they were addressed to?'

'The Emperor, I imagine. Or, given his advanced senility, his chief minister and heir. Who else?'

Of course. Justinian, then as now. An appeal, genuine or counterfeit, for the East to invade and overthrow the Goth. To restore Roman rule in Rome and re-unite the Empire. That would be grounds enough for treason in Theodoric's eyes.

I sat down again. It was worth a try. I explained the deletions in the text. Notably, the one that I found especially mystifying.

'A problem,' he agreed.

'Irritating,' I replied. 'Nothing the Chaldeans might be able to solve, I suppose?'

He shook his head.

'But I know someone who might.'

*

Paulinus scraped away at the vellum with gentle patience.

With each stroke of the strigil, he removed a layer, using his finger nail to pry up any stubborn fibre. Then he wet the next layer with thumb and sputum, before repeating the process.

We had taken refuge in the underground library, thinking that defacing a valuable book would most safely be carried out away from the eyes of others. Despite the warmth of the cellar, I shuddered with anticipation. But I still had little idea how he would achieve what was intended – to reveal the deleted phrase.

He had started by turning to the back of the page in question, and was scraping through from the rear. Eager as I was, I felt all he was likely to achieve was a puncture in the text on both sides of the parchment.

But eventually he stopped rubbing and, with a finger on each side of the hole, judged the thickness of the remaining membrane. He looked at

Josephus who smiled his approval. Then he took a piece of charcoal, gathered some soot on the tip of a finger and applied it to the back of the vellum. Then blew away the loose dust.

By now I was totally mystified and wondered whether I was simply witness to some necromantic rite.

Paulinus then took hold of the oil lamp that provided our light and help it up against the membrane.

I whistled my amazement. The impression of the deleted phrase was now clearly visible – white against the black of the coal dust. The only problem was that the writing was reversed.

Josephus obliged by producing a speculum, which he held at an angle to the page and the light. It was now possible to read what had been written.

I did not know whether I should feel elated or deflated.

Instead of the substitute, 'ab beneficium', Paulinus had revealed the substituted, 'de benefactori'. In the original he had been punished, not *for* his benefactions or services, but *by* his benefactor.

I stared at the text for a minute or two, urging it to yield more. The spell was broken by Josephus.

'I used to be able to do this myself, of course,' he said. Then he crooked his swollen knuckles. 'Arthritis. So I taught our friend here.'

Paulinus gave a rueful smile. I expect he had learnt the trick too late to employ it for illegal gain.

'Works well with keys too,' he said – to my bafflement. Which combined with my disappointment to produce a massive sense of deflation.

Josephus guessed how I felt, although it did not require a forensic investigator to do so.

'This mean anything to you?' he asked.

'Does it mean anything to you?' I countered with a degree of asperity.

He took my bitter disappointment in good part and gave the question some thought.

'Ultimately, his patron, his benefactor, was the king, of course,' he said.

I frowned. It was true that the king would be finally responsible for the punishment of a traitor. But then why the deletion?

A bell chimed faintly back in the files of my memory.

'Wasn't Boethius orphaned early in his childhood?' I asked.

Josephus gave an absent nod.

'Mm. He was brought up by the senator, Memmius Symmachus.'

146

'Who provided his education and sponsored his career,' I continued.

Josephus looked doubtful.

'They were the closest of friends.'

'The patron-client relationship does not imply enmity,' I declared with a confidence I did not feel.

'He was executed shortly after Boethius,' Josephus pointed out.

Perhaps to silence him, I thought. This time I did not share my idea.

But it really was time for a word with Basilius, I decided. On two counts now.

The Meaning of Charity

Whenever a man by proclaiming his good deeds receives the recompense of fame, he diminishes in a measure the secret reward of a good conscience.
Boethius

As it turned out, Basilius got to me before I could get to him.

I wondered if he had come fresh from a bout of self-flagellation. He seemed to be glowing with piety. For the first time, I think, he looked me straight in the eyes as he spoke.

'We wondered,' he began, without specifying who the other party or parties might be, 'whether you would be so good to accompany us on the rounds.'

Rounds?

'I think I got the general idea on our first tour of the premises,' I replied. Even though the parts I wasn't shown were much more interesting than those that were.'

He stared at me, then shook his head as if to clear it. When it settled back into position, it wore an apologetic smile.

'Forgive me. I fear you misunderstand me. I should have explained myself more clearly.'

Clearly.

While I waited for a further explanation, my eyes dropped to his hands. For once there was none of the usual invisible weaving going on. They were totally at repose.

'We have the custom here of visiting the needy and the sick, and distributing alms amongst them.'

'Very commendable, I'm sure,' I replied, not rising to the bait.

He gave a nervous cough, at which his eyes began to wander again.

'We thought....'

'We?' I interrupted.

'... Brother Isidorus and myself...'

'Aah....'

'... that as the new bishop of the diocese, you might...'

Now I cleared my throat and drew myself up to my full height.

'I have not yet been consecrated.'

A pre-emptive strike, I thought, congratulating myself. I had no great desire to hobnob with the down-and-out. I had acquired quite enough fleas at the monastery, and no wish to contract a more serious complaint. The plague had now passed on in most places, but there were still pockets....

'Nonetheless. It would raise their spirits greatly to be honoured in such a fashion.'

No doubt.

'They otherwise enjoy few blessings in this life,' he continued.

Apart from the periodic handouts, I expected.

'The poor souls have been abandoned by the rest of mankind. A blessing from your hands will in all likelihood be the last occasion many will have to rejoice.'

My shoulders drooped, and my stomach sighed. It looked as if my unsolicited pastoral duties were to begin sooner than expected.

Ah well. That is how the oatcake crumbles, I supposed. If my presence managed to cheer the poor, it might go some way to making me feel less wretched for having accepted the invitation with such ill grace. I might as well put a good face on it.

So I did. Then I followed the abbot and his colleague out on their 'rounds'. Sadly there was little chance I would be able to raise my other business with him while we were in the company of Isidorus.

*

The weather for once was clement as we crossed the grounds of the monastery, then made our way along a goat-path through the jagged stone outcrops and couch grass. Up, and then farther up we climbed, in the company of a mule, driven by Isidorus and laden with packs of what I assumed was poor relief. At one point I turned and looked down the path we had taken. I felt dizzy and began to sway. The abbot took my arm and looked into my eyes with concern.

I patted his hand to reassure him. Then recovering my equilibrium, I gazed down again and then scanned the horizon. The roar of the sea was hushed here to a gentle whisper by the shrill whistle of the breeze.

I pulled my cape more closely about me. At this height the air was chiller and we were more exposed to the wind. But still I could not take my eyes from the stark grandeur of the scene. The monastery was lost to sight behind the crags. We might have been the only men left in the world. Or the first. A part of Nature, rather than in constant struggle with it.

For some reason the thought cheered me. I smiled as I turned to the other two. The abbot's eyes smiled back, as if he understood what I was thinking. Then he placed his hand on my shoulder to urge me forward.

'Not far now,' he said.

We crested a ridge and then dropped into a shallow valley where the vegetation was equally parched and sparse. Goats grazed among the crags, seeking out clumps of fresh grass and raising their front legs to pull down branches where withered leaves had clung on through the winter.

At least it was more sheltered from the wind here. Marginally. That and the presence of the goats made me think we might have reached a human settlement. But as my eyes ranged the bottom and sides of the valley below the pinnacles of rock that towered on the other side, I could detect no sign of habitation.

I turned to the abbot in question.

He pointed up towards the almost sheer rock face opposite. I looked at him again, more puzzled than ever. He said something that I couldn't make out. The wind was still strong. He cupped his hands and shouted in my ear.

'The caves.'

I looked again. Sure enough there were holes in the rock that man or Nature had carved.

Castalius had been right. I was bishop of a congregation of troglodytes.

'People live there still?' I shouted back, desperately hoping we had come sight-seeing rather than sick-visiting.

The abbot replied with a nod.

'You might be surprised,' he said. 'Some....'

I lost the rest in the wind that once again roared along the channel of the valley. So much for it being more sheltered here.

We paused at the bottom of the path and took respite from the fierce gusts in a ramshackle lean-to, intended presumably to serve as a goat fold. Only then was the abbot able to complete his sentence.

'Some of the caves are quite cosy, in fact.'

I gave him a sceptical look.

Isidorus chimed in.

'They provide shelter from the chill of winter, and shade from the heat of summer.'

I wondered for a moment if he was trying to sell me one of the cavities. He looked all sincerity. But his words reminded me of the patter of the 'realtors', they called themselves. Wiry men with furtive looks that hung around in the taverns on the edge of Constantinople. Ever ready to prey on the landless and dispossessed that streamed into the city expecting the streets to be were paved with gold.

I too had fallen victim to their cant when I had arrived in town to take up my post with Gunthigis Baza. He had failed to mention in his correspondence that the position included rooms in one of the more upmarket quarters of the city. So I had at first looked for a place myself and been escorted to what the 'realtor' in question had called a 'bijou pied à terre in a desirable suburb'. The property proved to be a basement in a crumbling and presumably condemned tenement deep in the red light area. It was to be shared with a heady mix of whores and highwaymen.

Meanwhile, the abbot was nodding his agreement with Isidorus' assessment.

'Then again,' he shook his head, 'times are hard.'

Perhaps the bottom had fallen out of the hole-in-the-wall market, I thought to myself.

'What with the war, and then the plague...,' Isidorus took up the refrain.

'And then the war again,' the abbot added. 'Bad enough that malaria's endemic to the whole area. But then on top of that....'

'Malaria?' I exclaimed. 'At this altitude.'

'The rains come with the spring and don't drain off. The valley becomes a swamp.' Isidorus this time.

The abbot nodded in confirmation.

'Then through the summer, the miasma rises with the dawn.'

I shuddered. I had been infected once. It had struck me down somewhere in Eastern Thrace and I had endured the fits at intervals for a year afterwards. I had no desire to repeat the experience.

Thankfully, however, it was winter now, so there was little chance. But clearly I had little reason to envy the denizens of this pocket-Paradise.

My heart sank further as we rose to the first opening in the cliff-face. I could see no reason why anyone would choose to live in such an unforgiving environment. Unless, of course....

I stopped in my tracks. The other two stopped in theirs and looked back down at me.

'Not lepers, by any chance?' I asked, catching my breath.

Basilius gave me a look that was part relief, part amusement.

He shook his head.

'Just refugees from civilisation.'

'From which, the Good Lord spare us,' Isidorus added quietly.

I wondered what exactly had given rise to his comment but decided there was little point in holding a philosophical discussion on a scree-ridden dirt track.

In the meantime, I followed the two of them up the remainder of the track and into the first cave. Before we entered, I took a deep draft of the good clean air outside. I expected it would be my last for the duration. Then I looked up at the honey-combed cliff-face again.

As my eyes returned to the opening in front of me, I looked down and noticed that a hollow had been cut in the rock parallel with the ground. In it, someone had placed a very roughly-carved stone. It appeared to be man-made, but I had difficulty making out what it represented. I lifted it out of the cup and ran my hand along the side. There was no question about it. Someone had taken time to cut and polish this indeterminate shape.

Only when I stooped to replace it did I realise what the cylindrical object portrayed. It was a stone phallus.

I wiped my hands on my cape, as if the fetish had been real.

It was obvious these people were not just refugees from civilisation. They had never been a part of it, in any meaningful sense.

But to my surprise, there was little to take exception to in the depths of the cavern. There was a faint but not disagreeable animal smell, which was only natural if they had to take in their livestock at night for fear of the wolves. And if their livestock consisted entirely of goats then it was remarkable that the stench was not greater.

Otherwise, the interior was not much different from any other self-respecting peasant hovel, and cleaner than most. The floor was covered with what looked like a mixture of sawdust and sand, while a fine covering of soot coated the walls. The source was not hard to detect. A fire burned in a hearth below a man-made flue that led most of the smoke out above the entrance. Beside the hearth stood a number of rough clay pots and wooden cooking utensils.

I could see little in the way of furniture. Small piles of straw lay on the floor here and there, presumably serving as seating or bedding, depending on the time of day. But the straw itself also looked clean, as if it were changed daily.

In conclusion and in defiance of my expectations, the place was warm, relatively dry and almost cosy.

The only thing that was lacking were people.

Basilius sought to remedy the lack by calling out. If what he called was a name, then it was one I had never heard. If it was anything else, then the language was unknown to me.

The response came from deep in the darkness of what I had taken to be the back of the cave. It sounded the same as the original call, so I assumed it was a greeting of some kind. And that some primitive tongue survived in these mountains. If so, the abbot was familiar with it.

He followed the call to its source and Isidorus and I followed him. Astonishingly, the cave extended far beyond what I had taken to be the rear wall. As we turned a corner, the faint glow of a rush-light became visible and cast vague human shadows against the wall. We seemed suddenly to be in an underground amphitheatre of considerable proportions. Basilius' voice echoed into the distance as he exchanged what I took to be the greeting with what I took to be the members of the family that inhabited the cavern.

There must have been about a dozen of them gathered in a semi-circle against one of the sides of the cave. As I came closer, I could make out what had captured their attention. A rough mattress. The size of it suggested that it usually served the whole of the immediate family. For now there was just one figure lying there.

A shudder ran through me. Not from the cold. Although we were now far from the fire and although there was no visible source of heat, the large space was warm enough. The chill I felt was came from being in the presence of the dying. This was not something that I had been told. There was no need for that.

Basilius muttered something in the same barbaric tongue as before and waved a hand in my direction. A murmur went up from the throng and a stooped and wrinkled old woman approached and kissed my hands, holding them between her own. Then she looked up at me with glistening eyes, placed the hands on either side of my face and gently pressed. The first gesture was the first deference that I had experienced due to my new position; the second, the first affection that I had experienced for a very long time. I was both touched and thrilled. A welcoming hum rippled round the rest of those present.

'My new flock,' I said superfluously, and made the sign of the cross.

Basilius gave an embarrassed cough. I looked over at him. His face was lit strangely by the faint light cast by the rushes and tallow – his cheekbones thrown into such sharp relief they seemed to be hewn from the same rock as the cavern itself.

'I may have misled you.'

'How so?'

'These people are old believers.'

'Pagans?' I demanded as if I were offended, although I had half-guessed as much from the fetish by the entrance.

He nodded.

'I introduced you as my Master.'

I felt I should be outraged. And I would surely have to reprimand him for taking liberties later. But this was not the place for it. In any case, I was still oddly moved by the tenderness shown to me. Regardless of my creed or my mission, I had been accepted without question.

'They would be grateful if you would hold his hand.'

'I am no faith healer,' I snapped back, thus dispelling the feeling of well-being in which I had been basking.

'To ease his passage,' he replied.

What could I do? To do so was wholly at odds with everything I had learnt to believe. And yet, the man was dying. If it made his death more acceptable to him, then I supposed vaguely it might make him readier to meet his Maker.

I made my way forward and knelt by the bedside. I could now see that he was not as old as I had assumed. True, his sunken cheeks bore the signs of decrepitude. But then he had no teeth, so what else were the cheeks to do? The hand I took, however, though rough and torn was that of a younger man.

Sensing my touch, he turned to look at me. As he did so, a trail of saliva dangled like gossamer from his lips, and landed like a lifeline of the ground below. A faint sparkle came into the eyes and the lips formed a grotesque smile. I felt a responding pressure on my palm.

I placed my free hand on his brow and muttered some nonsense. It mattered not what, I guessed. He would take it as an incantation and a solace. So, feeling like a fool and a charlatan, I conjugated the Latin verb *benedico*. Over and over. Until his hand slipped from my grasp.

I expected a wail to go up that would drive me out of my mind and out of the cave. Instead, when I turned to face the others, I saw they were embracing each other, tears in their eyes, smiles on the lips.

I could do no better than follow their lead. After all, as St Ambrose advised, when in Rome....

While I was enduring the last of the interminable series of hugs, I wondered what had happened to my companions. Wiping my eyes to clear my vision, I realised that the person I had been embracing was the abbot. He gave a smile that hovered between apology and rapture.

'And Isidorus?' I asked.

He nodded towards the passage we had entered by. There I could make out the hunched figure of the ex-mason. He was crouching in the half-light surrounded by a semi-circle of children who were gazing down into the space between them and the monk.

Curious, I moved forward so I could discover the object of their fascination. But the light was so poor that I had to stoop to their level. The children shuffled around a little to admit me to their circle. Then my eyes followed theirs to gaze on the objects that Isidorus had created.

Marvellous, I thought. If I had been a child, I would have been captivated. As an adult, I was still full of admiration for the skill of the craftsman.

Puppets, they were. But not just any puppets. Carved from wood, these were the most lifelike that I had ever seen.

There were regular shows in Constantinople – crude affairs by comparison, with rough-hewn manikins that usually represented martyrs of the faith. The dexterity of the puppeteers and the stories they re-enacted were equally amateurish.

But Isidorus had not only exquisitely carved and painted his figures. He handled them with extraordinary grace and vitality. I was unable to follow the story closely, since it was delivered in the children's own barbaric tongue. But the actions of the puppets demonstrated quite clearly that his figures were also enacting a morality play, even if the identity of the protagonists was not obvious.

At the end of the show, he stuffed the dolls back into a bag – to the disappointment of the audience. But they cheered up considerably when he produced some similar unstringed models from another bag – no doubt for them to re-enact the story on their own and thus imprint it on their young minds.

As he rose and brushed off his tunic, I asked him which morality he had been performing.

'The trials of Julian of Eclanum,' he said with a gentle smile.

I was unfamiliar with that particular martyr, but chose to nod rather than reveal my ignorance.

Isidorus detected my evasion.

'An apostle of the teaching of Pelagius and Caelestius.'

'Aah,' I said.

By now, I was more than familiar with the heresies of Pelagius, since every time I came across the mason he insisted on propagating them. So I should have guessed what he was up to here.

I frowned my disapproval and decided to take the matter up with him at a more convenient juncture.

For now, I had to content myself with helping the mason and abbot distribute the more material offerings in the mule packs.

As we left, I commended the abbot on his charitable work.

'It may help to delay further deaths of the kind we witnessed,' he replied with a sad shake of the head.

'Starvation then,' I concluded with a sage shake of my own.

'Who knows? His constitution was already damaged beyond repair by the plague and the miasma of the area.'

I sighed.

'I wonder only that people choose to live in this inhospitable territory.'

'They have little choice,' he replied, 'if they are to avoid the depredations of others.'

'The war,' I nodded again.

He shrugged.

'War or peace – it makes little difference.' He paused. 'But the family we have just seen avoided the war at least. They have lived here for longer than I have been on this earth.'

This atavism reminded me of my episcopal role.

'It is a pity,' I said, 'that you should be more diligent in your alms-giving than in your propagation of the Gospel.'

'The right Gospel,' I added as an afterthought, with a reproving glance at Isidorus who followed a few paces behind us.

The abbot pondered the issue for a moment. His fingers began weaving their invisible tapestry.

'I suppose they have a God, or Gods, that most befit their circumstances,' he concluded.

'I should not have to remind you,' I snapped back. 'The Christian God is a God of charity. And charity is what we have dispensed to them.'

Basilius flushed and fidgeted with renewed vigour.

'I was thinking rather more of what forces they have to propitiate.' He halted and waved his hand around him. 'Here you see little sign of a good God. You see only an apparently indifferent Nature.'

'But…,' I began.

'Which they see preferable to the active malevolence of life in the coastal towns and villages. In any case,' he paused to study his hands and still them, 'I do not conceive charity to be a bribe.'

'And I do not apprehend your meaning.'

'In my view, Christian charity should not be limited to members of the faith.'

Well, there we had it. The deeds of the abbot might well be exemplary, even if it was the Master's money he was so liberal with. But it now turned out that this steward of Christian alms-giving was a pagan, and his sidekick a heretic.

The rest of our visit followed a similar pattern. We were not witness to any more deaths, but we did see much suffering, self-inflicted or otherwise. My hand was grasped many times by grimy hands and kissed by grimy lips. Basilius dispensed more of the Master's Christian bounty to infidels, while Isidorus indoctrinated the youth of the area with heterodox moralities and morals.

And the farther we progressed into the cavernous slums, the more slum-like they became. The hands and lips filthier, the stink greater and the general sanitary level more abysmal.

For some reason, the abbot gained some perverse satisfaction by pointing out that these latter caves were inhabited by the more recent incomers – those fleeing from the armies that plundered the coast during their passage. These 'refugees from civilisation' at least paid lip service to some hybrid version of Christianity and showed due deference to myself as a prelate of that faith. But that did little to redeem the stench of their clothes and bodies and the general squalor of their quarters. By the end of our rounds, I almost found more in sympathy with the more hygienic paganism of the older inhabitants.

But no matter how wretched the premises and the inhabitants, we were always received with warmth and in some cases with affection. Indeed, when we reached the last of the caves, the host insisted on us remaining to share their evening meal. The abbot looked quite embarrassed when I declined, citing a previous and pressing engagement. Despite his blandishments and the regrets of the host family, I felt myself drawn back to the monastery. Josephus was due to cook that evening and I felt that both my health and my appetite would be better served there.

Reluctantly, Isidorus was assigned to guide me back. Basilius, meanwhile chose to risk food-poisoning in his quest to save souls. Or propitiate the pagan gods. Whichever you prefer.

It was just as well I had a guide. The light began to fade earlier than normal. It looked as if a levanter was coming. Grey clouds scooted across to the west to be replaced by black ones. We would be lucky if we managed to get back without getting soaked to the skin and frozen to the bone.

Noting the change, Isidorus maintained a blistering pace. It was all I could do to keep up with him, let alone draw him into conversation. Still, I wanted to take advantage of the absence of the abbot to try to correct the error of his beliefs. I had no desire to antagonise him from the outset. So I started by commending the charitable work of the abbot and his community.

'The Father Abbot is a saint,' he replied unoriginally.

This I very much doubted. However much of his time he devoted to the care of the poor in the area, the man seemed plagued by his own inadequacy and troubled in his faith. Still, I trod gently.

'The Master would also qualify for canonisation, I imagine, given the amount of charity dispensed in the name of the order.'

Isidorus' response was an uncharacteristic snort.

'No matter where it comes from. It is the abbot that chooses how and where to bestow it.'

'Well, I suppose the giving of alms is not the only yardstick of piety,' I observed, seeking to save face.

Now he paused for reflection.

'Granted,' he said eventually. 'But it is surely that which pleases God most.'

This was of course in line with the heretical Pelagian views that I had previously detected in the mason.

'If we are to be saved from damnation,' I insisted, 'it will be by God's grace alone.'

I felt myself growing by the minute into my new episcopal role. To my dismay, the mild chastisement was greeted with a further snort.

'God's grace manifests itself wholly in the gift of free will, which in his mercy he has bestowed upon us. It is then up to us to employ that freedom for the benefit of others.'

I felt the hackles on my neck rise.

'What of Original Sin then?' I replied. 'Only God's grace can wash away that stain.'

He looked at me with a species of pity in his eyes.

'My God is not a usurer that summons me to pay the debts of my father. Is yours?'

I stared at the hunchback of the little mason as he walked on. I suspected he had simply trotted out a few articles of faith that he had been forced to commit to memory. Still, at least he had produced it at the right moment. So I was as surprised at his grasp of dialectic as I was disappointed at my own inadequacy in that field.

For in a few words he had effectively defenestrated centuries of accepted Christian doctrine, and denied the authority of the blessed St Augustine.

I fumed as I strove to keep up with his retreating figure. Meanwhile my mind was rewriting the script of our conversation. I would have to be better prepared in any future encounters with heresy. If only for the sake of my own self-respect.

I decided to practise on my servant when I got back.

I should have known better.

*

He was making a pretence of sweeping the floor when I walked in. The floor showed no sign of any previous cleaning, so I suspect he had started only when he heard me approach. Besides, his eyes were still rheumy from sleep.

'You must be exhausted,' I said. 'Take a break to speak to me a while.'

He wiped some non-existent sweat from his brow and squatted on his haunches, facing me while I sat on the only chair.

'What can I help you with, guv?' he asked.

'What importance do you attribute to good works in the struggle for salvation?' I demanded.

He muttered to himself in British for a moment and glared at the floor. Finally he detected one of the many pieces of muck that had escaped his ministrations and chucked it out of the window.

'Come again?' he said at length.

'How do we get to heaven?' I clarified with a sigh.

'By being good little boys and girls,' he answered with a touch of primness.

Not for the first time with him, I felt I was being made fun of in some subterranean manner. Still, in for a penny....

'And you feel able to be good without some kind of help?' I urged.

He thought about it for a moment, I grant him that.

'So far as it's up to me, of course.'

Now I felt we were making progress.

'So there are limits to how far your own free will can take you,' I prompted him again.

'Obvious, innit?'

'How so?'

'You can't be too choosy when you're in service.'

'I suppose not. But most people are not in your unenviable position of being paid to serve others.'

'Most everyone's got Masters, right? And it's the bosses as calls the shots.'

I felt he was getting off the subject a little. But I could not let the matter rest there.

'Most men are free. You can always choose to leave. You're not a slave, you know.'

I was almost tempted to put the theory into practice. He was, after all, a hopeless servant. And a totally unresponsive respondent.

'Tell that to the Kings and Emperors,' he said. 'Let alone the Generals.'

He gave me a wink.

'Not forgetting the bishops. Way I see it, they make our decisions for us. In most things anyways.'

He thought for a moment.

'Though, to be fair, I guess some people don't mind having others calling the shots. Like it better that way, see?'

Not an affliction my servant was ever likely to suffer from, I thought. I decided to sidestep the issue.

'But you can hardly do away with some chain of command. Some law and order,' I replied. 'Otherwise, things would just fall apart.'

He made a great show of looking puzzled.

'You mean like we'd all be fighting each other all the time.'

I began to understand where I was being led. By the nose, to boot.

'We were talking about religion, not politics,' I pointed out, unable to disguise the desperation in my voice. For I knew what was coming.

'What's the difference?' he said.

At least I had the satisfaction of having predicted his next sentence. There had been an air of inevitability about it.

A Sense of Eternal Loss

We learn but that we have forgot.
Boethius

As he accompanied me in to dinner, Owen seemed buoyed by his latest subversion of my authority and determined to undermine it further.

'You've got a bloom on your cheeks, boss,' he said. 'Been sampling the totty of the village?'

'Totty,' I repeated.

'Ready wenches.'

Suppressed anger and open embarrassment increased the bloom considerably. One day soon I would have to administer a beating, I felt sure. I felt less sure of the outcome of any such attempt.

'I am vowed to celibacy. As you are well aware,' I replied.

'I am also well aware,' he said, imitating my own accents, 'that not everyone in your position abides by the vow.'

This was true enough. The Emperor had recently made yet another attempt to enforce the interdiction. To little effect. No doubt the injunction would have been more persuasive if it had been issued by someone that wasn't married to a pornographic celebrity. For my own part, I felt the sanction easy enough to observe. As my age increased, my appetite diminished. For sexual congress, that is. The aromas wafting towards us from the refectory reminded me that my lust for good food remained as strong as ever.

'If you must know,' I replied at length, 'I was accompanying the abbot on his rounds.'

He looked at me with new interest.

'With Izzie?'

'Isidorus, yes.'

'Up to the trogs?'

'We visited the caves, if that is what you mean.'

'Good bloke, the abbot,' Owen commented.

That remained to be seen. I had urgent business with him, during the course of which I should be able to confirm or deny that understanding of his character.

'He may have a less commendable past. As I pointed out.'

'And he may have made up for it, as I pointed out.'

I grunted.

'Which is more than can be said for his charges.'

Now he grunted. I might as well have employed a pet parrot.

'You might at least try to get to know them better,' he concluded.

By now, we had reached the entrance to the dining hall, and I had more important things on my mind than researching the archives of a rogue's gallery.

As we entered, I was distracted by the prospect of having my palate tickled once again by Josephus. If good cooking could gain a man entrance through the pearly gates, then Josephus might attain redemption. I could not speak for the rest of the monks. Nor did I greatly care to.

I marched briskly into the room and towards my usual place on the communal bench, vaguely aware that we were not the first to arrive.

As I did so, I heard a seat slapping back, and feet clicking to attention. The familiar sound sent me back to my military days and triggered the trained response. I crossed right arm over my breast in salute. This was enough to break the spell.

I could now see Arminius and Uldin standing like triumphal statues, their arms like mine lying across their chests.

For a moment we gazed at each other in embarrassment. Then, at about the same time, we all burst into laughter.

'At ease,' I said.

They breathed out and relaxed their pose.

'Biarchus 1st class Arminius, 2nd Herculi limitanei,' declared the German, as if he were on a parade ground.

'Biarchus 2nd class Uldin, 1st Iovia limitanei,' echoed the Hun.

'Scythian legions,' I observed. 'Perhaps we have crossed paths before.'

'You were stationed in the region, Sir?' Uldin asked.

I nodded.

'I was tribune to Gunthigis Baza, magister militum of the 1st Armeniaca. You will have heard of him?'

The two of them exchanged a look.

'Our loss surely, Sir.' Uldin was obviously the spokesman of the two. 'Where were you stationed?'

'We had a roving brief, following trouble round the Caucasus chiefly.'

'Kept you busy then,' said Uldin. 'No shortage of trouble in that cesspit.'

I nodded a smile.

'No shortage in the Black Sea area, in general,' I said. 'Fact is we were ordered a few times to Pontus to help quell uprisings.'

'We know Pontus well enough not to miss it in a fog.' This time Arminius chimed in.

'Who knows then? Perhaps we have shared a mess before,' I said.

'Who knows? Though to be honest, Sir, me and Arminius here were stationed in the same area cheek by jowl for years and never met before we came here.'

'What's more, you were an officer, Sir. Noticed it for the first time when you marched in, military-fashion just now. Not likely to mix with the riffraff.' Arminius again.

Well, that explained their response when I entered. I had reverted to habit and they had followed suit. And as I have pointed out, I made it a practice to mess with 'the riff-raff', as did others in our regiment. But in some places it was frowned upon.

I recalled of a sudden that we three were not alone. I turned to see Owen taking all of this in. No doubt to use against me on some future occasion.

'You ever serve, Owen?' I asked in an effort to pre-empt any such attempts.

'Not in the military, Excellency.'

I blushed at my lack of tact. What is more, for once he had got my title right.

'Though it was rumoured my father was a centurion,' he continued.

That dispelled the embarrassment. All four of us laughed heartily. The others knew as well as I did that every bastard in the Empire claimed descent from a Roman officer.

I settled into my place on the bench opposite the military couple, wondering if indeed they were a couple. Either way, I had chosen to sit on the other side of the table from Arminius since my first meal at the monastery.

I was looking forward to this one. The fragrances from the kitchen were even stronger here and my stomach was rumbling.

Too bad.

Josephus appeared from a side door and, like an apologetic head waiter, wrung his hands.

'I regret to say there will be a delay in the scheduled mealtime,' he said.

My stomach sank with my heart.

'The abbot has been unavoidably detained,' the Jew explained.

My organs rose to their normal level again.

'He is eating elsewhere,' I announced.

'And, given the elsewhere he is eating, he will most certainly wish to supplement his diet by the time he gets back,' the Jew replied and, pivoting about, returned to his own elsewhere.

I heaved a sigh. Frustrating. I would have to wait to satisfy both my stomach and my curiosity. Apparently both depended on the presence of the abbot. So I turned my attention back to Uldin and Arminius.

'So how did you both wind up here, then?' I asked, thinking to pass the time until the food arrived. As it turned out, I had opened Pandora's box.

Arminius looked at Uldin, who gave a shrug.

'Let the old toga-lifter have his say first,' said the Hun. 'Only hope it doesn't spoil your appetite.'

'It's a long story,' Arminius explained. 'And not a nice one.'

There it was. I had invited it. I was, after all, going to find out considerably more about the inmates than I would have wished.

'Don't know who my Dad was. Probably a centurion.' He grinned at Owen. 'Nor my Mum. First thing I recall, I was in a home of some kind, run by priests. Banks of the Danube. Dark woods. Deep snow in winter. Fuck-load of insects in summer.'

Uldin snorted.

'Fuck-load of insects year-round, you ask me. Fucking priests are like fucking insects. Present company excepted, Sir,' he added, nodding to me.

'Say what you like,' Arminius continued, 'but they weren't a bad lot mostly. If you didn't mind the praying and the beating. A couple of mean bastards but you learned to keep clear of them.'

'As for the rest, they told us that they – the beatings, that is – were to help us learn. Not that they did much good. Three things we had to learn, as it turned out. Numbers, which was just common sense. Latin, which I could never get my head around. As you can see,' he added with a grim smile.

Despite his comment, I thought his command of the language compared favourably with many of the barbarian auxiliaries that I had had dealings with. Many of these had understood two words only. 'Kill' and 'Stop'.

'What was the third thing?' I asked.

'To be 'good'.'

Owen gave a dirty laugh. I gave him a dirty look.

'Seemed like being good was what they called 'suppressing the flesh', which mainly involved putting a lid on what you really wanted. First off, this came down to eating what little they gave us and not asking for more.'

He clapped his ample belly, on which the skin was stretched as tightly as on his face. It responded with a hollow boom like a drum.

'Made up for it since,' he said with a grin. 'As a kid, starving was even harder. I got my share of floggings.'

Uldin nodded. I guessed he'd also felt the lash on more than one occasion.

'What was more of a problem came later,' Arminius went on. 'When I was about twelve or thirteen, I guess.'

He looked down between his legs with a rueful expression on his face.

'You know, how it is. When you get hairs beginning to grow round your *gladius*.'

I looked at him blankly.

'Your cock,' Owen explained in my ear.

It was a new one on me. A sword was a penis apparently. And I had led an all-too-sheltered life as an officer.

'Then I began to understand what the flesh had to do with it.' Arminius had the grace to give an apologetic smile. 'And so did another kid, who'd also got the hairs early. Beautiful lad. Skin like fresh peaches. He'd look at me when we went for the annual spring bath in the river and he'd nod to the patch between my legs. I began to realise he knew something I didn't.'

By now I was blushing furiously, much to the delight of my servant.

'So he taught me. You know what I mean. Apologies, Bishop, Sir. How to touch yourself, that is. Best kind of teaching I ever had. And no beatings for getting it wrong. Not that I ever got it wrong, of course.'

He gave a surprisingly girlish giggle.

'Cut a long story short, we were at it together, not doing it to each other, I mean, just sharing the moment, when one of the younger priests looks in at the door of the dormitory.'

He paused, lost in the past, I supposed.

'Still remember his face. Looked as if he'd forgotten something. For a moment he just stood there. I could see him in the doorway. But I was too far gone to hold back. I just stared at him as I came.'

He shrugged.

'And that was it. The other kid didn't survive the beating we got. Me, I was given over to the next troop of legionaries that passed by. Never heard what they said to the commander. But they treated me like a slave. Beat me regular for no reason. Just for the hell of it.'

'Still,' he giggled again, 'made a man of me, if you can call it that. I got big quick, big as you see me now. And that put paid to most of the beatings that weren't ordered from above. I started to dish out a few of my own.'

'Time came when they began to see that they could make better use of me than getting me to clean out the privies. And I was pretty good at killing, even if I say it myself. Worked my way up to *biarchus*, like I said. Even managed to get my end away off and on. Strictly in secret, understand. I'd got a taste for the forbidden fruit, as the priests called it.'

'You preferred men,' I said. Might as well call a spade a spade. And a bugger a bugger.

'On the nail. I heard somewhere there was a time when this used to be encouraged in the army. Specially with the Greeks way back. What I heard, they used to pair up, one old, the other young. Look after each other – to the death.'

He gave a regretful sigh.

'Not any more, I can tell you that. So I kept my so-called weakness to myself for the most part. Just slip off to the nearest brothel, when we were in town, and order what I wanted.'

He swallowed with an effort.

'What happened next?' I prompted, more in an effort to expedite the end of the story and hopefully the arrival of the meal than out of any real interest.

'Word got out. Don't know how. But it did.'

He paused.

'Should have smelt a rat when the centurion sent me out in charge of a bunch of the roughest squaddies in the whole century. Recon mission, he called it, giving me a weird look. Heard there was some funny business afoot in the *limes*. First I'd heard of it. Thought the borderlands had calmed down. What he didn't tell me was that the funny business was yet to come.'

'Bastards!'

This from Uldin. Arminius acknowledged with a nod.

'Soon as we were out of sight of camp, some of the squaddies grabbed me by the arms, while the biggest bastard took out his *gladius*. And I mean the weapon this time. Not what you've got between your legs.'

I cringed at what was obviously going to come next.

'And what I haven't got no more.'

I breathed a sigh of relief that he had had the sensitivity to spare us the gory details.

'That 'suppressed the flesh' all right. Would have done away with the fleshly part of me completely if a passing Thracian hadn't taken pity on me and fixed me up best he could with herbs, poultices and some weird kind of chanting. Good Samaritan, like. Those 'comrades-in-arms' of mine just left me there bleeding out in the middle of nowhere. Saying they could sleep safely now. Like as if I'd ever tried it on with one of them. Or ever would've dared.'

To my surprise, my disapproval of the sodomite and the anticipated cringe at his castration had been replaced by something like pity. Not an emotion I was in the habit of experiencing. And not one I felt comfortable with. Even more surprising, I began to feel a sneaking admiration for the resilience of the German.

'So how did you manage to survive, deprived as you were of your livelihood?' I asked.

He had slumped down. But now he drew himself up again.

'Made do. What else was there to do? I was still a big boy and I knew how to put it about. Leastways when I'd recovered enough to be able to walk the walk and wield the sword again.'

He shrugged and looked to the doorway of the hall, as if in some way this would prove his claim.

'There was always a call for protection. Leastways while some folks got more brass than others. And want to keep it that way.'

'So you gained employ as a bodyguard?' I asked.

'Yeah. Small stuff at first. Hired thug basically. Till I ended up saving a bit of posh skirt from a fate worse than death when her *lectica* was set upon in the backstreets. Needless to say, her bearers all pissed off quick as lightning when they saw they were outnumbered. I'd just come back from a bit of wet work for a guild-master, and my sword was still dripping blood. Didn't take too much to persuade the bandits to piss off and leave well alone.'

'So the damsel in distress was so grateful and impressed that she gave you a more respectable position,' I suggested, genuinely interested now.

Arminius snorted.

'Damsel, my arse. Spoilt wife of a silk merchant. Rich as Croesus they were. Younger than him, she was. But that's not saying much. Fancy clothes and snotty attitudes, both of them. Still, it was a fair notch up from what I had before. Better pay, better conditions.'

'So why did you leave?' I asked.

He took a deep breath and exhaled noisily.

'Fucking bitch. Decided she liked the cut of my jib. Called for me late one night while her husband was away on business. I didn't want to go. Knew she was in her chamber and had a pretty good idea that whatever she was up to was not likely to do a great deal for my career ops. But what could I do? If I'd disobeyed, I'd've been out on my arse anyway.'

'Extracurricular services,' I muttered.

'Is what?' asked Owen.

But Arminius knew.

'She wanted what I couldn't give no more. Wouldn't accept 'no' for an answer, either. I should have simply showed her that the cupboard was bare. As it was, she was mighty pissed off that I wouldn't oblige. And shouted the house down, screaming I'd tried to violate her 'honour', she called it.'

He spat to the side.

'Fucking word, that is.'

I couldn't help but agree. It had always seemed to me that it was a term used by the upper classes to give each other a pat on the head for doing what any decent human being would do, but what they weren't usually in the habit of doing themselves.

'Not the smartest thing to do, I admit. But I panicked. Made a bolt for it.'

'You could have proved your innocence easily enough,' I pointed out with a grimace.

He gave me a wan smile.

'Thing is, the loss of your tackle doesn't take away your appetite. Just your ability to satisfy it. Wouldn't have helped you see. Common knowledge.'

I nodded reluctantly. I had heard similar rumours about the court eunuchs in Constantinople.

'And here then? How did you end up here?' I asked.

'Praise be to whoever's up there.' He duly raised his eyes to the ceiling. 'There was a price on my head, so I got as far away from Scythia as I could. Made it as far as these hills, thinking somehow to stow myself onto a ship bound for the Vandal kingdom on the other side of the sea. By the time I got here, fucking Belisarius had taken Africa back for the fucking Emperor of the fucking East.'

He glanced at me for a moment.

'Pardoning my Greek, your worship.'

I sighed. It had been one of Justinian's most successful campaigns. So far the only one that had completely come off.

'I was desperate. Nowhere left to run. But I'd heard of sanctuary and thought it was worth a go.'

Tears began to well up in his eyes.

'Every day that goes by I thank Him upstairs for the Master of this place.'

'Who you've never met,' Owen pointed out – rather gratuitously, I thought.

'I've never met the Almighty either, but I still give thanks to him,' Arminius replied with grace and a certain logic.

I bowed my head to him in silent acknowledgement of his travails and the confidence he had entrusted me with.

The effect was seriously undermined by the all-too-audible growl of my stomach.

The aromas coming from the kitchen had now reached a pitch of perfection. I could not smell fenugreek this time. But there was something among the more familiar herbs that set my senses tingling, almost erotically. A suggestion of exotic lands, dark skins and sinuous movements. And most bizarrely, a melancholy nostalgia for a mother I barely remembered. A musky spice that warmed and cradled me. And moved me with a sense of eternal loss.

While Arminius had been talking, most of the other monks had trickled in, individually or in pairs. Only the abbot was still missing.

Finally Josephus emerged with a steaming cauldron.

'I call this a homage to the Indies,' he said. 'A goat kari. Ecce capra!'

He lifted the lid and tears rose to my eyes. I could not tell whether this was due to the pungency of the vapour, the poignancy of Arminius' history or the evocation of a lost childhood.

'The abbot has returned then,' I declared. 'Finally.'

Josephus nodded.

'He will be with us shortly. He just has to sign off on a delivery.'

'A new hair shirt, maybe,' Uldin suggested. 'The old one must be pretty much worn out by now.'

He exchanged a grin with Arminius.

'Apparently not,' Josephus replied. 'Books. Masses of them. They're unloading them as I speak.'

I sat up in my seat. Then heaved a very deep sigh. It seemed there was to be no end of the impediments put in the way of my dining today.

Cui Bono?

To think of a thing as being in any way other than what it is, is not only not knowledge, but it is false opinion widely different from the truth of knowledge.
Boethius

I followed the sound of voices to the atrium, where the abbot stood next to several stacks of crates. Beside both, there was a short, stocky man with pockmarks. Everywhere his skin showed, craters glistened with sweat.

Basilius too was perspiring freely. I assumed he had helped the carter carry in the consignment. But now he was moving his eyes between the papers in his hand and the boxes on the ground.

As I arrived, the carter was speaking. I caught the word 'Germanus,' and saw the abbot give a weary shake of the head as he continued to count.

'Everything seems to be in order,' Basilius said eventually.

'If you could just put your mark on the bottom of this then, your holiness,' the carter replied, producing what I took to be a receipt.

'Seal or signature?'

The carter shrugged.

'Whichever you like. The dispatcher knows who the abbot of this place is, I guess.'

'And who, may I ask, is this dispatcher?' I said, stepping out of the shadows.

Basilius flushed guiltily, noticing me for the first time.

The carter ran his eye up and down me and decided that I was a person that had a right to ask, or at least someone that it might be hazardous not to answer. He consulted the dispatch note.

'One Flavius Magnus Aurelius Cassiodorus Senator, to be exact,' he replied in one breath, adding 'Your Worshipfulness,' to be on the safe side.

Then for some strange reason, he winked at the abbot. Basilius did not respond to the show of familiarity. Instead he suffered a bout of the twitches and flicked his eyes everywhere but at me.

Another mystery. No matter. The main thing was that the infernal books had arrived. Somewhere amongst them had to be the one I needed and had awaited so long.

'If you could…,' Basilius said eventually to the carter. 'This way. The parlour. The seal, you know. Kept there.'

As the two of them moved out of sight, I took the opportunity to examine the crates. Fortunately for me, each was labelled with its contents. So it did not take me very long to discover what I wanted. I extracted the crate from its pile and the contents from the crate. They were loosely wrapped in waxed linen and bound more tightly with coarse twine.

It turned out that the histories were contained in three separate labelled packs. I was on the point of making off with all of them (to be on the safe side) when the abbot returned with the carter, the latter with his signed and sealed receipt in a roll.

The drayman tipped finger to forelock, turning to Basilius and then myself, then left the building.

As soon as he had gone, Basilius, showing surprising strength, wrested the packages from my arms and replaced them on the top of the crate I had removed them from.

'Forgive me Your Grace, but I have strict instructions….'

'To what effect?' I demanded.

'This consignment is to be deposited in the closed stacks. It is not open to public view.'

And there I was thinking he had guessed my nocturnal visits there. Out of sight, out of mind, I supposed.

'And how might one gain access to the closed stacks?' I asked, although I knew several answers to that question. Basilius gave me the first.

'Written application to the Master.'

I provided him with a second.

'I regret to say, your first vow of obedience is to your pastoral superior,' I replied. 'Which is to say, myself.'

I felt a pang of guilt. I am not, I hope, a bully by nature. But half a life spent in army service had accustomed me to having my orders obeyed.

I gestured for him to hand over the packages. As I did so, I noticed Uldin had appeared at my shoulder and was glaring at the abbot with open contempt and a more veiled threat of violence.

I'm not sure whether it was my air of authority or Uldin's physical presence. But the abbot entrusted the parcels into my keeping. You would have thought he was parting with his parents for the last time.

With the packages finally in my own possession, I made to return to the refectory. I didn't fully trust the abbot. So they would remain in my sight as I ate. And for some time after that.

But as I was about to walk away, a thought came to me and I turned my head to look back to where the abbot was standing as if orphaned.

'What was that about Germanus?' I asked.

'Dead,' he said. 'And with him all hopes of an early peace.'

*

As I made my way back to the refectory with my heavy load, I found my heart was also heavy, and my appetite no longer what it was. The way I had treated the abbot weighed on my conscience. Moreover, the death of Germanus was a bitter blow to any hope of a return to normality. As I mentioned, his planned marriage to the Gothic heiress to the throne could conceivably have served as the basis of a peace agreement between East and West, Goth and Roman. Moreover, unlike his Imperial cousin, he had an open and, dare I say it, honest demeanour. For which he was loved by all.

So rapt in thought was I, I hardly noticed that Uldin was walking by my side and talking to me until we arrived at the threshold of the dining hall.

Then two things brought me back to the present. And to a halt.

The first was that the hall was now empty.

The second was the phrase 'fucking civilian' that Uldin had more or less spat out at me. Followed swiftly by 'no fucking balls'.

Wiping the residue from the front of my tunic, I asked him who he was referring to. Germanus hardly qualified. Arminius certainly did, but they appeared to be good friends and he wasn't a civilian. I truly hoped he hadn't meant myself.

'Fucking abbot,' he garbled from his wretched excuse for a mouth.

Still feeling guilty for my own treatment of the poor man, I mumbled that I was sure he meant well.

'You mark my words,' Uldin replied, pointing at the bottom of his eye. A word to the wise, I suppose. Though I was none the wiser.

Despite the absence of fellow diners, or perhaps because of it, I felt my appetite returning a little. Besides, the aromas still lingered.

So I took my place and waited for Josephus to reappear with what I hoped would be the substantial leftovers of his latest creation. Uldin must also have missed his meal in his generous, if unnecessary attempt to help me out, for he sat down next to me. Despite the conviviality of our recent conversation, he still made me nervous. I'm not sure whether it was his ferocious manner or his poor collapsed face that disconcerted me most.

'Thing is…,' he began.

Fortunately Josephus entered with a no longer steaming tureen and rescued me from the Thing That Was. For the moment at least.

He deposited the bowl on the table with a resounding thud, then brandished a ladle at us.

'I wait all evening for the abbot to turn up,' he says, 'and then he decides he isn't hungry after all.'

'Looks like everyone else was,' I consoled him. The thud of the tureen had been depressingly hollow. And so was my stomach. His words had nudged my sense of guilt to life again.

'They refused to wait any longer,' he explained. 'No doubt they were privy to information that had been withheld from me.'

He crossed his arms.

'Then they just bolted it down.'

'A testament to your fine cooking,' I offered with perhaps too much of a question mark.

'How anyone could truly have appreciated the subtle blend of the spices,' he tapped the tureen with his ladle, 'is beyond me. They just opened their throats and….'

'I will try to do it greater justice,' I said.

'Five hours to prepare. Five minutes to devour.'

'There is a lesson in that somewhere,' I replied. I was at least unlikely to devour it in that time, especially if the build-up was included.

He pivoted on his heels and positively flounced back towards the kitchen. Then just before disappearing, he pivoted back to us.

'It is enough to make one take up accounting,' he concluded with a grin. I didn't see the joke but threw a smile of sympathy back to him.

The floor-show over, I spooned some of the '*kari*' onto my plate and for extra pleasure stooped over the dish to run my nose across it a few times before I tasted.

'Usual dogshit,' Uldin commented. 'He'd been cooking in the army, they'd've mutinied. Before stringing him up.'

'You prefer more traditional fare,' I said, in an effort to shut him up and let me get on with my dinner. Meanwhile I rolled the food round in my mouth prior to allowing it to charm its way down my gullet. 'Home-cooking, perhaps.'

'Too fucking right,' Uldin exclaimed, depositing some morsels on my tunic as he spoke. 'Give me Isidorus's tucker any day of the week.'

I mumbled a response that could reasonably have been taken as agreement. Isidorus' idea of fine cuisine was do dump everything he could find in a pot and let it boil merrily away until all moisture, taste and texture had disappeared. This was probably the reason the toothless Hun preferred it. The reason for him choosing to sit next to me rather than opposite also became apparent before long.

He cleared his plate, and, despite his misgivings, licked it clean by rolling it round as he held his tongue stationary. Then he leaned into me. This would have been a deterrent to the appetite at the best of times. The constant spatter that issued from his mouth was accompanied with a breath so foul that even the spices of the Indies could not disguise it.

'I promised to tell you my story too,' he whispered in a confidential tone.

Threatened would be a better word, I thought. It seemed as if suddenly the whole monastery had been granted a licence to subject me to their personal tragedies. Perhaps word had got around of my assumption of the role of father-confessor to the anonymous inmate.

'You promised to explain how you came to reside at the monastery,' I corrected him, in the vain hope that this might restrict the narrative slightly.

'It's a long story,' he said.

My heart sank. I helped myself to more of the *kari*, in an effort to ward off boredom and poisoning by halitosis.

To cut the long story short, Uldin had, unlike his friend, enjoyed a cheerful and fulfilling childhood in one of the breakaway Hunnic tribes that followed on the disintegration of Attila's empire after his death. The tribe had settled on the Black Sea coast and paid a tribute of crops and men to the Eastern Emperor in exchange for the protection provided by the Imperial troops.

'No missionaries this time then?' I asked glibly.

He gave me a grim smile.

'Not for long. They tasted too bloody good.'

I shuddered, regretting the question. I hoped he was joking.

At the onset of his manhood, Uldin had become a part of this annual tribute and been enrolled in the border auxiliaries. He confessed to enjoying every moment of his service. Cracking skulls and carving limbs were for him obviously prerequisites for job satisfaction, and entailed skills with which he was admirably equipped. So much so that he worked his way up the ranks to become an NCO.

He had taken less kindly to being sent with his legion to Italy to support Belisarius' stuttering campaign against the Goths. For, when he arrived, he realised that this involved him fighting fellow-Huns. Indeed there were in fact more Huns fighting with the Goth army than with the Imperials.

'Nothing against kicking the fucking shit out of the Slavs and the Parthians. But fuck me blind if I was going to do the same to my own blood.' As he put it.

I conceded he had a point. As much in the hope that this would hasten the conclusion of his story, as out of human sympathy. Instead he fell into a kind of meditative trance.

'So what did you do?' I prompted.

He looked up at me for a moment in confusion, then recovered the track of his story.

'Asked for a transfer back to the Euxine – to another legion,' he replied. 'Piece of cake, I thought. Our tribune was also a Hun. Had been rather. When I managed to get in to see him, I found he'd been replaced by some bright young spark straight out of the military academy in Constantinople. One of the *scholae*.'

He snorted his disgust. The members of the Imperial Guard had never been popular with the rank and file. Even in my day. 'Spit, polish and curls' was the nickname they went by. It seemed Uldin's new commander conformed to the stereotype. He turned down the request without ceremony and without even removing his attention from the mirror the barber held in front of him.

When Uldin had protested, the young officer turned to his adjutant and muttered a few words. Within a moment or two, Uldin found himself being dragged out of the officer's tent by a group of elite NCOs and hauled onto a platform that was usually used for parading the legion's eagles.

A trumpet and a drum summoned the remainder of the legion to witness the spectacle. Once the crowd had gathered, the officer emerged from his marquee and addressed them. Uldin meanwhile remained pinioned by the *scholae*.

The tribune had then delivered a short speech, full of rhetorical flourishes, about the need for utter loyalty and obedience to the Empire and the penalties for failing to render unto Caesar.

He had then sounded a softer note.

'Where there are compelling reasons for not engaging in combat with the enemy, a financial indemnity might be acceptable – in full conformity with barbarian law.'

This appeared to be quite popular with the auxiliaries, many of whom presumably shared Uldin's qualms about fighting their fellows. A buzz hummed round the assembled troops.

'Allow my assistants to demonstrate,' the officer said.

'Twenty years, I'd been saving my pay,' Uldin interpolated. 'Put my money where my mouth was, you could say.' He grimaced. 'Safest place to put it when you're always on the move. Like when you're in the army. Same with our tribe too.'

The *scholae* had then, in full view of the auxiliaries, clubbed out the Hun's gold teeth.

Uldin spat the words out as if he were reliving the rape of his mouth.

I was stunned into silence. I lowered my spoon to the dish and rested it there. Then held my hand over the other arm to stop them both trembling.

'And that was how you left?' I asked.

'That was why I deserted,' Uldin replied. 'Middle of the night. Not before I knocked the teeth out of the bastard that took mine. In conformity with Hun Law.'

He smiled grotesquely.

'So you ended up here,' I declared, hoping this brought the grisly story to a close.

He leaned back on the bench.

'Ran into Bro Arminius in the market down in the village. And Bob's your uncle.'

Someone else that had run out of land and life, I reflected.

*

I pushed my dish away. This business of getting to know more about the inmates of the asylum was turning out to be a harrowing ordeal.

There was something about teeth. And toes for that matter, but that is by the bye. Uldin's story set my teeth on edge, in a manner of speaking. Obliterated the appetite. And brought on nausea.

I was obliged to visit the *latrinum* on my way back to the room, carefully depositing the contents of the packages on a ledge before depositing the contents of my stomach in the bowl.

All in all then, it was quite late by the time I got back to my cell. I might have guessed. Owen had already called it a day. So I carried my precious load out to the scriptorium and lit one of the lamps. The hour might have been advanced. But so was my curiosity.

I wrapped myself in a sheepskin that had been abandoned by someone that had already turned in for the night and probably bearing the name of Josephus. Then I ripped open the parcels, and, finding the one I wanted, set myself to skim through the missing volume of the *History*. I would get down to the business of summarising it the next day. For the moment, I wished to satisfy my own needs rather than those of Castalius. I was tormented by the mystery of Boethius' trial and would not be able to rest until it was solved.

Despite my urgency, I decided to adopt a systematic, if perfunctory approach and began from the start. Which, of course, consisted of a blow-by-blow account of the career of Theodoric. To my surprise, it wasn't long before I ran into annotations again. I flicked forward and found they pervaded the whole text. Deletions, additions and scribbled notes.

The amendments were distracting, so I tried to focus my attention on the original text. But my curiosity, and irritation, soon got the better of me. For it wasn't long before the history referred, as Ennodius' eulogy had, to Theodoric's education at Constantinople. This had been heavily deleted, though not obscured, and edited to the effect that the future king was 'agrammatus'. Admittedly, I had myself been under the impression that Theodoric was illiterate until I had read the eulogy. And it is true that Ennodius himself could have been guilty of misrepresentation. His intention, after all, was to flatter the king.

But for this history to assert one thing, and the annotation the opposite, suggested conscious falsification. It would seem that the editor of the history had a diametrically opposed interest to that of the writer of the history. To say the least.

The farther I read, the more convinced I became, that the editor's intention was to blacken the name and memory of the Goth king. On each occasion that the historian had something positive to say about Theodoric, the editor had deleted and corrected this to a negative. Thus, in the original, the king had consciously cultivated the Roman population and striven to maintain a balance between the demands of the Gothic settlers and the Roman natives. In the revised version, this was altered to suggest a clear favouring of the former over the latter.

And the farther I read, the more irritated I became. Not so much for the character assassination that was taking place. I was, after all, hardly a devotee of the usurper. What really made my hackles rise was the sheer disregard, ironically enough, for the rules of grammar and orthography. Not to mention calligraphy. For the annotations were written in an almost illegible scrawl. If anyone was 'agrammatus', it was the editor of the history, not Cassiodorus himself.

After half a reign of regal vilification, I could restrain myself no longer. I flicked forward again and searched for mention of Boethius and his trial. Strangely enough, the reverse practice seemed to have been observed in the case of the philosopher. Where the history had him as conceited, over-ambitious and scruple-free, the 'corrections' clearly desired to convey the impression of almost canine devotion and loyalty. And, by extension, Theodoric's eventual treatment of him as treacherous and a masterclass in ingratitude.

So that the trial, which had originally been represented as a just and righteous example of judicial process, was now portrayed as a cavalcade of trumped-up charges and false testimony. Those that witnessed to Boethius' guilt, including the mysterious Basilius, were alleged to have been suborned by the king himself. And the public prosecutor, Cyprian, who claimed to have been handed the incriminating documents, was portrayed as a scruple-free careerist. Meanwhile, the letters – whereby Boethius was supposed to have been in secret correspondence with the Emperor – were, of course, forgeries.

I could have torn out my hair in frustration had I any left to spare and enough to grab hold of. I had been waiting more than a week now to complete the history, get Castalius off my back and carry on with the rest of my bleak existence. Besides that of course, I had been longing to find out what had really happened to Boethius. And here was the result. With all apologies to Euclid, I was presented with two parallel but widely divergent histories of the same course of events.

I drew a deep breath and tried to collect my thoughts. When all was said and done, my commission had been to summarise Cassiodorus' *History*. I now had the *History*, so all I had to do was summarise it. *QED*. The annotations had nothing to do with my assignment, even if they represented the factual truth.

I settled back on the seat and exhaled my relief.

Until another thought came to me.

This volume was the private property of the author. And while it is true that I managed to get hold of the earlier volumes, this had only been achieved with great difficulty and by the most devious of stratagems.

The chances of anyone else ever having gained access to this volume, while possessed of the leisure and effrontery to deface it were minimal.

Ergo, it was in all likelihood the author himself that had made these changes.

I rolled up the edge of my tunic and inserted it into my mouth to stifle a howl of rage.

Why, in the name of all that was holy, had Cassiodorus changed his mind so totally? He must have been, if not a direct witness to the events he described, at least as well qualified as anyone else to judge what had really happened. Had he not himself held the highest positions of public service during the reign of Theodoric?

Unless, despite all the laws of probability, someone else had contrived to borrow Cassiodorus' books behind his back.

*

My head began to spin. I needed fresh eyes and a fresh mind to look at this. It would have made most sense for me to wait until the next day when the fresh eyes would be my own. But, having come so far, I couldn't contain myself.

I considered returning to my cell and kicking my servant awake. I could at least rely on him to give a new perspective on matters even if I didn't always care for the result.

Then I recalled the Jew's evening researches into the occult. He had the advantage of having been relatively close to the events outlined in the *History*. The cellar, meanwhile, had the advantage of being warm.

I dropped the sheepskin back where I had found it, shivered along the corridor, then basked in the warmth of the cellar doorway and stairs.

Josephus looked over the top of his lenses as I approached and gave a questioning smile.

'More midnight browsing?' he asked.

'Actually,' I replied, 'more a wish to avail myself of your greater experience and superior judgement. If I am not imposing too much on your time.'

'Superior judgement, eh? How could I refuse? Though I won't ask superior to what or whose.'

He removed the lenses and placed them on the desktop.

'How may I be of service?'

I explained as briefly as I could the mystery of the parallel texts and the contrasting versions of history they purveyed.

'And on which question would you like my advice exactly?' Josephus asked.

'Which account should I believe and why are there two opposed versions from, apparently, one and the same author? An author who was, I assume, a witness to the events in question.'

He looked privately amused.

'That was two questions.'

I shrugged.

'Then choose which you like best.'

'I feel privileged that you should appoint a Hebrew to judge which text should be admitted to a canon of orthodoxy.'

I looked at him with dumb eyes. It was too late at night for this tomfoolery.

'I find canonicity a fascinating subject,' he continued.

'Enlighten me,' I said.

'The Gospels, for example. The Holy Mother Church chose only four, when there were any number to choose from. Why were those four deemed more trustworthy than the others, I wonder?'

'I have no idea,' I sighed. I had not come down to the cellar to be party to a lecture on Christian theology. From a Jew, no less.

'I have always favoured the Gospel of Judas Iscariot, myself. Very lively and awfully poignant.'

I scowled.

'Then again,' he rambled on, 'why as many as four? Why was one not enough? Three, at least, would have had a pleasing symmetry with the Trinity. But four?'

He beamed at me.

'You Christians are too subtle for me, I feel.'

'Can we get back to the question?' I asked in the end.

'The questions. Plural, as I recall,' he said, 'though I suspect there is a connection between the two. For the 'why?' may lead to the 'which?'. And both perhaps beg the question 'when?''

The spontaneous generation of questions confused me.

'When what?' I asked.

'Ah, now we have a 'what?' as well,' he chuckled. 'When were the two versions written?'

I had not thought about this before. So I had to think about it now. I checked the end of the manuscript.

'The original must have been written towards the end of the reign, I should guess,' I replied. 'It includes the trial of Boethius, but not the king's death. I don't think Theodoric survived his minister by long.'

Josephus nodded.

'Not by more than a couple of years, no,' he agreed. 'I have another question, then.'

I sighed. I had little patience with the Socratic habit of answering questions with further questions.

'*Cui bono*?' he asked cryptically.

'What do you mean?'

'Who do you think would be most pleased with the first version?'

'Theodoric, of course,' I said. 'Or his heir.'

Then a thought struck me.

'You mean the writer couldn't afford to tell the truth while the king was still alive.'

I almost moaned with self-satisfaction at having worked this out.

'Or he couldn't afford to tell the truth after the king died,' Josephus said, deflating and confusing me in equal measure.

'So who would be most pleased with the second version?' he continued, relentless.

'Anyone who wished to blacken the memory of Theodoric and the Goth legacy,' I replied after a moment. The answer was so obvious that I suspected a trick.

Josephus smiled broadly, as if to a clever child.

'And who *imprimis* would that be?'

I shrugged, struggling not to lose my temper.

'You tell me, if it's so bloody obvious.'

'Forgive me,' he apologised, 'an old weakness for the dialectic. Put it this way. Who took advantage of Theodoric's disputed inheritance?'

I gave him a blank look, preferring not to follow where he was leading.

Now it was his turn to sigh.

'Who has been fighting the Goths for the best part of twenty years now?'

I drew myself to my full height.

'I have little love for the Emperor. But there are no grounds for accusing him of being party to such underhand dealing.'

Nonetheless, I carried on with the argument in my head.

Cui bono, indeed? The name of Symmachus came back to me and the suspicions that he might have been party to the conspiracy. The deleted 'benefactor'. But he would have been long dead by the time it came to the writing of the original let alone the revised version. He had to be out of the equation.

Cassiodorus himself too, of course. Currying favour with the king while he was in service in Ravenna. Then with the Emperor when he was in captivity in Constantinople.

Suddenly I recalled a further scrawl on the back of the final page. I had noticed it when I checked the end of the history but not given it much thought. I resisted the impulse to examine it more thoroughly in the presence of the Jew.

I glanced up at him again. He was grinning broadly now.

'I have had personal experience of the Emperor's animus, if that is the further evidence you require,' he declared.

I recalled he had lost his job on account of Justinian's attempts to rid his administration of Jews.

'The edict was not directed at you personally,' I pointed out.

'But I felt it very personally,' he replied.

I felt there was more to the story than he was letting on. As a qualified and experienced public administrator, he would surely have obtained more lucrative alternative employment than a factotum in a monastery at the end of the world.

'Even if I was the prime instigator of my own downfall,' he admitted with a rueful smile.

There we have it, I thought.

He leaned back in his chair as if challenging me to ask the question.

I contented myself with raising the statutory eyebrow.

He leaned forward again.

'Gambling was my special vice,' he admitted with a cheerful grin.

My eyebrow rose higher – this time in surprise. It would not have been my first guess.

'I was rather good at it,' he continued. 'All a question of probability, you know. And I'd always been fascinated by mathematics. Not to mention numerology. A great help with deciphering the Kabbalah, by the way.'

Proficiency in a vice hardly excused it, I pointed out.

'True,' he conceded, 'but it can make it more lucrative. The problem was that sometimes the laws of probability that I had constructed failed to hold.'

'You lost heavily,' I suggested.

He nodded.

'So I was compelled to take a small advance on my salary.'

'Small?'

'Sometimes not so small,' he agreed. 'But I always paid it back in time.'

'In time or on time?'

'In time. For the annual audit. Carried out by a little man who did the rounds.'

'Regularly and predictably, no doubt.'

'As clockwork. Usually.'

'But not always.'

'Not when you play regularly and predictably with a bitter rival and a bad loser. And when that bad loser has enough clout to call for an extraordinary audit.'

'In which case....'

'In which case, a fine would normally be in order. At worst, dismissal. Unless....'

'Unless you are a son of David,' I guessed.

'You have hit the nail on the head,' he said with overdrawn satisfaction. 'Even if I had, long before, converted to your faith out of a profound sense of civic duty.'

Poppycock, I thought. Enlightened self-interest at best.

'In which case,' Josephus continued, '...the case of a Judaic offender that is, one is subject to prosecution, along with all kinds of cruel and unusual punishments ensuing.'

'So you fled here?'

He nodded again.

'I heard the abbot was in need of a bookkeeper. He was kind enough to ask no questions. Not even a single reference.'

Not a bad deal for the abbot, I thought. He got a gardener and cook thrown into the bargain. Though I'd had no idea that it was the Jew that kept the accounts. I wondered if I had on occasion mistaken his bookkeeping for his obsession with numerology. If so, he had taken delight in my misunderstanding for he had deliberately compounded it.

'So there you have it,' he concluded. 'My life story, to date at least. In all its sordid detail. If you should feel the need to turn me in...'

'Out of a profound sense of civic duty?'

He gave a brief, enigmatic chuckle.

'... I would be grateful for a little advance notice.'

I gave a brief and enigmatic chuckle. He pursed his lips and looked at me again over his lenses.

'You had a second question. In point of fact, the first.'

'I think I am now in a position to work that one out,' I replied.

'We are happy to be of service,' he said, inclining his head.

*

Back in the scriptorium, I lit the lamp again and turned to the scrawl at the end of the history. Here, I felt sure, would be a clue as to which of the versions was the more accurate.

The unknown editor had indeed added a post-mortuum postscript. To the effect that the pre-mortuum Theodoric had announced the forthcoming closure of all Catholic churches in Italy and their conversion into Arian ones. This was merely a prelude, the writer told us, to a full-scale persecution of the faithful.

The scrawl then informed us that shortly afterwards the king was terrorised by a talking fish-head. To the presumable embarrassment of his dinner-guests, the king had struck up a conversation with a poached cod that had been placed on the table. The nature of his (one-sided) dialogue suggested that he imagined the head to be that of the executed

Symmachus. It was, apparently, soon after this that Theodoric himself died.

I put the book down and inhaled deeply. The addendum had not taken me much farther. It had simply followed the pattern of character assassination established by the rest of the annotations.

Perhaps I could consider it as a 'question of probability'. I knew little of the science, if you could call it that. But I would try.

Firstly, it was extremely unlikely that a dead fish would be able to talk, when, alive, it had not possessed that faculty. Miracles aside, and just for the sake of probability, Theodoric clearly imagined it had talked. Which would seem to indicate that he had lost his reason. A classic sign of guilt, I supposed.

Secondly, his threats towards the Catholic Roman community were a sign that he was reverting to barbarian and heretic type after years of controlling his savage instincts.

On balance, the revised version seemed more credible. The original, then, had been written under duress – a bespoke eulogy, you might say. And the penalty for failure to satisfy would be the same as it was for the unfortunate Boethius and Symmachus.

Theodoric was the key, then. The instigator of the conspiracy against, and the judicial murderer of Boethius.

Probably.

And probably more reason than ever to press the truth out of Basilius.

Illumination the Fifth
Fish-head on a Silver Platter

AD 526

Theodoric looked at the over-sized cod that the servant laid on the table before him.

He hated fish.

He looked at it again. It stared back at him with glazed eyes.

He hated this fish in particular.

He turned to the other guests. They made no sound. Their mouths just gaped. Like the mouth of the fish. And closed again.

He checked the fish. Now its mouth was closed too.

He must be going mad.

That would explain the headaches. They never left him these days.

Everyone else had left him.

His beloved wife had succumbed to the miasmic ague some years before. As had his beloved heir.

Theudis, his oldest and best friend was in Spain. He never visited now. Just sent cheerful notes while he carved out a kingdom for himself there. Contrary to orders.

Then there was Boethius. Was.

These people here were strangers to him. Except Cassiodorus, of course.

He turned to his first minister.

'Tell me, Magnus Aurelius. Do you sleep at nights?'

Cassiodorus' mouth gaped and closed.

Theodoric slapped himself on the ear.

Cassiodorus exchanged a look with the other guests. Theodoric knew what that look meant.

'Be so good as to repeat what you just said,' Theodoric asked.

'I said insomnia is an affliction of age, Sire. It will come to us all in time.'

'You dream then?'

'Only of serving you, Sire,' the minister said with a smile.

Theodoric dreamed awake. He wished he didn't. Manlius Severinus visited him regularly at nights, rendering sleep impossible.

'Do the dead speak to you, then?' Theodoric asked again, interrupting Cassiodorus in full flow.

Again that knowing sideways glance.

'I do not have that privilege, Sire.'

The minister wiped the edge of his mouth with a napkin.

'They say it is a gift granted only to the most saintly of us,' he added. He bowed his head, and looked up only with his eyes to check the reaction.

But Theodoric was studying the cod again.

'The fish could not speak even in life, Sire.'

And if it could have done what would it have said of us? Theodoric wondered.

'It would have said that we lose our nature by falling into wickedness.'

He heard the voice clearly. Without having to slap his head.

He looked around to see who had spoken. They were still listening to Cassiodorus.

He looked at the fish again. It was a skeleton now. But its head was still intact.

'Is that you, old friend?' he asked.

The fish said nothing. But Theodoric recognised the words as those of Boethius. From the little handbook he had on his bedside table. The *Consolations* that saw him through the sleepless nights.

Theodoric checked with the others again. Now their mouths had stopped moving. They were all looking at him. The king ignored them.

'Tell me, old friend. Why can I not sleep? Why does my head ache so?'

'If to care and want you are prey, no king you are but slave.'

Theodoric nodded. This was true. He felt more and more the chains of his office.

'And why am I a prey to care and want?' he asked.

'You know why. Because evil men prosper,' Cod's-head Boethius replied.

Theodoric did know this. They had been betrayed.

'I am so sorry, old friend,' he said, feeling the tears course down his cheeks.

The fish-head rocked forward.

'The greatest misery in adverse fortune is once to have been happy.'

'What can I do to put it right? To end this screaming in my head?' Theodoric asked. The ringing in his ears now approached a pitch that threatened to quite unman him.

The fish's mouth broadened to a smile.

'I think you know the answer to that too.'

Theodoric did know the answer to that.

A bolt of light flashed across his inner eye.

Then there it was. What his old friend called 'The Dark Without'.

A Rose by Any Other Name

Man is brought lower than the beasts if he lose self-knowledge.
Boethius

'The winners,' Owen said. 'It's them as calls the shots.'

'Does what?' I asked. I had yet again made the mistake of asking my servant's opinion – this time regarding the respective credibility of the two versions. I had made my own decision. I sought confirmation only.

'It's them as decides what's the truth,' he explained.

I heaved a sigh.

Owen wiped the soap from his face and slapped the towel down on his mattress.

'So there is no absolute truth then, according to you? Just stories?' I asked.

He nodded.

'And the only stories that count are those told by the high and mighty?'

Another nod.

'If you think about it long enough, you'll see I'm right,' he said. 'When you're in service, it's a fact of life.'

'And in this case,' I persisted, 'whose version counts? The one that favours high and mighty Theodoric? Or the one that suits higher and mightier Justinian?'

'Just have to wait and see, who comes out on top,' he replied with a grin.

I wondered how long we would have to wait before we saw. As Josephus would have put it, in the long run the odds were heavily on Justinian and his minions.

Owen interrupted the next stage of his ablutions.

'You know, you should have a word with that old geezer. The one what comes into dinner with his own personal waiters,' he mumbled, waving a birch twig in the air before returning it to his mouth and continuing to brush.

'And why is that?' I asked, not managing to disguise the irritation I felt. I had after all already confessed him, albeit it to little effect. So it was annoying to acknowledge that once again my servant had stolen a march on me and had managed to find out something I hadn't.

'He should know a thing or two about what you're wanting to find out,' using the chamber pot now as a spittoon.

'I have so far experienced great difficulty in finding out anything from him. I don't even know his name.'

Owen grinned the grin again. The one that enjoyed superior knowledge.

'It is 'not to be said',' I explained.

'You could try asking him who his father was,' Owen replied.

*

Time for another confession then. My heart sank.

It could not be long before *nones* by now. I wasn't sure whether the 'old geezer' was in the habit of confessing every day. It seemed unlikely. Given his age and his location there was little he could get up to that would require absolution in the first place. On the other hand, for the same reason, confession might be his idea of entertainment. In the absence of any other avenues of conceivable enjoyment, so to speak.

I made my way out into the garden just in time to see the abbot making his way into the church, and hurried across to intercept him. As I approached, his shoulders fell.

'You feel the need to shrive the poor man's soul again, I take it?'

I gave him a cursory nod.

And yours, I thought. But first things first.

*

The nameless one gave me a similar nod when he entered the confessional.

'She's back again,' he said.

As I had entered the church, I had tried to refresh my memory and call to mind again the eccentric grammar of the person I was about to re-confess. I recalled that I was 'he' to the old man, while he was 'we'. I had just about got the hang of it by the time our previous session had closed.

So I was taken unawares by his opening and cast my eyes about outside the confessional for a woman. Not that I had seen one since I arrived. But he had sounded convincing.

'She must be getting to like him,' he continued, looking straight at me.

192

Clearly I still had some work to do before I cracked the code. Especially if it kept changing like this. And if it kept changing like this, I might end up questioning my own identity. Or my sex.

'She must be,' I replied, playing along with an ingratiating smile. 'But she needs to examine his past more closely to make sure nothing has been missed.'

He looked puzzled.

'Whose?'

I pointed at him, wondering what pronoun he was awarding himself today.

'Missed?'

I tried another pronoun by way of experiment.

'There may be some peccadillo in your past that the abbot has not managed to dredge up. If so, she will be unable to absolve you.'

Now he looked amused, as if I had suggested we play a game of knucklebones.

'New rule?' he asked.

'New rule,' I confirmed with an inward sigh of relief. The idea of a changed procedure seemed to appeal to him. As did the subject pronoun.

'Direct from the Holy See,' I continued. 'Let us take it from the very beginning.'

'Us?' he asked.

This was likely to be very heavy going.

'They,' I corrected myself. 'When were you born?'

'Who?'

I pointed directly at him with more than a touch of irritation. There was after all a reason why grammars evolved as they did.

'A very long time ago,' he said with a note of satisfaction.

I scratched my head.

'What else happened in the year you were born?' I asked in the end.

'He doesn't remember. He doesn't remember being born either.'

Well, it was a silly question, I suppose.

'Understood,' I said. 'What do you remember about your childhood years, then?'

'Uncle Ernak was very kind to him.'

He seemed to have a lot of kind uncles, I decided. I was about to ask about his father when I froze. Ernak? I had read the name somewhere. Then I recalled he had been mentioned in an earlier volume of

Cassiodorus' *History*. The Goths, like most tribes, had had dealings with the Huns. Ernak was one of the sons and successors to the terrifying Attila.

'King Ernak?'

He nodded.

The little old man did not look like a Hun now, and it was hard to conceive he had ever done.

'What were you doing at Uncle Ernak's court?' I asked. A hostage perhaps.

'His father worked for Uncle Ernak.'

I stared at him for a moment wondering if he was making fun of me beneath the imbecilic disguise.

'And what did your father do for Uncle Ernak?'

He thought about it for a moment.

'Wrote letters and things.'

A *notarius* like myself? I wondered.

'And took soldiers into battle,' he added.

Not so similar then. As a tribune, I could have been required to lead men into battle. But my commanding officer was wise to my shortcomings. Or prized my strengths too highly.

Still, this was all most extraordinary. His father had either been a high-ranking Hun or a captive of such ability that a Hun chieftain had found a use for him. A Latin secretary? I doubted I would have ever heard of him, but I asked anyway.

'Did his father have a name?'

He looked at me as if I was stupid.

'Everyone has a name.'

I took a deep breath as an alternative to throttling him.

'And what was his name?'

'Orestes. The Great.'

I had to think about it. Apart from the ill-fated avenging son of the Greek tragedy, I could think of only one other of that name. And he was neither Greek nor Great.

'Great?' I asked.

'Very great.'

He was biased. Understandably. One would expect nothing less of one's son. But the Orestes I had in mind was nothing more than an ambitious warlord. True, he had sounded the death knell of the Western

Empire back in the previous century. But otherwise he was a short-lived upstart.

How Orestes might have got from the Hun court to such a position of power in Ravenna, I had no idea. Perhaps he had been left behind when the Hun's army retreated from its unsuccessful attempt to take Rome. But that would have to have been before his son was born or there would be no memory of the Hun court. And, if that was so, the man in front of me would have had to be older than Methuselah.

Whatever the truth of the matter, 'Great' was not an epithet I would have used to describe a man that banished the last legitimate Emperor, then brought down the curtain on a thousand years of glorious civilisation by installing his own puppet on the throne. A puppet that was not only ineffectual and barbarian but his own ....

I looked up again at the old man in front of me. Not Methuselah, exactly. But still. He would have to be almost a hundred years old to be....

'And what was his son's name?' I asked.

He tittered as if I had caught him out. Then he mumbled something.

'Repeat, please,' I demanded.

'Little Romulus,' he said, rocking his arms as if they held a baby.

I stared at him, incredulous.

Could I really be in the presence of the last Emperor of the West? Or was this grotesque simply a demented geriatric with delusions of grandeur?

'And how did little Romulus survive all these years?'

'Uncle Odo was very kind,' he mused.

Odo? Theodoric had had a general of that name. Or so I had read. Though his reputation was definitely not that of a benevolent uncle. Then again, a Hun hardly fulfilled the benevolent avuncular stereotype either. Let alone a son of Attila.

I drew a deeper breath as the realisation came to me. Orestes had been beaten in battle and supplanted by his own henchman. Odovacar. Who in turn had lost out to Theodoric.

'How was Uncle Odo kind?' I pressed further.

'When his Daddy died, he gave him a little house of his own, and servants to look after him. A pretty little house. Up there.'

He pointed vaguely northward.

'Crotona?' I guessed.

He shook his head.

'Very cold.'
'Neapolis?'
He grinned.
'Warmer.'
'I give up.'
'Lucullanum.'
He began swinging his imaginary baby wildly in his arms.
'Lucullu… Lucullu… Lululu… Little baby, sleep in peace.'
Then he held out his arms as if for me to take the non-existent child.
Now I shook my head. I was more than a little anxious. The man was clearly out of his mind.
'She's not very good with children,' I said.
He pouted.
'Uncle Manlius always took care of the baby.'
It was beyond my powers of reason to work out who Manlius was, or what he might have been to the creature in front of me. I needed a break. Not just from the ravings of the senile last Emperor, if that was who he truly was. I also needed to settle my own mind before I ended up as patently unhinged as the man in front of me.
I rose to leave but was prevented from doing so.
'Are his sins gone this time then?' the penitent asked.
I had in the heat of the moment forgotten what the ostensible reason for the interview was.
I nodded. He looked relieved. I felt guilty.
'I absolve you, in the name of the Father, the Son and the Holy Ghost,' I said, wondering at the same time whether I should have said 'I absolve him…'
I made the sign of the cross. It wasn't his fault, after all, who his father was. Or his many uncles, for that matter. Whoever they were.
But the most immediate question that came to mind was the following:
If all the old fool had told me was true, how, in the name of all that was holy, did the last Emperor of the West end up in a monastery in Scylletium almost eighty years after he disappeared from history? And what was the purpose of the guard that was posted at the door of the church as I exited? To prevent flight or protect from harm?

*

I slumped down into a chair in the scriptorium feeling defeated.

I wasn't sure what Owen had intended by directing me on another wild-goose chase, nor even how he had been made privy to the identity of Romulus. But the diversion had done little to enlighten me, and a great deal to confuse me further. It seemed the farther into the history I waded, the muddier the waters became.

I glanced across at Josephus, who was seated in his favourite draught-free corner, scribbling and every now and then pausing for thought. As I had entered, I had passed close and caught sight of a series of figures. Numerology or accounting? I wondered.

No matter how much I needed a shoulder to cry on, I had no desire to get involved in further discussions of esoteric codes. So I decided not to risk striking up a conversation.

Instead I reached over to a book lying on the opposite side of the table, figuring that it might provide the distraction I needed from my own morbid thoughts.

No such luck.

It was the copy of *Consolations* that I had purloined from the cellar and carelessly left in the scriptorium after our decoding exercise.

With a sigh, I opened it at random in the vain hope that it might indeed provide me with some kind of guidance, or at least some form of consolation. Perhaps inspired by Josephus' occult example, I closed my eyes and stabbed down with my finger. It was Boethius' chance to speak to me from beyond the grave. When I opened my eyes, I read the philosopher's words of wisdom.

'What hope of freedom is left us?'

Very true, I thought. And not in the least helpful.

I flicked the book closed in disgust. It sprang back open at the title page. I had never bothered to examine this before, since the title and author's cognomen had been on the binding.

Now the author's full name stood in front of me.

Anicius Manlius Torquatus Severinus Boethius.

Manlius?

I had never understood why the Roman patrician class needed quite so many names. Perhaps they had one for each level of intimacy or formality. To me and posterity in general, he was known only by his cognomen. To Romulus he had perhaps been known as Uncle Manlius.

Assuming we were talking about the same Manlius. But it was not the most common of names these days. And I had never been a great believer in the power of coincidence.

If, then, Romulus was indeed on close terms with Boethius, what could possibly have been the reason?

*

Unsurprisingly, the main product of my deliberations was a blinding headache. I nodded in parting to Josephus, who was still deep into gleaning significance from meaningless or meaningful numbers, and made my way back to my cell. I prayed that Owen would be occupied elsewhere, since I had an urgent need to lie down in darkness and silence, neither of which could be guaranteed in his presence.

As I pulled open the door of the room, the first thing that caught my attention was a fragrance of lavender. And something else that I could not immediately identify, overpowered as it was by the scent of the flower. Eventually I worked out what it was. Another flower. Attar of roses. Delightful. And soothing to my head.

Until I realised that it denoted the presence of someone other than my servant. He was pottering about on the far side of the room with what looked like studied innocence.

It was not too difficult to work out that he had been enjoying the company, if that is the right word, of a member of the opposite sex. I had not seen a woman since we arrived. But trust my resourceful manservant to find a female in a monastery.

I pinched the bridge of my nose between my fingers in an attempt to focus my eyes and mind.

'You realise, I assume this is a celibate establishment?'

He feigned a look of surprise as he folded up a towel that was well past the stage of benefiting from such treatment.

'Funny,' he replied, holding his head on one side. 'I don't recall taking any vow to that effect.'

Then he made a great show of picking up a bowl and sprinkling water around the room. Rose water and lavender.

Once again he had made a gull of me. Nonetheless, I reflected, the use of such fragrances did not rule out the presence of females. On the contrary, they could be used to conceal more obvious tell-tale odours.

Again I was pre-empted.

'No offence intended, boss,' he said. 'But it was getting a little funky in here.'

I flushed. The word was new to me, but the gist was obvious.

I had not bathed since we arrived. I gave a furtive sniff to my armpits. But in the best traditions of poor personal hygiene, I would be the last person to know. The stench I carried round was too familiar to me.

'Don't worry, boss,' he continued. 'Where I come from we take a bath regular as clockwork – every summer solstice. So I'm used to it.'

He treated me to a disarming smile that along with the sweet smells of the room seemed to have dispelled my headache. Thus filled with gratitude, I once again made the mistake of taking him into my confidence. A theory had been forming in my mind and I wished to test it out.

'Fire away, boss,' was his response. Boss again. This was a new one. He seemed to have any number of means of addressing me. This one, however, was at least more accurate and so preferable to most.

'You seem to have been particularly well-informed as to the identity of the mysterious older figure,' I began.

'The geezer?'

I nodded, assuming we were referring to the same person.

'Keep my ear to the ground, that's all,' he continued with a shrug.

'If what he claims is true,' I continued, 'then as the last Emperor he would have had a superior claim to the throne of the West. Superior to all the rulers of Italy that followed him.'

I anticipated a nod of agreement but got an inscrutable stare.

'And would thus have been a threat to Theodoric. A threat he would have wanted to dispose of.'

The same blank face.

'But Boethius, out of the goodness of his heart, took the imbecile under his wing, providing for his daily needs and concealing his existence from the barbarian king. To protect the poor idiot, as it were.'

Owen wagged his head from side to side, as if weighing up the evidence so far.

'His existence came, despite the efforts at concealment, to the attention of Theodoric. And Boethius had just about enough time to spirit Romulus away before the axe fell on the cretin's head.'

A purse of the lips this time.

'The axe then fell on Boethius' head instead. And....' Another thought came to me. 'So Theodoric was obliged to fabricate a set of treason charges against his minister. Since he wished, of course, for the existence of the rival claimant to remain hidden.'

The satisfaction I felt at the neatness of this explanation was undermined somewhat by Owen's cool reception of it. Still, I felt that in the absence of any other evidence to the contrary, the theory held water. I wasn't sure how all the corrections to the various manuscripts entered into the equation, but that would no doubt become clear now that I had a hypothesis to work with.

'All due respect, boss,' he said in the end. Not a good omen. He seemed generally oblivious of how much respect was, in fact, due. 'I don't get where you're coming from half the time.'

I was, as usual, unfamiliar with this idiom, which was probably of his own making and designed to confuse me further. It succeeded, although I divined a negative thrust. I gave an ambiguous grunt.

'I mean, Theodoric was a barbarian. Granted. But so am I. And so are you. So how come you're always down on them so much?'

I opened my mouth to speak but nothing came out.

'For all you know, Theo might have been protecting the bloke himself. Or simply providing him with a pension. Using what's-his-face as his agent.'

I took a moment to decode this. And was forced to concede the possibility.

'I mean, I can't figure you out,' he said. 'You ashamed of where you come from?'

I felt my lips and nostrils tighten.

'Must be really tough living with yourself, in that case,' he concluded.

I stormed out of the room. I had no wish to let my servant see my reaction to what he said. It would have undermined what little authority I had left.

Illumination the Sixth
Lucullanum

527 AD

He sat on the ramparts of the castle and looked out over the sea.
He hummed to himself.
'Lucullu..lu..lu..lu..lu.. Lucullanum.'
He spotted a sailing skiff. It was fishing just off the rocks the castle stood upon. He waved to the fishermen. They waved back. He smiled a sad smile. He would like to be on the boat, and sail far away. Back home. To see his Daddy. Feel Uncle Ernak tousle his hair. Romp and wrestle with his cousins.

Away from the castle and the monks. Especially away from the abbot. The abbot never smiled at him. Never waved to him. Nor did the monks. The abbot did not like smiles.

Uncle Manlius smiled at him. Hugged him when he came. But Uncle Manlius hadn't visited for a long while now. Romulus missed him. He missed a lot of things now.

The children used to smile at him. Allowed him to join their games. Spinning tops. Sailing small boats in the pools besides the rocks. Wrestling on the sand.

The abbot had stopped that. Said he was too old for that. Grown-up people understood so little. He would never grow up. Grown-up people did not understand how to play.

In fact grown-up people did not understand how to have fun at all. He wondered why they bothered to grow up. The abbot, for example. He could do what he wanted, go where he wanted. But he stayed here all the time. Looking miserable. Talking about someone called Augustine. Telling Romulus he was born bad. So why was the abbot so surprised and angry when Romulus did something the abbot said was bad?

Like sailing boats in the pools. And spinning tops. What could be 'bad' about that? 'Wicked.' 'Evil.' It wasn't hurting anybody. Neither was wrestling. He liked wrestling with the boys. He liked wrestling with the girls better. But that had made the abbot even more angry. That had stopped the games.

He had asked why wrestling was bad, when he was good at it. That earned him a beating from Brother Paulus. Brother Paulus was old and ugly. He had a very hard hand. Afterwards, the abbot showed him a Bible.

'Adam and Eve,' he said. 'We carry their original sins.'

'Why?' he asked.

'Because we are fallen.'

'Where?' he asked. 'Fallen where?'

The abbot spread out his arms.

'Here,' he said.

Romulus looked around the bare room with damp walls.

'We are being punished?' he asked.

'Chastised for our sins,' the abbot had agreed.

The abbot had given him a book to read. It was called *Confessions* and would explain everything, he said. It was very boring and had no pictures. But there were a lot of original sins. Romulus felt sorry for the writer and wondered why he had confessed.

'To get rid of his sin,' the abbot had explained.

So that was all right then. You could sin as much as you liked. Then you confessed.

*

Romulus looked down again at the sail boat. The sailors were shouting to each other as they hauled at the net. They were saying bad words and laughing. He wondered why they were not being chastised for it. Instead they were laughing. Enjoying themselves.

He shifted slightly on the seat. It was hard. His bottom was sore. Now he looked out over the land. The rain had come and made everything green again. He wished he could be in the fields. Men were working in the fields. Gathering corn. Picking fruit. Beating olive trees with sticks, then picking up the olives.

They were too far away. He couldn't hear if they were happy. Couldn't see their faces. But he would like to be with them. Playing ball. Or knucklebones. Scrumping fruit. Wrestling in the grass.

But he was stuck here.

The bell rang. Time for church, he thought. Good. He liked church. He liked the singing. He liked the pictures on the walls and the screens. The abbot said they were to remind him of his sin. But they made him happy. They were beautiful. So was the singing.

And after church there was always breakfast. Or dinner. Unless it was Friday. Was it Friday? he wondered.

'Lucullu..lu..lu..lu..lu... Lucullu.'

Suddenly he felt very sad. Nobody came to see him anymore. Where was his papa? Where were his uncles? Uncle Manlius always brought cake with his smiles. Why did he not come?

Why could he not go home?

*

'You have a visitor,' the abbot said, as the man-child walked out of the church.

Romulus' face brightened until he saw another grim-faced monk in a dark brown robe. He had hoped, at last, it would be Uncle Manlius.

'I leave you with him. I do not approve,' the abbot said to the monk. 'You may tell your master that.'

'We are born in sin,' the monk replied with a nod. Romulus nodded too. He knew that.

The strange monk took him into the parlour of the monastery, grasping his hand firmly as if afraid he would run away. Once inside, the monk sat him on a stool.

'Your time here is over,' he explained.

Romulus' heart leapt. They would take him back to his papa now. To his lost childhood.

'Where are we going?' he asked, suddenly unsure.

The monk looked angry.

'Where we all go in the end,' he replied.

'To heaven?' Romulus exclaimed, clapping his hands. Heaven was filled with apples and grapes, and romping with angels. He knew this.

The monk looked at him.

'They did not say you were...,' he began, then paused. 'How old are you really?'

Romulus screwed up his face and began to count fingers. Then he looked thoughtful.

'And some more,' he said.

The monk sighed.

'And yet you are a child.'

Romulus clapped his hands, gave a smile and nodded hard.

'They did not tell me.'

The monk fidgeted with the sleeve of his tunic, folding and unfolding again. He would not look at Romulus.

Then he seemed to come to a decision.

'Come. Let us go,' he said, rising from his own stool.

'To heaven?' Romulus asked.

The monk shook his head.

'Show me your cell. We will pack your clothes. You will not need them here anymore.'

'What should I call you?' Romulus asked as they left the room together.

'You may call me, Father Venantius,' the monk replied with a grimace.

'Father,' Romulus echoed with a smile. The old man slipped his hand into the long fingers of the monk.

Father Venantius winced.

'And what do they call you?' he asked.

'They give me no name,' Romulus said.

'That is as well,' Venantius said, 'for where you are going.'

Confessions

That which each seeks in preference to all else, that is in his judgment the supreme good.
Boethius

I was still in a furious temper after my humiliation at the hands of my servant when I noticed the figure of the abbot slink into a room off the atrium.

I decided it was finally time to confront him with what I had so far found out about his so-called flock of brothers. And, realising that I was in just the right frame of mind to intimidate him to the full, I followed him into a tight cell without windows. The abbot had lit a lamp that threw shadows onto the floor and angled up the walls. He was in the process of changing into white vestments for yet another office of the day.

As I entered, he looked over at me with an uncertain smile.

'Peace be with you, brother,' he said, 'on this day of days.'

Perhaps it was his birthday. I was in no mood to offer my felicitations.

'I feel obliged to reveal that I have discovered the identity of your prisoner.'

His face lost all colour. For a moment I thought his legs were about to give way beneath him. He leaned his hand against the table-top for support.

'Prisoner?' he repeated in a faint voice.

'Romulus,' I prompted. 'You can't have forgotten him. He was for a very short while Emperor of the West – much good that it did him.'

'Much good indeed,' he parroted again and turned his head to the side.

'This much I have discovered,' I confirmed. 'What I don't yet know is why he was visited by Boethius prior to his incarceration here.'

'Incarceration,' he repeated. It was like having a conversation with myself.

He raised the courage to look me in the eye at last. His eyes had become rheumy. As I had anticipated, the man lacked moral fibre. It should not be difficult to squeeze the rest of the truth out of him.

'Boethius was a good man,' he said eventually.

'That much, I had worked out for myself.'

'His wife's estate lay nearby. And he was charged with securing the comforts of the ex-Emperor,' he continued. 'Which he did with the utmost diligence.'

'And that diligence cost him life.' A suggestion only, but I delivered it like a challenge, defying him to deny it.

It had its effect. A look of panic flashed across his face.

'You know, then.'

I was not sure whether this was a statement or a question.

'I do not know why the ex-Emperor was brought here. Or on whose orders he was locked away,' I said.

The abbot composed his features. A line of resolve now settled on his lips.

'You presume too much,' he replied.

I was puzzled but decided to stand my ground.

'I presume nothing. Have you forgotten your vows? Do you not recall who I am?'

His face softened.

'*Assume* is probably the term I should have used,' he said.

'And what exactly am I assuming?'

'That he is here against his will.'

Now it was my turn to fumble for words.

'I suppose he is here for his own good then,' I said with heavy sarcasm.

'His own protection,' the abbot nodded. 'He was no longer safe in his previous … residence.'

His attendants were bodyguards rather than warders then?

'Lucullulum,' I said. I was playing for time. I wasn't sure how I could square this with my findings.

He nodded, but his attention appeared to be wandering.

'So how did you know he was no longer safe there?' I demanded, although I had a good idea of what the answer would be.

'It was rumoured…,' he began before his voice trailed off. He looked at the floor.

'What was?'

'Orders had come for his removal.'

'Removal?'

'Execution.'

'Murder,' I said.

'Murder,' he agreed with an absent nod.

'From whom?'

'I cannot say.'

'Theodoric,' I decided to answer my own question. 'The last Emperor's existence having come to his knowledge.'

A smile flickered across his face. He aimed it at the floor.

'From whom, then?' Now it was I that was reduced to repeating what I had said.

'I cannot say.'

'I command you as your bishop.'

He remained silent with his head bowed.

I could have torn out my hair. An answer to that question would surely be the answer to the whole mystery.

'Well, how did he end up here, then?' I asked, thinking this was at least a question that would not risk compromising anyone.

He shook his head.

'I cannot say.'

He then looked up at me again. Now he seemed to exude an aura of peace and acceptance. Indeed there was a quiet dignity about him, almost a beauty, such as much have blessed the faces of the early martyrs.

A joyous peal of church bells broke the silence between us.

He pulled on his white robes.

'And now if you will excuse me, my Lord Bishop,' he said, 'I have more important business to attend to.'

'What could be more important,' I demanded, 'than the truth?'

'Celebrating the birth of Our Saviour,' he declared. And with a whisk of his vestments as they brushed the wall and door, he left the room and myself.

I had completely forgotten.

It was Christmas Day.

*

I put on my best face and hurried out into the garden and across to the church, pulling down the cowl of my tunic as I walked to fend off the snowflakes.

I must have been among the last to arrive, for the church was nearly full by the time I took my place alongside Josephus. The Jew gave me a sardonic grin as I shuffled into position. I noticed he had smuggled in a book that was far too large for a missal. Some esoterica probably, with which to divert himself during the long mass. And, no doubt, an equally long sermon.

I shook the snow from my hood prior to removing it, and looked around. It was the first time I had seen the villagers present in the congregation and assumed that there was a tradition of inviting the whole community up to the abbey church for the festival, plague or no plague. I raised the edge of my cowl to my face.

The abbot was praying before the altar – desperate, I supposed, to remove the taint of sin prior to celebrating the holy mass. A sin of commission in defying his bishop. One of omission in withholding the truth. The need for confession was clear.

As we waited for him to begin the service, I wondered how much deeper the stain of his sin ran. He had claimed to know much about the fate of Boethius, and once again I asked myself how deeply he himself had been complicit. Had he indeed been one of the informants that had betrayed the philosopher? If so, was it not also likely that he had been involved in the abduction and immurement of the ex-Emperor? For I was not entirely convinced that Romulus was here as a free agent.

A creature of Theodoric, no less.

A murmur ran through the congregation as the abbot rose to his feet, and then the liturgy began. For once we had a choir. I had no idea where the abbot had procured it. Perhaps from the chapel in the valley. For none of the monks were present amongst the choristers.

As the exchanges between priest and choir droned on, I began to drift off into my own thoughts and reflections. But no matter how I shuffled the facts, I always came to the same conclusion. The key to all the mysteries lay with the fate of Boethius. And the barbarian king was the prime suspect in creating the fog of secrecy that I was fumbling through. A fog that was surely designed to conceal Theodoric's own culpability.

I became aware of a change in the world outside my head. The litany had ceased and the abbot was mounting the podium. For a moment I was further affronted by the failure of the abbot to invite me to preach. Though, given the frame of mind I was in, the delivery would have been uncertain and the message hardly uplifting.

He had taken Paul's *Epistle to the Corinthians* as his text. An obvious choice.

When I was a child, I spoke as a child, I understood as a child, I thought as a child; but when I became a man, I put away childish things.

I yawned, wishing I had a seat to slouch and slumber into. Then something woke me up completely.

'When I became a man, I did many things that I would never have considered as a child. I fell into sin.'

Then he listed the sins 'he' had fallen into. Without being too specific about the details. Was he talking about himself? I wondered. Or was he reprising Augustine's *Confessions*?

I became more convinced that he was paraphrasing Augustine, when he came to the moment of repentance. This took the form of *seeing the light*. Of course.

'And with repentance comes trust in God. And with trust in God comes faith.'

I relaxed a little and began to drift off once more. The sermon had attracted my attention for a moment, but now it was drifting off into formulae.

My interest was aroused again by a protracted moment of silence. Had he finished already, I wondered – more in hope than conviction. Then a roar came from the abbot. I would never have guessed he had it in him.

'What 'good' are repentance and faith,' he demanded, 'if we do not *make* good? And how do we do so, other than by doing good? And what *good* is atonement, unless we do it with a good heart?'

Augustine had suddenly been ditched in favour of Pelagius, it seemed.

'And how can we have a pure heart without looking into it and coming to terms with what we find there?'

'For, only by accepting who we are, will we be able to accept what others are. Only by trusting ourselves can we learn to trust others.' Which seemed to bring us to the edge of heresy and tip us over the brink. Into paganism, even. Wasn't that a Socratic formula?

I looked directly at the abbot. He seemed to be looking directly at me.

I wondered for a moment if the whole harangue had been improvised with me in mind. I looked into my own heart and found it raging. Who did he think he was talking to? By what right?

Somehow from there, he managed to bring us back to St Paul.

And now abide faith, hope, love, these three; but the greatest of these is love.

Love was not what I was feeling at that moment. At least, not towards this insubordinate and subversive cleric.

Descending from the podium, he consecrated the Host and the Wine and invited the congregation to partake. I remained where I was. My mind was in turmoil and my heart in no state to accept the Body and Blood.

Josephus also stayed in his place, although I suspected other motives. As the congregation lined up to take their turn, the Jew laid two fingers on my arm to attract my attention.

In his other hand he held a book open – the book that was not a missal. He passed it to me. It was the collection of Cassiodorus' epistles. I raised an eyebrow in question.

'I took the liberty,' he said. 'You had left the book in the scriptorium.'

I was none the wiser.

'Look at the names,' he whispered. 'I thought they sounded familiar.'

The book was open at a transcription of a letter from King Athalaric, Theodoric's grandson and successor, to one Opilio on his appointment to the position of Count of the Sacred Largesses.

The name was familiar to me too. But I couldn't place it and began to feel my choler rising. This was neither the time nor the place.

My face must have betrayed me.

'One of the informers against Boethius,' he explained.

'The same Opilio?'

He nodded.

'Brother of Cyprian, the state prosecutor.'

He flicked to another page. Cyprian too had been appointed to the same position after the trial. The family had been awarded the post in perpetuity, it seemed.

But I failed to see the point

Again Josephus prompted me.

'What did Boethius say about Opilio?'

I tried to recall. Something uncomplimentary, for sure. Then it came to me.

Boethius had claimed that he, like his fellow informers had been sentenced to banishment for his crimes.

Yet here was Theodoric's grandson appointing him to one of the highest posts in the West.

I shrugged at Josephus. Assuming Theodoric had commissioned the conspiracy against Boethius, it was hardly surprising that the conspirators should be rewarded. This just made the whole family party to the plot. It was also no great wonder that the barbaric taint of the father should be passed down to the son.

I said as much to Josephus.

'The family of Opilio and Cyprian was not the only common factor,' he replied.

He had lost me again.

'Athalaric was no more than a child. His mother, the regent, not much older.'

I shrugged again.

'They would in all likelihood be acting under advisement in the appointments they made.'

This was more convincing. It was sufficient to raise questions in my head that I would have preferred elsewhere.

But it had to be Theodoric, I decided finally.

I looked around at the rest of the congregation, as if defying them to challenge my conclusion. My defiance was wasted. I was alone in the church. I had been so deep in thought that I had not noticed that the service had finished. Even Josephus had left me.

The cold made me shiver. Not only the cold perhaps. But the door to the church was swinging open. Still, my mind was focused. Rubbing the life back into my hands, I braced myself for a day of judgement with the damned abbot. It was time to see what his own reward for bearing false witness had been. Appointment as head of Vivarium, perhaps? I would waste no time finding out.

*

Or so I thought.

*

As I re-entered the main building, I heard a rumble of voices from the direction of the atrium, and made my way towards them. The closer I came, the stronger grew the aroma of spices. Cinnamon, definitely. Cloves maybe, but if so, just a hint. Something subtle underlying the more pungent herbs. Saffron, then. And an overlay of sweetness. Honey! That was it. Perhaps the monks enjoyed their Christmas dinner within the monastery itself rather than in the more usual refectory.

But when I came closer, I was forced to correct my first impressions. A sourness assailed my nostrils. *Conditum paradoxum*, then. Spiced wine. And instead of the anticipated collection of monastic habits, I beheld the grubby tunics of the villagers. Some kind of party thrown for the great unwashed, therefore. Commendable, no doubt. But my mission took precedence.

I approached the throng, and noticed Isidorus hovering on the fringe, a beatific smile on his face. When he saw me, his expression changed to one of concern. He held out an arm to bar my way forward and, with gentle determination, propelled me back into the *scriptorium*.

'The Xmas alms-giving,' he said, assuming this was some kind of excuse for manhandling his bishop. 'The abbot has few such pleasures.'

I drew myself up so that I towered over the hunchback.

'Far be it from me to begrudge him his indulgences, but my business is urgent.'

He cocked his head on one side, adding to the grotesqueness of his appearance.

'For those receiving, the matter is also important,' he replied. 'It will help them survive the winter. Is your business as important as that?'

I flushed.

'It is all too easy to be openhanded with other people's money,' I responded, my self-esteem piqued.

Now the little mason looked puzzled.

'Whose money?' he asked.

'The Master's. Who else?'

'But the alms come from his own pocket,' he replied after a moment's thought.

I was taken aback, but snorted my disbelief.

'Or so he claims,' I responded.

'You may check with Josephus.'

'The Jew?!'

'Being in charge of the accounts for the monastery, he will be able to confirm. Not only the alms-giving but also the entire maintenance of the monastery and the support. All these come from the revenues of the abbot's estates.'

'If that is so, not all of the monks appear grateful,' I persisted, thinking of the disrespect Arminius and Uldin had shown towards the abbot.

'Not all of the monks are aware of the fact. Only Josephus has known from the beginning. I only learnt of this when I questioned an invoice for building materials.'

I found nothing to say.

'The abbot does not like to broadcast his charity,' Isidorus concluded.

I suddenly felt all the fight go out of me. Perhaps I had got everything upside-down. For I certainly could not square this new image of Basilius with the one I had constructed of him as a corrupt informer.

But, as usual, I decided to bluster my way out of my loss of face.

'I imagine he has read somewhere that it is easier for a camel to pass through the eye of a needle than for a rich man to enter the kingdom of heaven,' I said, though even I felt the feebleness of the response.

It served at least to stir the mason to what he no doubt considered rightful indignation.

'There is precious little of his estate left by now so he should have little trouble on that score,' he replied. 'Besides, you have seen for yourself that the abbot's good works are not limited to dispensing largesse.'

I had indeed. I wondered if I would take my pastoral duties so keenly when I was installed as bishop.

'What is more, all of us are here due to his good graces,' Isidorus continued.

Again he astounded me.

'How so?'

'We are all refugees of one kind or another, fleeing from injustice and persecution. Or 'the march of progress', as some would have it.'

I had some difficulty digesting this. But on reflection, I could see that there might be an element of truth in the claim, given what I had learnt of the histories of some of the monks.

'I had thought the Master...,' I began.

Isidorus snorted.

'The Master does next to nothing for us or the abbey. Barring perhaps his decision to limit himself to a peppercorn rent for the use of the property.'

I fell silent for a moment.

'So you live on the abbot's charity,' I declared, out of spite as much as anything else.

Isidorus replied with a smile and:

'You could put it like that. Although we all contribute to the running of the monastery.'

I supposed he was right. I had had some experience of how they did so.

'And we are all beneficiaries of the abbot in a more important way,' Isidorus persisted.

'How so? I can imagine nothing more important than being kept alive.'

The mason granted me an indulgent smile.

'The bishop will allow that saving a man's soul is more important than saving his body, I hope.'

I blushed.

'I was on the point of committing the cardinal sin of destroying the life God gave me,' he continued.

'Because of your excommunication as a heretic.'

He nodded.

'My soul had been cast into the pit of despair.'

I tried to look sympathetic. But I was impatient to be gone and to confront this benefactor of crippled souls. The owner of the most crippled soul of all.

'And so it was with the rest of the brotherhood, then,' I suggested in an effort to summarise matters and bring them to a close.

He nodded.

'Brother Arminius…'

'I have heard about Arminius.'

'Brother Paulinus….'

'… was a housebreaker who had a change of heart and now keeps housebreakers out.' I prepared to take my leave and force myself on the abbot, even at the cost of humiliating him in front of the villagers.

'… was a housebreaker who was witness to the murder of a householder by another member of the household. Naturally he himself was accused.'

'And sentenced to be put to death until the abbot rode to the rescue,' I concluded for him.

'From a treadmill in the salt mines,' Isidorus corrected me with a gentle smile. 'The abbot knew the real murderer. He had confessed him.'

Well, then. He had me there. I was obviously not the only one to use the confessional for ends other than the ones it was designed for.

I could only pity the gullibility of the abbot if he assumed that all his sinners were now truly repentant. But the insight also cast doubt on his own involvement in the judicial murder of Boethius. Naivety was perhaps the man's besetting fault rather than duplicity.

I was about to thank the mason for the unsolicited biographies when I was pre-empted by a familiar guffaw of laughter. I had not noticed that Owen was also in the scriptorium. For the first time, I am sure. I looked over, curious as to what could have brought him to a place of study and devotion. He was peering over the shoulder of Anacreon as the cretin doodled, chuckling and nudging him as he worked.

Isidorus looked over at him with tenderness in his eyes.

'The boy-child jumped ship in Tarentum. He was neither a boy nor a child when he did so.'

The way he looked now, it was hard to imagine him ever doing anything remotely as sensible as escaping from what was most probably a pirate galley.

'The abbot and I had travelled up to the port to buy some marble and tufa for repairs to the buildings. We came across the boy sheltering in the harbour, scared out of his wits.'

His wits had also very sensibly jumped ship, then. They cannot have felt at home in such a poor creature.

'He was still coherent but it was clear how badly he had been treated.' He hesitated.

'His injuries went beyond the usual beatings.'

'He had been sodomised,' I guessed.

The mason blushed.

'Almost to the point of death. His other wounds were superficial. But that... had caused internal damage. Which brought on a fever. That, in turn, rose to the brain.'

'Since which time...,' I said.

'... he has been here in the care and protection of the abbot.'

He once again gazed fondly over at the cretin.

'Such a lovely lad he was. Now look at him.'

I did as instructed. He was certainly most unlovely now that idiocy had descended upon him. Despite myself, I felt a wave of pity thrill through me.

'One at least,' I said, almost to myself, 'that doesn't contribute.'

When I looked back, I found Isidorus' eyes on me. They were smiling.

'You'd be surprised,' he said.

'I have had the doubtful pleasure of witnessing his efforts at illuminating manuscripts.'

Now the mason's mouth stretched into a smile.

'It depends on the manuscript. You should take a look at how inspired he becomes when illustrating Augustine's *Confessions.*'

'As he is doing now, I assume.'

For it was true. The cretin's face glowed as if filled with the Spirit. But I could not understand why Owen would find the procedure amusing.

I made my way over towards the desk he was working on. The laughter faded as I approached, but Owen's eyes showed lingering amusement.

'You'll love this, boss,' he said. Which was enough to persuade me I wouldn't.

And I didn't. But even though I had been forewarned by my servant, I was still shocked by what I beheld. The sins that the pagan, as-yet-unrepentant Augustine had indulged in were vividly and pornographically illustrated by the idiot. In the most minute anatomical detail. The standard of draughtsmanship was superb and worthy of excommunication.

I looked up and glared first at my servant, which only amused him the more, then over at Isidorus, who also appeared diverted, if in a more sedate fashion. I wondered for a moment how he squared his disrespect for the Church Father with his own strong if misguided faith. Until, that is, I recalled how Augustine had been pre-eminent in denouncing the mason's beloved Pelagius as a heretic.

The sacrilege had totally dispelled the spirit of charity that had begun to settle upon me. The little that remained, I myself consigned to oblivion. I scowled my disapproval at all present, and was just about to pronounce anathema on them all when the abbot entered the *scriptorium.* Which did at least solve the problem of deciding whether anathematisation was within my purview.

*

Basilius looked, as usual, harassed beyond endurance. He was fumbling with the edge of his cape, trying to restore it to its normal position. Flakes of snow fell to the floor and melted into the gaps between the tiles. By which token, I deduced that he had been outside and that the weather had taken yet another turn for the worse.

He caught sight of me and flinched.

'You were waiting on me, I take it. A thousand apologies, your Excellency. First the Xmas duties. Then a message from the outside world.' He smiled broadly, though without conviction.

Not more news, I thought to myself. Don't tell me the Emperor has died this time. Not that I had any great love for Justinian. But I was in awe of what he represented. I had no wish for the collapse of the Empire.

'Not bad tidings, I trust?'

'No, only good. Very good, in fact.' His face told a different story. Clearly he wasn't referring to the demise of the Emperor. Anything else could wait.

'So how can I help you?' he asked.

'I had a couple of questions.'

Actually that was a conservative estimate. And I expected the answers to the questions would breed others exponentially.

'I am at your disposal,' he replied. The shifty look returned. 'But perhaps we should adjourn to the vestry so I can change out of my vestments.'

I followed him back into the small cell. But first I scooped up a pile of books – the *Consolations*, and Cassiodorus' *History* and *Letters* – intending to refer to them as evidence if necessary.

I laid them down on a side-table, as the abbot began to disrobe and I began to cross-examine.

'This time I really must insist on an answer from you.'

He assumed a look of innocence. Not with a great deal of success.

'Who ordered Romulus' execution? And how did he find asylum here?' I demanded.

His lips remained tightly closed – so tightly, in fact, that they lost all colour.

'Allow me to answer the first question myself, then,' I persisted. 'You may merely nod to confirm if it makes you feel any better.'

He did not even nod to this suggestion.

'Theodoric ordered his death. Astonished to discover that his first minister had been harbouring a rival and more legitimate claimant to the throne of the West, he ordered the death of the claimant and the show trial of his minister.'

As before, his response was the shadow of a smile. Then words.

'Theodoric had already been dead some time when the order came,' he said. 'As, of course, had his minister. It was, in fact, the king that consigned Romulus to Boethius' care, in the first place.'

That stopped me in my tracks for a moment.

'Then who, in the name of heaven, gave the order?'

'I cannot say…'

I interrupted him. I was, by now, a man possessed. Or obsessed. As if my own identity rested upon revealing the identity of the mastermind behind the conspiracy.

'In that case, you will perhaps enlighten me as to who lay behind the false accusations and false witness that consigned poor Boethius to an early grave.'

'I cannot…'

Again I interrupted him.

'I am by now sure beyond all reasonable doubt that you were one of the said false witnesses, Decius Basilius Venantius. That is your full name, is it not?'

I was, as you will note, in full inquisitional flow.

The abbot bowed his head. I chose to take that as both a nod and an acknowledgement of guilt and shame.

'So much is clear to me,' I continued. 'As is the identity of your accomplices, to wit one Opilio and one Gaudentius.'

Despite the confidence of my tone, I had little to go on but bluff. There was little doubt and less brilliance about this particular piece of detection though. The names of Basilius and his two confederates were, of course, in *Consolations* for all to see.

Still the abbot said nothing, his head hung low.

'More important, I am absolutely sure that you three were neither the only nor the chief conspirators. To wit, there was someone else who was working behind the scenes – pulling the strings. As it were.'

The abbot made a choking sound.

'My question to you should be clear by now. Who was this puppet-master?'

The abbot finally looked up at me. Tears coursed down his cheeks. I felt a twinge of remorse nudge at my soul. However hardened in wickedness he may have been in the past, he was clearly now made of less stern stuff. Eventually he threw his eyes up.

'I beg your forgiveness, Lord,' he said. I thought for a moment he was talking to me. 'As I have begged for twenty years and more.'

'Why?' I asked in a gentler tone.

'I had, in the foolishness of youth, contracted debts,' he said. 'And as was common practice, had taken public office in an effort to hold off my creditors.'

'And no doubt channel some public funds into your own pockets in order to repay them.'

'God forgive me,' he said. 'For Manlius Severinus...'

'Boethius, that is.'

He nodded.

'...took his duties more seriously than most.' He thought for a moment. 'He was a difficult man. But a good one.'

Now I nodded to urge him forward.

'He brought me to trial for corruption.'

'For which you were sentenced to banishment.'

He looked up in surprise. But it was all in *Consolations*.

'All in all then, I suppose you were particularly receptive to any suggestions that might discredit Boethius.'

A further nod.

'But I had no idea that....' He stopped short. Yet again.

'... that he would suffer the ultimate penalty,' I finished for him. 'Of course not. But still it ended happily enough for you. Your sentence was revoked and your career prospered.'

He looked up at me sharply.

'Never suppose that it ended happily for me,' he quoted back at me.

'You were appointed abbot of a prestigious monastery,' I said.

'Do I look happy about it?' he asked in return.

I thought for a moment.

'I suppose not,' I said. 'But at least you found God.'

'I wish only that He had found me too.'

'So you have been punishing yourself ever since. In a spirit of atonement.'

'I cannot presume...,' he began, then made an effort to pull himself together. 'I cannot presume to have atoned.'

'With God's grace?' I suggested.

'I cannot presume on God's grace.'

That broke my momentum. Augustine would have disagreed, I feel. True repentance for the Bishop of Hippo brought with it assurance of God's forgiveness. But was that not, I wondered, in itself presumptuous?

I felt suddenly drained. And, despite my intentions, filled with a degree of pity for the abject creature in front of me.

'Can you not see,' I said, again gently, although I had to summon up my resolve to speak with such calculation, 'that part of your atonement would lie with your telling the whole truth?'

'Your meaning?'

'Who was it that orchestrated the conspiracy?' I pressed him further. By now, I was in no doubt that the abbot had rescued the ex-Emperor. As he had rescued others since. But still....

'Was it not the same person that ordered the murder of Romulus?'

He shook his head. It was difficult to work out whether this was a refusal to answer or a denial of my suggestion. Again I stiffened my resolve.

'Or perhaps we should take it to the confessional.'

By now, the abbot was kneeling in front of me. But not in supplication so much as desperation, I guessed.

Suddenly, there was a commotion that issued from the atrium. Sounds of tables being overthrown, running feet, voices of protest. And one voice that rose above the others.

I turned back to find Basilius now looking up at me.

'You will find the Master better qualified to answer your questions than myself,' he said.

That, presumably, was 'the message from the outside world'.

Illumination the Seventh
The Justinian Code

AD 524

Cyprian paused for a moment at the entrance to the Great Hall of Daphne. Partly to catch his breath. He had lost count of the steps that he had climbed on his way up to the entrance of the Palace.

Partly also to recover his senses. The heat, the stench and the noise of the street had all been overpowering. He had to assume that the temperature was normal for Constantinople at this time of year. It cast the Ravenna summer quite into shadow, he thought, allowing himself a narrow smile at his own wit.

The foul odours were also a novelty. The parts of the Italian capital that he chose to frequent were spotlessly clean. Rubbish was collected regularly, and sewage carried away by the ancient pipes that had been repaired and were now efficiently maintained under the Goth King. Here, on the other hand, everything appeared to be consigned to the centre of the street, be it household garbage or human waste. Several times during his conveyance from the dock, the litter bearers had had to swerve to avoid being coated in effluent flung from above, and voiced their displeasure in a demotic that was unfamiliar to the young Roman. And even on the short walk from the litter to the steps he had had to fight his way between scavenging dogs.

As for the noise, his ears were still ringing. It was obvious that the infamous races were in progress in the Hippodrome. The cacophony raised by the rival Blue and Green supporters had traumatised his aural faculties. The eerie silence that had greeted him once he entered through the grand portal had done little to remedy the damage. It had served merely to convince him that he had suddenly become stone deaf. It was only the sound of his own breath and the echoing patter of his sandals on the geometrical tiling that persuaded him otherwise.

To add to the discomfort, he was still struggling to cope with the fact that he, inexperienced and lacking in authority as he was, would have to meet the second most important man in the Empire alone. For some inexplicable reason his more senior companions had been detained at the dock by an officious functionary claiming their papers were not in order. Even though, as far as Cyprian could see, they were identical to his own. The other members of the embassy had been obliged to return to the ship pending his return. When, he supposed, they would all sail back together to Italy.

As he drew closer to the end of the chamber, he marvelled at the scale. Ravenna too had its fine monuments – the churches and palaces were surely masterpieces. But compared to this, they were masterpieces in miniature. Plated with marble and porphyry, the walls seemed to soar to the sky. Meanwhile, the pillars and pilasters that lined the hall appeared to be designed to stop the sky from falling through the cupolas. These piers, in their turn, were laminated with agate and a green stone that Cyprian had never seen before but that reminded him of mould on cheese. Nonetheless, the surfaces were spectacular. He wondered, wryly, what lay beneath.

At last, he arrived before the screen beyond which no man would go. Not if he valued his life. The effect, he was forced to admit, was awe-inspiring, as if one were approaching the throne of God. The impression was accentuated by two gigantic mosaic figures that towered above the partitioned area on the wall behind. Cyprian squinted to make them out, then gave a tight smile. He had seen similar mosaics in Ravenna devoted to the saints and apostles, and of course the Pancreator. The man and woman that these portrayed had not even achieved the divinity of Empire. Yet.

Cyprian sensed his heart begin to race. He had arrived without his senior colleagues, it was true. But this had the consolation of providing an opportunity for him to shine. A chance to burnish his credentials and advance up the career ladder. More seriously, perhaps, he had also arrived without the customary gift-tribute. That too had been impounded at the dock. All of a sudden, he felt naked and instinctively moved his hands to his groin. Equally suddenly he became aware that someone was standing at his shoulder. Or not quite. When he looked round, he had to lower his eyes by a span or two to make out the figure.

He found himself looking at a bald patch on a very short man. Then the face looked up at him, eyes glistening with intelligence and amusement, cheeks covered with feathery down, even though the man was in his middle years.

'Welcome, Count,' the man said.

Cyprian struggled to smile at the mistake. Instead he burst into a fierce sweat.

'You take me for someone else, I fear,' he said. No doubt, one of the party detained at the docks.

The eunuch nodded.

'Forward of me, I know. But we see great prospects for your career.'

'We?' Cyprian asked, confused.

'Allow me to introduce myself. My name is Narses, and I serve as steward and minister to the Consul.'

Now he nodded to the screen.

'As such it is through me the Consul speaks.'

By telepathy? Cyprian wondered. And why, for Heaven's sake?

'The Consul prefers not to have direct contact,' Narses added, answering Cyprian's unspoken question, and so compounding the supernatural impression.

Cyprian gave an involuntary glance in the direction of the screen. Two seated and shadowy figures could be made out behind the diaphanous drape. Justinian and his whore, he supposed. Then corrected himself. 'The Consul's consort', of course.

'The restrictions on contact also apply to the ocular variety,' Narses pointed out.

If Cyprian had felt uncomfortable before, now he felt wholly unmanned. He tried to repress the surge of panic that coursed through him. Having quelled the urge to run for his life and sanity, he then found himself trying to stifle the urge to laugh. The situation was absurd.

The Consul, it was true, was almost certain to succeed his childless uncle as Emperor. And it was also true that the Emperor Justin was infirm in mind and body, and that his nephew had in all but name already assumed the real power. But still... These demands and this protocol would not have been out of place at the palace of a Persian potentate.

Still, it was best to play safe. Cyprian mentally promoted himself to Count and the Consul to Emperor, and addressed the dwarf accordingly.

He began with 'Serenest Highness' and got no further before he was stopped.

''Excellency' will do fine for the present,' Narses said. 'We would not presume so much.'

'Excellency,' Cyprian resumed, face twitching with the effort of restraining a smile, 'I bring you the greetings and obeisances from the King in Ravenna.'

He bowed to underline the point.

Narses looked at him with gentle reproof, then shook his head.

''Governor' would be more appropriate. 'Loyal servant' is customary.'

Cyprian began to feel the sweat flowing again.

'Moreover, it is also customary to prostrate oneself at this juncture,' Narses added.

Cyprian looked down with dismay at the ornately-tiled but none-too-clean floor. Then sank to his knees and lay face-down. He was still unsure what he should direct to whom, so positioned himself at an angle that pointed somewhere between the minister and the Consul.

There was a pause before Narses bade him rise, then a nod from the same source to urge him to continue.

'Your most loyal servant begs to inform you of his continued fealty and to ask you to inform your esteemed Uncle and his revered Emperor of the same.'

It was bad enough having to speak through one medium. To tell Narses to tell the Consul to tell the Emperor was ludicrous. But he was committed to playing the game.

After another chain of compliments and honorifics, Cyprian was about to embark on the real business of his mission, when he was once again interrupted.

'It is also customary at this particular point to submit one's material tribute.'

'Aah.' It was not so much that Cyprian had sought to evade the issue. But rather that he had forgotten about the omission in the confusion.

He turned towards the screen again before being tutted by Narses and turning back to the eunuch.

'Excellency, it is with the most profound apologies that I appear naked before you. Without the conventional tribute. And without the more senior legates.'

'A fit of absent-mindedness, perhaps?' the minister suggested.

Cyprian caught the sound of a stifled chuckle from behind the screen. The 'consort', he supposed.

'To my lasting regret and humiliation, they were detained at the docks. Both the other legates and the tribute.'

Narses cocked his head to the side and appeared to give the matter some thought.

'Papers not in order, I imagine. Combined with an over-zealous public servant.'

Cyprian nodded and swallowed hard.

'Still, the tangible manifestations of Theodoric's homage will, I dare say, eventually find their way to their rightful destination. As will your colleagues, no doubt,' Narses suggested.

Cyprian gave an over-eager nod. By now, he wished only to join his company on the ship home. As soon as possible. In the immediate absence of a ship to re-embark upon, he chose instead to re-embark upon his mission.

'Your loyal servant,' he began, 'the one in Ravenna, that is, regrets to inform His Most Eminent Excellency...'

The minister gave an encouraging smile.

'... that it will certainly escaped your attention that those adhering to the Aryan faith have been subjected to the most abject treatment at the hands of the Orthodox....'

He shuddered to a temporary halt and glanced to the screen, fearing the repercussions of such temerity. When he turned back to Narses, he was greeted by a mirthless smile.

'... within the confines of Your Realm,' the legate concluded.

'That should read within the realm of the Most Serene Emperor Justin, if I may make so bold,' Narses said. 'And it is presumptuous to claim that anything escapes the attention of his most attentive nephew.'

Cyprian gulped, repeated the given formula and then ploughed on, wondering where his head would be in respect of his body this time next week.

'Your loyal servant wishes to point out that within his own sphere of authority...'

''...beneficently awarded domain of temporal jurisdiction.''

'... that Catholic and Aryan...'

''faithful and heretic'...'

'... are treated with equal respect, both legally and in terms of civic usage...'

It was Narses turn to glance towards the screen.

'... and your loyal vassal entreats you to accord the same privilege to both, um, both varieties of the faith, here in the East...'

The minister's eyes remained on the screen for a moment before returning to Cyprian.

'You make your case most eloquently. But the matter is not one for a temporal authority. This is for the Almighty to decide. It is out of Our hands.'

Cyprian felt himself floundering again, and once again longed for the company of his more experienced colleagues. The minister's claim was arrant nonsense, of course. The Emperor, or his proxy, was quite capable of enforcing freedom of worship if he wanted to. But this was not something that he was empowered to point out. Even if he had dared to.

With an overwhelming sense of relief, he commenced the formulae that he hoped would be sufficient for him to take his leave.

He began with a deep bow, trusting that one prostration would suffice.

'Most Honoured Excellency, I will convey your pearls of wisdom to my own liege lord and take the liberty of expressing his eternal gratitude for your generous courtesy in receiving his humble supplicants.'

When he stood upright again, Narses was smiling his approval.

'Such eloquence. Such grace. You have a great future ahead of you, we can see. ...Count.'

Cyprian returned the smile with a sickly grimace, then turned to leave.

His departure was arrested by the minister.

'We have ways of helping you assure that future.'

Cyprian halted in mid-stride. He felt the perspiration turn cold on his back, then turned round to face Narses again.

'Your official title at present is that of *referandius*, we understand,' the minister continued.

Cyprian gave a weak nod and wondered where all this was going to lead.

'Perhaps you could remind us of the nature of the position.'

The *referandius* was sure that the Consul and heir-apparent were more than familiar with 'the nature of the position'. But he was in no position to point this out.

'My duties are to bring to trial, and prepare and present the case for the prosecution of malefactors.'

Narses nodded and gave a smile of fellow-feeling.

'Such is human nature,' he replied, 'there must be as many malefactors in your domain as in ours.'

'And there are a corresponding number of prosecutors,' Cyprian pointed out.

'But only one *referandius*.'

Cyprian nodded, although he was none the wiser as to the aim of the questions.

'The cases I deal with tend to comprise the more grave offences.'

Narses looked interested.

'Offences against the state, chiefly,' Cyprian explained.

'Peculation, perhaps?' Narses suggested.

'From the state coffers, certainly.'

'Heresy?'

'Theoretically, yes, although we have few such prosecutions.'

'You are truly blessed.' Narses shook his head. 'We are cursed with more manifestations of the affliction than one could imagine.'

There was another chuckle from behind the curtain. Theodora, the consort, was a notorious Monophysite, Cyprian recalled, but for obvious reasons had escaped persecution herself.

Cyprian was well aware that the lack of prosecutions for heresy in Italy was more attributable to Theodoric's policy of tolerance than any conformity of belief. But he felt it inadvisable to mention the fact in the present company.

'And treason, of course,' Narses continued.

'Of course.'

'If you were to hear of such an instance, you would then be obliged to take action?'

'There are channels of investigation, but I would most certainly set them in motion.'

'And such is your sense of duty that you would feel bound to do so, if the matter was brought to your attention,' Narses persisted.

Cyprian drew himself upright.

'Most certainly.'

'Even if it concerned a person of rank.'

The *referandius* hesitated a moment, before answering.

'No-one is above the law,' he said with a touch of primness.

'Not even one of the highest station?'

Theodoric himself? Cyprian wondered, before dismissing the thought from his mind. It would be absurd to bring a case before the King that touched the King himself. And technically, the only person the King could commit treason against was the Emperor. Another chill ran through him, before he realised that would then be out of his own jurisdiction.

'Do you have someone in mind?' he asked, for want of anything else to say.

'Your chief minister,' Narses replied, studying Cyprian's face for his reaction. 'It has come to our attention.'

The sweat on Cyprian's back turned icy cold. He had no love for Boethius. The man was a supercilious prig. But he was favoured by the King and not reluctant to use his power in favour of the Romanising faction. Cyprian meanwhile had nailed his flag firmly to the mast of the Goth cause, figuring that this would most easily lead to advancement.

But he was astonished by Narses' accusation. Boethius, despite his sympathies was famously and scrupulously honest. Not to mention, despite his own sympathies, totally faithful to his master.

Still, such a case, if successfully concluded, would most certainly be a feather in the *referandius'* cap. And a huge step on the ladder of offices.

On the other hand, if the conclusion was less than successful…

'In the event of failure,' the minister continued, as if divining his doubts, 'who knows where the axe could fall.'

Exactly, thought Cyprian.

'The effects could be quite counter-productive,' he pointed out, reassured by the understanding eunuch.

'In which case, we would have to settle for a lesser figure. If such suspicions came to our attention, of course.' Narses gave another sympathetic smile. 'A state prosecutor, for example.'

Cyprian hesitated for a moment to allow his heart to resume its function.

'For such a prosecution to succeed,' he began, struggling to quell the tremor in his voice, 'witnesses would be required. Particularly where such a senior figure as a first minister were concerned.'

Narses nodded.

'Many witnesses. Of reputable standing,' Cyprian added.

Narses nodded again.

'Of high social standing, at least,' the eunuch said.

'And irrefutable evidence,' Cyprian continued.

'All this can be made available.'

Cyprian began to understand why his colleagues had been detained at the port. But he still failed to comprehend the purpose of what was clearly a conspiracy against a loyal servant of both the King and the Emperor.

'Such a move would almost certainly undo all the work that the King has devoted himself to through the years,' he pointed out.

Narses looked up at him in expectation.

'This would open an unbridgeable rift between the two communities,' Cyprian said. 'Goth and Roman, Aryan and Catholic.'

There was a period of silence, during which Narses simply stared at him while giving no sign of responding.

In the end, Cyprian could stand the silence no longer.

'I myself would have to be above suspicion,' he said.

'As Caesar's wife.'

Now a guffaw that was rapidly choked off issued from behind the screen.

Narses turned and scowled at the curtain.

A shudder ran down Cyprian's spine as the enormity of what he was committing himself to sank in.

'This could cause the kingdom to fall apart,' he said.

'In which case you will find the Emperor has a long memory and infinite gratitude. In the meantime, your so-called King can be guaranteed to demonstrate his own gratitude to the saviour of his so-called kingdom,' the eunuch replied, before appending 'Count' once again to the statement.

Cyprian took a deep breath. He certainly hoped so. The King could equally well take the opposite stance. Still, Justinian's guarantee offered some kind of insurance. And if all went well, he would win out however the dice fell. For the moment, he felt the need for further reassurance.

'This evidence you mentioned.'

Narses nodded willingly.

'And the witnesses. All is in hand.'

'You already have an agent in place?' Cyprian asked, surprised.

Narses inclined his head again.

Somewhere outside, the watch called the hours. It should have been a cock-crow, the prosecutor thought.

'He is due any minute. You might like to discuss the further details with him.'

Cyprian became aware of the patter of footsteps coming down the great hall – towards them.

Are we not all men?

They want most who possess most.
Boethius

I was staring in the direction the commotion was coming from, when the door burst open to reveal a massive figure. It was wearing a long robe skirted with silver braid and flecked with mud. Over the robe was a knee-length jacket of dark fur, which I guessed to be sable. Above the jacket was a red face framed by flowing white locks and beard. And crowning the whole was what looked like an Astrakhan hat.

The wearer, whoever he was, obviously had no objection to appropriating clothing habits from barbarians where he judged it convenient. If he was not a barbarian himself.

His eyes searched for the abbot and, having located him, locked on. The wretched head of the monastery looked even more cowed than usual. He seemed to curl in on himself in an effort to achieve invisibility. The newcomer's eyes had skimmed over me without apparently absorbing my presence.

''My house shall be called the house of prayer; but thou hast made of it a den of thieves,'' he said, raising a declamatory finger towards the abbot.

This was, I assumed, the Master. And the quote was accurate enough, barring the fact that he had identified himself with Christ. Going by his appearance, he would have made a more convincing representation of Jehovah.

He advanced on the abbot, his feet making no sound as he moved. By the time he halted he was almost touching Basilius. Only his paunch came between them.

'Old friend,' he began, 'how good to see you after all this time.'

He placed his hands on the abbot's shoulders as though about to squeeze Basilius even tighter than he already was.

'The years have treated you well,' he continued. 'The mountain air, no doubt.'

He breathed in deeply as if to savour its health-giving properties, although the abbot had never looked a picture of health and was certainly no advertisement for converting the monastery into a thermal spa.

Then he wagged a finger so close to Basilius' face that it almost flicked his nose.

'But you have become a little lax in your duties, old friend.'

Flinging out his arms in full thespian manner, he cast his eyes about the room and its other occupants – once again without seeming to take them in.

'I arrive, careworn and foot-weary from inspecting my Sicilian estates, having longed for months, nay years, to see what you have made of the Order I ordained. And what do I find?'

The abbot raised his head, then lowered it again.

'A choice selection of scribes and academics, perhaps?' Again the theatrical appeal to an unacknowledged public. 'Alternatively, a band of brothers devoted to a life of pious meditation and contemplation of the divine mysteries?'

Now he raised the huge hands to the abbot's face and applied pressure, distorting the features.

'No. I find a plague of parasites, rogues and imbeciles.'

He dropped his hands once again, threw one arm over the abbot's shoulder and moved alongside as if speaking in confidence.

'I left you with a monastery, old friend. And with a set of clear rules.'

He shook his head as if disappointed in a wayward son.

'You have made of it a refuge for the scrapings and scum of the earth.' Again the squeeze of the shoulder. 'Tell me, dearest, oldest. What am I to do with you?' Again the shake of the head.

At this Basilius raised his eyes to meet those of the Master.

'We have created a sanctuary,' he said with quiet dignity. 'For the unjustly persecuted and abandoned.'

''Come all ye that labour and are heavy-laden, and I will give you rest,'' I quoted with a touch of smugness. I had decided it was time to make my presence felt. Whoever this Master turned out to be, as titular head of a monastery he was my ecclesiastical subordinate.

He turned, as if noticing me for the first time.

'And who might you be?'

'I was about to ask the same.'

'Flavius Magnus Aurelius *Cassiodorus* Senator,' he replied. 'Lord of Scylletium and Master of this abbey. And my own question still stands.'

On reflection, this all made some kind of sense. But at the time, I had no opportunity to reflect. Instead I remained silent for a moment. I suspect my mouth and jaw hung loose as I did so. I suppose I should have felt truly honoured. And, in some distant part of me, I suppose I did. But for the moment I was conscious only of being overwhelmed by the sheer size of the personality and the person before me. And, not least, the revelation of the identity of the Master. Then I came to my senses a little and began to realise that this introduction was just what I needed to answer the many questions my commission had posed. But first of all I had to assert myself.

'Jordanes, Lord of Tauris,' I replied, awarding myself an origin and title of dubious provenance. 'Bishop of Crotona.'

It was Cassiodorus' turn to be surprised, though he managed to disguise the fact better than I had, I am sure. He hardly broke stride. But his eyes alighted on the copies of his own letters and the final volume of his history, which I had brought with me into the vestry to challenge the abbot if he had continued to deny his involvement in the conspiracy. Cassiodorus then glanced with meaning at Basilius before returning his eyes to me.

'Dear boy!' he exclaimed, his face lighting up as though he had won the Saint Sophia lottery. 'If you could only imagine how much I have been looking forward to making your acquaintance.'

He came over and grasped my elbow. Gently but firmly.

'You know, it seems like only the other day that I was dining with our good Emperor when he brought your name up and assured me that he couldn't have imagined a better appointment to such an important see.'

I looked for signs of sarcasm but could find none. I would be surprised if the Emperor had heard of either the diocese or its new Bishop.

I mumbled my appreciation, as he began to shepherd me away from the abbot and out of the room.

'Come you must join me at dinner. I can't wait to discuss some of the finer points of the Nature of Our Lord with one as erudite as yourself. You know the Emperor was saying only the other day (he's remarkably well informed on all matters of doctrine, astonishing really when you think he has a whole Empire to take care of), that....'

I lost track of his words and took the opportunity to study him more closely. This was not a simple matter, given how much he had invaded my space. What surprised me most, I suppose, was his sheer magnitude. For some reason I had imagined him as slender and elegant. Perhaps he had been in his younger days. Or perhaps I had simply over-exercised my fancy. With the benefit of hindsight, it was easier to visualise a man of his amplitude delivering the pompous speeches and writing the over-ornate prose I had ploughed through.

Still, it was gratifying to be taken up in such cordial fashion by a man of his standing, even if the days of his power and reputation were most likely long behind him. Indeed, I should have felt honoured. But some vague doubts kept nagging at my brain.

As he swept me through the library (open stacks, of course), I noted the absence of the usual monks. In their place were a number of figures clad in more orthodox habits than our little brotherhood usually managed. That was about the only thing that could be said in their favour. I have rarely seen a more wretched and shabby bunch.

They were pallid and undernourished, and their ignorance of bodily hygiene was probably detectable as far away as Crotona. All cut from the same cloth, they seemed to be weighted towards earth by their cares. Everything seemed overextended. Long faces drooped to longer bodies; cheeks hung loose and down, as if they had lost some internal support and padding.

As we passed by, they turned their eyes away. Strangely enough. After all, they had presumably been recruited and transported hither by Cassiodorus himself. I assumed they were clerks, perhaps failed patronless applicants to the Civil Service now to be employed in transcribing and copying (correctly) Cassiodorus' words of wisdom for the benefit of future generations. Since I supposed he had selected them, they should have been on at least bowing terms with the Master. They seemed instead to be either embarrassed or intimidated by his presence.

I duly averted my own eyes. They were not a pleasant sight. Indeed their abjectness prompted a faint but agreeable longing for the exuberant irreverence of the former patrons of the premises.

*

I had assumed we were headed for the refectory, since I had been invited to share dinner. But we passed through the scriptorium and skirted the dining hall. As we left the main building of the monastery and stepped out into the garden, I asked my companion whether he had indeed personally selected the new recruits. This entailed me probing for a gap in the constant flow of his discourse and rushing to plug it before the torrent resumed its flood.

For a moment, he looked confused. Then he explained. The rest of his 'pitiful' life was to be devoted to a new project for monasticism. This aimed to spread the light of learning rather than just encourage the inner light of the soul.

'This was why I was so upset with poor old Basilius,' he said. 'I hope he didn't take it too hard. The riff-raff he had collected were hardly likely to qualify as missionaries of the sort I had in mind.'

I assured him that the abbot would accept the rebuke in the spirit it was intended, and with all due humility. I omitted to mention that he had had plenty of practice at my own hands.

The Master stopped for a moment and grasped my elbow more firmly.

'The soul requires nourishment, don't you think? And I speak not just of those souls that inhabit such cloistered institutions as this.'

He waved his hand at the buildings behind us by way of demonstration. Then his head fell forward.

'Ah, this pestilence, this war. Will they never cease?'

He stopped speaking and I wondered if he was really expecting a reply to what I had taken as a rhetorical flourish.

'So many bridges burnt,' he continued after a moment. 'I like to think this establishment will do something to restore them. Barbarian and Roman, Catholic and Arian, Greek and Latin – are we not all men?'

By now we were at the entrance to the Master's house and I realised it was there we were to dine.

I had never been inside and was immediately struck by the contrast with the dilapidation of the rest of the monastery. Opulent drapes trimmed in elaborate brocade hung on almost every wall, rugs with raised pile and floral patterns coated each floor. I couldn't help noticing traces of mosaics peeping from the edges and corners of the coverings, and wondered what abominable pagan practices they had been intended to hide.

In similar fashion, the furniture was sparse but select, and threw into stark relief the artefacts that it supported – bowls and urns of great antiquity and exquisite design, lamps, candlesticks and incense burners of hammered gold and silver. True, everything was in need of some dusting and polishing. But a crew of servants had already started on the household chores necessary after a long absence.

Moreover, needless to say, the whole place was very well-heated.

Without interrupting his discourse or releasing my elbow, Cassiodorus shepherded me into the dining area. I had stopped listening some time ago and his words either passed over my head or bypassed my memory as soon as they had entered.

Candles had already been lit in the room in anticipation of our arrival. I inhaled deeply. Not the stench of rotting flesh emitted by melting tallow. These must have been made of beeswax. Not even my previous employer, the esteemed, corrupt and thus fantastically wealthy Gunthigis Baza, had made use of these.

The Master finally relinquished his hold on me as we approached the huge banqueting table. I prepared to seat myself opposite him wherever he should choose to sit. For it appeared that we would dine on our own. Instead he continued past the table. I found myself guided by a tall maggiordomo (not Gorgeous Giorgos, thankfully). He was dressed in a green silk tunic embossed with heraldic arms, and endowed with an air of long-suffering condescension, and led me to one of a pair of *klinai* at the far end of the room.

He indicated that I should recline on the couch and then retreated – now with an air of affronted self-esteem. The number of embroidered cushions made it difficult to find a comfortable position that was also dignified, and which still allowed me access to the small dishes by the side of the couch.

Cassiodorus greeted me from the other couch with a raised little finger.

'I like to maintain the ancient traditions,' he said. 'The high Roman style seems to me so much more elegant than the practice of seating oneself as if one were about to complete an exercise in parsing Classical Greek.'

He looked at me eagerly.

'Don't you think, dear boy?'

I was not used to such luxury and felt myself quite out of my depth. I simply gave a weak nod.

'You'll have to forgive Lucius,' he continued.

'Lucius,' I repeated.

'The butler. New to me. Came highly recommended. But what's that worth these days? I ask you. Could be just a means of offloading unwanted baggage onto someone else.'

I knew the feeling.

He cocked his head to the side.

'Or perhaps you would prefer to be served by your own man?'

I imagined Owen consorting with this company and could barely restrain the giggle that rose to my lips.

'I bow to your superior discrimination,' I replied in the end.

He looked at me with interest, as if he had suddenly discovered a new species of beetle.

'Jordanes, you say?' he said. As if he hadn't already heard the name a thousand times in the company of the Emperor, I thought with wry satisfaction.

I nodded.

'A Goth name, is it not?' he asked. 'Slightly adapted for consumer use, I imagine.'

I nodded again. It had been my old master, the General, who had chosen the name for me, finding the original too difficult to master and too long to serve on a regular basis.

'Thought so. Splendid chaps, the Goths. Greatest admiration, dear boy. Really made something of yourself, haven't you? Wonderful what a pinch of education will do. And a sliver of civilisation, of course.'

I winced. It looked like it was going to be a long evening. Only my respect for social convention and for my host's reputation prevented me from excusing myself from the invitation. There was also the chance that I might be able to find the answers to some questions, of course. I gritted my teeth and forced my mouth into a tight smile.

He reached over to his side table and extracted something from a platter, then dropped the something into his mouth – all without removing his eyes from me.

I glanced over at the contents of my own table. One of the salvers held what appeared to be small rodents, depilated, rolled in poppy seed, and glistening with honey.

'Local dormice,' Cassiodorus apologised, dropping another into his mouth by its tail. 'Not as bad as you would think. But hardly in the same class as those harvested from the north shore of the Euxine Sea. As I'm sure you're aware.'

I had a suspicion that this was a joke at my expense. I had never eaten a dormouse and wasn't about to start doing so now.

I fumbled for what looked like an olive on another tray. It turned out to have been stuffed with something that tasted like rancid offal.

Cassiodorus gave an approving nod.

'Goldcrest hearts,' he pointed out helpfully. 'Dash of garlic and nutmeg.'

He opened his mouth wide and picked his teeth with a long little-finger nail, extracted a shred of rodent and held it up for inspection before flicking it to the floor.

'Interesting mythology surrounding the bird,' Cassiodorus continued. 'Pliny called it the king of birds, you know.'

I did not but nodded anyway.

'Which is why some call it the kinglet.' He belched softy and patted his stomach. 'The pagans believed it was killed every winter to be reborn in the spring. Connected with some kind of rebirth rite, I suppose. Some barbaric sacrifice or another.'

A louder belch to underline the point.

'All because it's got a golden crown, I imagine,' he concluded.

I became aware of someone standing by my shoulder. It was the emerald tunic again, this time holding a carafe of wine about the size of a fish-sauce amphora. I nodded. Anything to get the taste of the poor bird's entrails out of my mouth.

He poured no more than a mouthful into the goblet. I looked down into the beaker in disbelief. Given the sybaritic nature of the appetisers, I had assumed that there would be ample wine on offer. And I had intended to take full advantage to dull the pain.

When I looked up again, Cassiodorus was smirking.

'He will taste it for you, if you are in any doubt,' he said. 'Otherwise, you are expected to taste it yourself and signal your approval or rejection of the vintage.'

I flushed, tasted, nodded, and drank half of the large beaker at a gulp.

In the meantime, my dining companion instructed the butler to taste his wine first, waited for a moment while he studied the servant's face, then made a sign for his own goblet to be filled. Finally he waved a finger to dismiss the server.

He took a sip and grimaced.

'Devilish difficult to get any decent plonk round here,' he concluded. 'Vines must be blighted, as the rest of the country seems to be.'

More like plague than blight, I thought. And the war. I had seen grapes still standing shrivelled and frozen on the vines as we travelled to the monastery. Plenty of grapes. No one left to pick them.

I shuffled amongst the cushions trying to negotiate a more comfortable position. Cassiodorus seemed to have no difficulty finding a posture that allowed him to talk, look at me and fill his mouth at the same time. The benefits of inherited civilisation, I supposed. I furtively shoved a couple of the offending cushions to the floor. When I next twisted my neck to look over at my host, he was paring a wishbone with his teeth, prior to dropping it once again on the floor. I noted the side-dishes had received reinforcements. The chicken looked innocuous enough. There are, after all, a limited number of ways in which one ruin the taste of a fowl.

I tentatively tore off a strip with my fingers and dropped it into my mouth. I have never liked fish sauce. The Romans drown everything in the condiment, presumably in the hope of disinfecting the food, or disguising the taste of putrefying flesh. But at least I was used to it. What made the food stick in my throat was a flavouring that reminded me of nothing more than the bile that comes with vomit. Eventually I managed to force it down without regurgitating it. When I had done so, I wiped the sweat from my brow and glanced over at Cassiodorus. He was studying me with unconcealed amusement.

'Another resurrected tradition,' he explained. 'A recipe from Apicius. Laserwort is the herb you're probably wondering about. Apart from imparting a distinctive flavour, it has a number of beneficial side-effects.'

As an emetic, I thought to myself.

'Pray tell,' I said to him.

'It enhances the process while suppressing the product.'

Now I was completely mystified.

'It is claimed to be both an aphrodisiac and a contraceptive.'

'I'm sure it would be invaluable if I weren't in holy orders and in the sole company of men.'

I could not forbear. And even if I had been about to take part in a week-long orgy, that would not have excused the vileness of the elixir.

Cassiodorus broke into hearty laughter.

'Just so, dear boy. Just so. A worthy response. I won't be repeating the experiment.'

He called for his emerald boy and the next course.

'Pheasant,' he explained. 'More conventionally spiced. Another from the same classic recipe book.'

'Apicius?'

'The very same. Something of a gourmet from the time of the unfortunate Emperor Tiberius. Now the book is a bit of a collector's item. I have an extra copy if any of the dishes strike your fancy.'

'You are too gracious.'

He chuckled again.

'I would offer to show you my private library. But it appears you have already had the pleasure.'

I felt my cheeks redden. So he had recognised the books I had with me when I confronted Basilius.

'And I left strict instructions that the private collection was to be off limits,' he sighed. 'Poor fellow,' he continued. I assumed he was referring to the abbot. 'The responsibility is obviously all too much for his meagre shoulders.'

The pheasant now arrived along with its splendid plumage, which had been reinserted into the rear of the cooked bird. The Emerald Immaculate dispensed it in tranches from the main table.

'But what is one to do,' Cassiodorus mumbled through his meat, 'when the bonds of ancient friendship override all other considerations?'

'A thorny moral issue,' I replied, as I played knucklebone with latest food that had been placed before me. By now I was longing for the elegant simplicity and understated flavours of Josephus' concoctions.

'His negligence does have its compensations,' the Master said.

'He is a worthy man. A pious man,' I muttered.

'No doubt, no doubt. And if it hadn't been for his oversight, I would never have known I was dealing with a fellow bibliophile.'

'Aah.'

'I am interested to know what drew your attention to those particular volumes.' He paused, then added another 'dear boy'.

I took a long draught of the wine, then decided my host had a point. It needed diluting.

'Your reputation as an historian precedes you,' I answered as I searched my brain for a better excuse.

'You are too kind.' But he was still waiting for a fuller response. I decided to fling caution to the wind. I also had mysteries to solve.

'I was astonished by the depth of the research as well as the richness of the prose.'

He was delighted by this response, but showed no sign of having had his curiosity satisfied. Unfortunately.

'You must have had privileged access to a great deal of information,' I added.

'Aah. One of the few perks of office, dear boy.'

''The Scribe's office is the great safeguard of the rights of man,'' I said, quoting from his letters. 'An office you appear to have occupied with great diligence for many years, given the extensive correspondence in your collected epistles.'

He inclined his head in gracious acknowledgement.

''The Scribe is more diligent in other men's business than they are in their own,'' I continued from the same source.

'You too seem to have little respect for others' privacy,' he replied.

I gazed fondly at the goblet of wine.

'The books were published. That is, 'made public',' I pointed out.

He continued to fix me with an unblinking gaze. Then relaxed and burst into laughter.

'You have me there.'

I emptied my goblet. Whether the wine was raw or not, I needed some help.

'I was even more astonished by the amount you chose not to include.'

The laughter stopped and the steely look returned.

'Well, you have been busy with your research. To what end?' he demanded.

'I have been commissioned to write a summary of your *Gothic History*.'

I was rewarded with a raised eyebrow.

'By the Emperor?'

'A bookseller called Castalius.'

A morsel of dead bird flew across the room as Cassiodorus broke into joyous laughter.

'To offset a debt, I take it.'

I nodded.

'Or else,' he added with a snipping movement of his fingers.

Another nod. Rewarded by a shake of the leonine head this time.

'Well,' he sighed, 'that is your funeral.'

'I trust not,' I replied. 'With the help of your magnificent library.'

Which had helped me to fill some of the gaps in his summary. Though I would still have to raise the subject again if I was going to fill the remainder. And get the complete story from the jaws of the lion in front of me. I would have to tread carefully.

'I can only marvel at the extraordinary quality and varied nature of your collection,' I added, by way of lubrication.

'Much of it came in the form of a bequest.'

'From a grateful client?'

A nod. I waited for a name to be dropped ever so casually.

'A much lamented friend and colleague.'

'Boethius?' I suggested. A stab in the dark really. But it hit home.

'The same.'

That explained the esoteric, not to say heterodox nature of much of the library. But not much else.

'A tragic loss,' I said.

'At least we have inherited some of his wisdom.'

This I was not sure of. But it provided an opening for the question I wished to return to.

'I regret to say that someone does not agree.'

'With what?'

'The wisdom of the philosopher.'

I could have sworn he snorted at the word.

'How so?' he asked.

'His *Consolations* has been defaced.'

His face changed colour.

'In what way?'

'Some passages have been deleted. Others have been commented upon. In uncomplimentary fashion.'

'Is that so?' Cassiodorus appeared suddenly lost in thought.

'Indeed some of your own texts have been subjected to similar treatment.'

'Indeed.' I wasn't sure if this was a question or a confirmation.

'Notably your own *History of the Goths.*'

'Outrageous.'

'My thoughts exactly. You may take some comfort from the fact that the graffiti artist was illiterate.'

His cheeks turned from pink to red.

'Couldn't spell to save his life,' I continued blithely.

Now they were Imperial purple. I failed to understand how my words could have given offence. But clearly they had. So much for finding the answer to my questions. At least now I might have a pretext to terminate the appalling dinner.

He muttered something under his breath.

'I beg your pardon,' I said.

'You might well do that. I said that it was a medical condition.'

I was bewildered.

'What was?'

'My spelling disorder,' he explained. 'It is in no way a reflection of level of learning or culture.'

I looked round desperately for a rock to crawl under.

'That is why I employ scribes.'

His level of colour fell as mine rose. He seized and fiercely consumed a piece of pigeon pie. I was left only with a large slice of humble pie. In looking to get the truth from the lion's mouth I had inadvertently stuck my head inside it.

'But why?' I stammered.

'Why what?'

'Why change what you had written?' Not to mention what Boethius had written.

HIs eyes flitted right and left. Then he relaxed, leant back and clapped his hands. Not, as I initially thought, in ironic applause. For his servant came running.

'More wine. And not this disgraceful vintage. Can't you see we have an honoured guest?'

The servant's face colour clashed with his tunic. He wheeled about and exited.

Cassiodorus gave a heavy sigh.

'O tempora, O mores!' he exclaimed. 'As difficult to find good servants as it is good wine.'

His quoting Cicero could not dispel the notion that he had chosen the first wine as an insult to my origins, and demanded a replacement because he wanted something of me.

'The same could be said of the, er…, corrections I was obliged to make, of course,' he added.

I failed to understand.

'How do you mean?'

'As spring brings green to the trees, so autumn brings brown, while this winter strips them bare. So also our own plumage fades, brown giving way to grey,' he fingered his own white mane by way of demonstration, although I was none the wiser as to his meaning, 'and so we fall from an age of heroes to an age of lead.'

'Very true,' I nodded, helpless. I guessed he had been referring to Cicero bewailing the times and customs rather than quality of the wine or the service.

'As the philosopher says, all is flux.'

I gave an inane smile of encouragement.

'To wit,' he concluded, 'the circumstances under which I wrote my texts are not the same under which I labour now.'

'Aah,' I replied. Now I was gaining a glimmer of understanding. 'But history does not change, does it?'

'I beg to differ. As circumstances change, so history changes. And all change is change for the worse, of course. A condition of our fallen state, as the venerable Augustine would have said.'

He paused for a moment and sighed.

'And probably did somewhere. Only God and his Truth are immutable. (Augustine again, I fancy.) And only by His grace can we find redemption from our inherited corruption and vicious appetites.'

So saying, he dropped a fistful of quail eggs into his mouth and belched.

'Thus the historian is compelled to make changes. You might call it a compromise with reality.' A benign smile. 'You will be aware I was captured by the Imperials when Belisarius took Ravenna?'

'And have since then languished in captivity in Constantinople.'

'You express it so well. In order to ease the bonds and travails of captivity, as opposed to, say losing some of my vital appendages, I was required to, how shall I put it, correct some of my more mistaken impressions of the course of events and their major agents.'

'To cast the Empire in a better light.'

'In a nutshell.'

'Which entailed casting the government of the Goths in a poorer light.'

'I would rather express it as redressing some of the imbalances of perspective.'

'Aah.'

'The Emperor wishes our vast culture to reflect the glory of God. And himself of course. Which necessitated alterations to the standard editions.'

An expedient therefore. And in human terms, an understandable one. But surely not all of the revisions were accounted for by the desire for self-preservation?

I was distracted from my thoughts as Cassiodorus continued.

'You will no doubt also find such discretion prudent when you come to write your summary,' he said.

I realised the force of the argument. I already had Castalius after me. Small fry compared to the Emperor himself. While I dislike conflict, I am not by nature a coward. But nor am I, I like to think, a total fool. And to invite persecution for fulfilling a commission not of my choosing would be totally foolish.

None of which diminished my desire to learn the truth. For my own satisfaction, if for no other reason. I looked over at the Master again. He was nodding slowly and looking at me.

'I am beholden to you,' I said. 'Yet I can't help wondering....'

He smiled in an encouraging manner. But not with his eyes.

'You referred to Boethius as your friend.'

The smile continued but the eyes narrowed.

''Client' would be perhaps more accurate. Though the relationship does imply a degree of intimacy, I suppose.'

I resisted the urge to whistle. So Cassiodorus had been Boethius' 'benefactor'? The word that had been expunged from the text and that Paulinus had managed to restore?

I pulled myself together and pursued the argument.

'Yet your marginalia in his *Consolations*, if they are indeed your comments, are quite damning.'

Not to mention his tampering with the text itself.

'How so?' he demanded.

'They contradict his own account of his trial. Indeed they seem to underline his guilt.'

'He was found guilty by his peers.'

'He claims to have been framed.'

He shook his head as if in disappointment.

'Alas, it requires a strong character indeed to maintain one's integrity in the face of death.' He leant back on his couch and picked up a single egg, examined it for a moment, then bit into it. 'Human nature is so frail, such is our fallen state.'

'I imagine the King was grateful to all those concerned with bringing the traitor to justice,' I said, changing tack.

He raised a suspicious eyebrow.

'What makes you say that?'

'I believe the *referandius*, Cyprian, was promoted shortly afterwards.'

He relaxed slightly.

'His prosecution was masterly.'

'And you succeeded Boethius to the post of first minister?'

The Master picked up yet another dead bird and peeled off a leg.

'I can really recommend the ortolan,' he said. 'You should try it.'

By now I was ready to take up Pythagorean vegetarianism.

As he chewed on the meat, he replied to my question.

'You are in essence correct. The King was obliged to rely on my humble services in the absence of more suitable candidates for the post. Few of your people, you know, had the benefit of the education you yourself received. And my fellow Romans... Well, many of them had fallen into the decadence that afflicts overripe civilisations.'

'And you served him loyally.'

'Dear boy. Just because a gentleman is obliged by circumstances to ride an ass doesn't make him less of a gentleman.'

I wriggled on the couch, as I recalled my own arrival at the monastery.

'And just because an ass is caparisoned like a horse doesn't make it less of an ass,' he concluded with a snort.

Now I squirmed. He had summed up my own feelings perfectly. Cassiodorus had made an utter donkey of me. Or simply revealed to me my own essence.

'It was shameful that Boethius did not show such sterling loyalty,' I commented in a desperate attempt to restore my self-respect. The irony in my remark was missed by my companion. Irony did not appear to find a place in his stock of rhetorical devices. So it bounced back on its progenitor. He had at least the grace to give the matter some thought.

'I suspect the poor chap was promoted beyond his capabilities. And found the temptations of office too great.'

I nodded my understanding, as he continued.

'He had, moreover, some abstract and outdated notions. The man was a pagan at heart, you know, as you probably found out for yourself when you read his so-called masterpiece. There was substance in the sorcery charge. That alone was enough to have him executed.'

'Though I imagine it was the attempt to enlist the help of Justin, the Emperor, to overthrow the King that really sealed the verdict,' I offered.

Again he stopped masticating for a moment, and fixed an eye on me as if checking for something.

'You really have missed your métier you know. Have you never thought of joining the *vigiles*?'

Now I raised an eyebrow. Elegantly, I hoped.

'All mention of that was suppressed,' he explained. 'In the interests of what Theodoric called laughingly 'national security'.'

I pursed my lips, gave it some apparent thought, then nodded.

'But I suppose it was Boethius' attempt to set up the previous Emperor of the West as a rival claimant to the throne that must have precluded any hope of clemency from the Goth King.'

I had the satisfaction of seeing Cassiodorus choke on his food.

'And which 'Emperor' would that be?' he asked when he had recovered.

'Romulus, familiarly known as Augustulus.'

Cassiodorus emitted a high-pitched whining sound that might have been an attempt at laughter.

'My dear boy, you will be the death of me. The poor wretch died long before that.'

I couldn't resist, even though it seemed against my best interests.

Strange,' I said. 'He seemed to be in the best of health last time I saw him. Given his age and a little softening of the brain.'

He stared at me as if his eyes were about to eject themselves and walk my way. I admit I gained great satisfaction from having stopped the smug bastard in his tracks. Even if it was only for a moment. He soon shook himself and recovered his poise.

'You will have your little joke with me. I must be getting a little weak in the head myself. Where on earth did you imagine you saw him?'

I began to realise that I might have made a mistake. I had wanted simply to puncture Cassiodorus' massive self-assurance.

'A monk with delusions of grandeur perhaps?' I suggested.

He nodded slowly.

'You should not believe everything the rabble Basilius has collected here tells you. Which reminds me. I promised to have a word with him.'

He rose heavily to his feet and wiped his mouth with a napkin. Then grabbed my elbow again as a prelude to shepherding me back out.

'In the meantime, do let me know if you need any help preparing for your onward journey to your diocese. We would love to entertain you further but there is likely to be some severe disruption to the routines from now on.'

He patted me on the back.

'We share an interest. For my part, having helped in my humble way to make history, I suppose, now I will have to devote my time to writing it.'

Or rewriting it, I thought to myself.

I wondered whether Augustine would have approved.

Mule on an Ass

Thus are all things seen to yearn
In due time for due return;
And no order fixed may stay,
Save which in th' appointed way
Joins the end to the beginning
In a steady cycle spinning.
Boethius

I sat outside the monastery waiting on a beast of burden different from the one I had arrived on. I had decided the donkey was more tractable than the mule that had brought me here and consigned the latter to the care of Owen.

The weather had taken a turn for the better, for which I was grateful. The wind had died down and the sun shone, warming my back as I waited for Owen to emerge. I did not understand how long it could take to pack our belongings onto the pack mule. Even if it was more clement, it was still winter, and I was freezing.

I clapped my hands together and rubbed them to keep the circulation going. My breath emerged as vapour. It reminded me of the clouds of prejudice that had misted my mind and blinded my eyes to the truth.

A mule on an ass.

For despite what the Master had claimed, there had to be, I was convinced, a history that was not contingent on expediency and circumstance. And that was not jealously guarded by God as his own prerogative. Had He not, after all, imparted to Man the blessing of His truth? There must then be a reality that was both tangible and immutable – one that was not constrained by the demands of the moment and the whims of the powerful.

The donkey stamped its hooves, perhaps for the reasons that I rubbed my hands, perhaps out of impatience to be gone. I patted its neck to reassure it. Owen would take the time necessary. I would have done better to rely on my servant's common sense throughout our stay. It would have saved me a great deal of trouble and anxiety.

As it was, I had chased here and there pursuing each *ignis fatuus* that shimmered for a moment and then vanished. And the greatest illusion of all was my own contempt for my barbarian origins and all that shared them. By extension, everything that was civilised had to be the true light, the real fire.

My meeting with Cassiodorus had at least served the purpose of disabusing me of that misconception. I had presumed, in my ignorance and despite all suggestions to the contrary, that either Boethius or Theodoric were perpetrators – the one of high treason, the other of massive ingratitude. Instead I was now convinced they were both victims.

My suspicions had been first aroused when it became clear that Cassiodorus was the Master of the monastery and thus logically the owner of the estate where it had been established. And the library. And thus the editor of the Boethius text.

This was the final absolution of the sins I had thought Basilius guilty of and their reassignment to the soul of Cassiodorus. The poor abbot had used the place as a sanctuary, while his master had intended it to be a *scriptorium* for the rewriting of history. Or a centre for the propagation of learning, as he would have put it. With his warped sense of justice, he might even have thought the abbacy a fitting reward for his penitent pawn, while the unrepentant Opilio and Cyprian were presented with more material prizes.

That Cassiodorus' revisionism was designed to placate the Emperor by vilifying Theodoric cast a doubt on the loyalty of his service to the Goth King. And his own trustworthiness in general. It also raised the possibility that he himself had been behind the fabrication of charges and evidence against Boethius. If so, he was probably acting at the instigation of the Empire. Meaning Justinian, of course. Although the latter had not yet assumed the Imperial throne, he effectively ruled during the senile last years of his uncle.

I had at first wondered what Justinian had to gain by such a conspiracy. His ultimate aim would have been, then as now, to reunite the Empire. But I was puzzled for a time as to how this stratagem would have helped achieve that. Then it came to me. The sight of a Goth King trying and executing a prominent and virtuous Roman, on the grounds that the public servant in question had been defending the 'liberty' of Rome and the Senate would be bound to drive a wedge between the two communities.

Thus causing a breach that Theodoric had spent most of his reign seeking to seal and Justinian would hasten to exploit.

The rift would be further deepened by provoking the King into a mass persecution of the Italian Catholics. The provocation, no doubt took the form of a mass persecution of Arians in the Eastern Empire – one that continued to this day. Happily, there was little evidence that Theodoric had actually fallen for the trap, or had had time to do so, apart from the now-questionable post-mortuum addition to Cassiodorus' *History*.

The Emperor-in-waiting would then have been able to come to the rescue of Rome, rid the West of its barbarians and ultimately rule a united Roman Empire. Unfortunately for him, and for Theodoric, the Goth King had died before such rifts could develop and such a pretext could be given. He had to wait years for another such occasion to arise. And then he claimed to invade Italy in order to avenge the murder of Theodoric's daughter and successor, after her son died. It would not have surprised me unduly if he had actually orchestrated her death himself.

As for Cassiodorus himself, I guessed from what he said that he had been driven by envy and ambition – envy of Boethius and ambition for his office. An office that Cassiodorus inherited and continued to hold under Theodoric's successors. I expect he had later ceased to operate as Justinian's agent-in-place, given the rank and power he had managed to achieve and maintain. Still, during his eventual capture and 'imprisonment' in Constantinople, he seemed to have been handled with kid gloves – not something the Emperor was renowned for.

And now we lived with the result of Cassiodorus and Justinian's plotting – nearly twenty years of warfare on the peninsula. God bless the Empire!

For Cassiodorus had done more than open my eyes to his own perfidy and that of the Emperor. He had also disabused me of all that I had most admired about Roman *civilitas*. His barely concealed contempt for myself and *my* people (I may now claim them with pride) was difficult enough to square with my belief in the infinite inclusiveness of the Empire. This contempt and his constant patronising air had driven me, to my eternal shame and regret, to reveal the presence of Romulus at the monastery. For I am sure now that it was he himself that had ordered the execution of the ex-Emperor of the West. Once Boethius and Theodoric had disappeared from the scene, Romulus would have been perceived only as a threat to Justinian's attempt to re-unite the Empire.

Furthermore, Cassiodorus' self-indulgence and cynicism slid the cover of the sarcophagus of my illusions into place. If the ancient Roman heroes, those paragons of self-reliance and self-denial that had been presented to me as models for life by my teachers were to be found anywhere now, they were more likely to be amongst the so-called barbarians. Theodoric, Totila. Alaric even.

Not myself. I had denied my birthright.

But much as it grieved me to admit it, Cassiodorus had read my character correctly. I lacked the moral courage to do what was right and honourable. I would, on arrival in my episcopal seat in Crotona, discharge my commission to Castalius. He would doubtless be disappointed at my summary, lacking as it was in salacious details. But that was his business. Even more to the point, the Emperor could hardly object to the uncontroversial, anodyne version of events that it would purvey.

To redress the balance, I decided I would insert at intervals above certain of my own monastic 'illuminations'. This in an effort to redeem Theodoric and his legacy, and more pathetically, to redeem myself – in my own eyes at least. But these corrections, as with the rest of the manuscript would be reserved for the eyes of the future, safe from the Justinian's spy network.

For the present, I would be content to write myself out of history and be left to fester unmolested in my episcopal seat. If I could find any further way to redeem myself by ministering to the poor or alleviating the ravages of the plague and the war, then I would do so with the greatest good cheer. If nothing else, it would salve my conscience and, I hoped, atone to some small degree for my pusillanimity.

I chuckled to myself and tickled the donkey's ears. I was beginning to sound like a Pelagian myself. I had, after all, little chance of winning heaven purely through repentance and grace. I was even beginning to wonder whether I had chosen the right God to worship. I had certainly chosen the wrong chariot to back in becoming so enamoured of Roman *civilitas*.

For I had come to doubt that Augustine was right in judging us to be inherently corrupt and thus in need of a faith and a civilisation to curb our wicked instincts. I now leaned more towards the Pelagian view, that we are born innocent. And if that is true, then we can only be corrupted by those constraints. In such case, it follows that it is civilisation that allows, even encourages evil men to prosper, as Boethius and Theodoric found to their cost. And that it is Roman *civilitas* that causes us to forget or deny our own essential nature. Here I was the chief victim.

As Owen put it, 'it's the bosses as call the shots and make our decisions for us.'

The ass pricked up its ears, and out of fellow-feeling I pricked up mine. Then turned my head towards the entrance of the monastery.

Owen was finally making his exit. He was followed by the pack-mule, which he had tethered to his own. I made ready to chide him in all gentleness and lifted my heels to urge my own mount forward. What I saw next made me recover my grasp of the reins. My vision grew blurred.

But I could still make out the figures of Arminius and Uldin, the latter on a mule that was radically out of proportion to his stature, the former beside him on foot and holding the bridle. Then Isidorus and Paulinus, also on foot. Josephus came next, waving to me as though renewing our vows of everlasting friendship, and leading a broken-backed donkey. Then Basilius, holding the arm of Anacreon for support. He stopped for a moment and looked back. I wondered if he was saying farewell to his home. I hoped he was waiting for Romulus.

No Romulus emerged. I feared the worst. My head hung low over the pommel of the saddle. More to atone for. Much more.

But the company would be good and would cheer the way. I hoped the brothers needed little persuasion to join me in Crotona. They had made a goodly community here in Scylletium and a self-sufficient one.

I felt my heart warm suddenly as if someone had blown on the embers of my dying spirit. If there was nothing else, not progress, not civilisation, not learning, there was at least companionship.

And I made my decision for myself.

As Bishop of Crotona I would call the shots and provide a home for others. One based on true community, rather than the false mores of this coercive society. In doing so, I would also find a home for myself. An end to drifting, buffeted by every wave that broke, finding a haven in one rock pool after another, none of my own choosing. I had hitherto mistaken aimlessness for freedom. What I needed I felt was a fixed point around which my universe could revolve. It could revolve to its heart's content. Myself, I longed for stasis.

Perhaps that would give meaning to the passing of time. For the rest is but the flying of dust across the wasteland.

Afterword

The events described in this book are chiefly lies. Some are not.

The last Emperor of the West is recorded as having been provided for by Odovacar and Theodoric after being deposed, latterly at Lucullanum. His death is not recorded. If he had lived to 550AD and been present at Vivarium then, he would have been about ninety years old.

Cassiodorus is supposed to have written a *History of the Goths*, which is now lost. He served a line of Gothic monarchs, was captured at Ravenna and 'imprisoned' at Constantinople, before retiring to Vivarium. He devoted the remainder of his life to writing. He died in about 585, which would have made him about one hundred years old at his death.

Jordanes wrote a history of the Goths, commonly known as *Getica*. He claimed to be summarising Cassiodorus' lost history. Somebody of the same name is recorded as Bishop of Crotona about the time of the main setting of this novel.

Theodoric, Boethius and Justinian are also, of course, historical figures.

A certain Basilius is indeed mentioned in *Consolations*, as one of the informers against Boethius. The other monks are my own invention.

There is no evidence of an Eastern-inspired plot against Theodoric and/or Boethius. But there is no evidence against it either.

Printed in Great Britain
by Amazon

56953331R00149